DARK RADIANCE

DARK RADIANCE

ALLISON ALDRIDGE

ALSO BY ALLISON ALDRIDGE

Dark Radiance Series:
Dark Radiance (Book One)
Dark Sacrifices (Book Two)

FOR MY PARENTS,

WHO ALWAYS TAUGHT ME TO

SHOOT FOR THE STARS & NEVER STOP

DREAMING.

CONTENTS

SIGN UP FOR THE MONTHLY NEWSLETTER

TO RECEIVE SPECIAL OFFERS, GIVEAWAYS, DISCOUNTS, BONUS CONTENT, UPDATES FROM THE AUTHOR, INFO ON UPCOMING RELEASES, AND OTHER GREAT READS!

WWW.ALLISONALDRIDGE.COM

PLAYLIST

FIND THE FULL PLAYLIST & MORE ON SPOTIFY:
AUTHORALLISONALDRIDGE

ANGEL WITH A SHOTGUN

THE CAB

SALVATION

GABRIELLE APLIN

BEDROOM HYMNS

FLORENCE + THE MACHINE

ANGEL ON FIRE

HALSEY

TILL I FALL ASLEEP

JAYME DEE

RUNNING UP THAT HILL

KATE BUSH

GLORY AND GORE

LORDE

HORNS

BRYCE FOX

CROSSFIRE

STEPHEN

Welcome to Idelwood

Chaos is an angel who fell in
love with a demon.
–Christopher Poindexter

PROLOGUE

Bedtime stories are just nightmares masqueraded as childhood fantasy.

The words slipped off my older brother Nathaniel's tongue. Our usual bedtime routine of a story in a dimly lit corner was my favorite time of night. Both of us were crammed in a small room with four other foster kids who resided in the current home we had been placed in. Nate had always told me the stories our father once told him, legends of monsters passed down for generations. I didn't have the comfort of meeting our parents. They had been brutally murdered in the front yard of our home days after my birth. The bed always dipped in rapid movements at night when Nate would relive the execution-style killing he had witnessed.

"Tell me one more, Nate." I choked back a yawn before it could slip out from my lips. The clock struck nine o'clock. Two hours past our supposed bedtime.

"You'll have nightmares again, Lilypad." Nate spoke quietly, careful not to disturb the sleeping boy who lay inches from the grimy mattress we shared. His arms circled my petite frame, pulling me closer to his chest. He leaned down and rested the top of his chin near my hairline.

My nightmares came from his tales — I knew that just as well as he did. Nate's stories were filled with wickedly beautiful creatures who roamed the earth under our noses, seeking a place to rest. They were terrifying. But still, I always craved more.

"Just one more please?" I looked up toward him, jutting out my bottom lip in a deep pout. Nate sighed heavily but quickly gave in to the pleading puppy dog eyes which I directed towards him.

"All right, one more, that's it." Nate allowed me to get comfortable once again before he began his story. "Back before Angels walked among us, they would sit on the edge of large clouds, feet dangling down into the blue sky as they watched mortals down below commit their daily sins against God. That's when he decided to send his most trusted soldiers to walk among the sinners. God called these Angels the Elite. The creatures' beauty was unprecedented to anything the mortals had laid eyes upon. This caused corruption within his ranks, forcing him to make a decision. Strip every soldier who defied him of their wings, cursing them to live alongside the mortals for the rest of eternity. They were labeled the Fallen."

Tales of the Fallen always sent an uneasy feeling spiraling into the pit of my stomach. There it would stay until I found peace in sleep. Quiet slumber was interrupted by vivid nightmares of fallen soldiers whose inhumanly vibrant eyes shone in the darkness of my dreams. Those eyes held true power. Just the thought of them sent chills up my spine. Quick flashes of those who defied God played on a constant loop through my everyday life. The images caused paralyzing fear to course through my veins as the creatures from Nate's bedtime stories held me in the scenes, releasing me only once they were done playing with my mind. The feeling fueled my love for the stories even more with each one I was told.

I continued to listen to Nate's soothing voice speak of the Angelic creatures that walked alongside us. I did this until my eyes grew heavy.

The next morning, I noticed the spot next to me on the small mattress was cold to the touch and unslept in. Peeling myself from the dirty mattress, I searched through the vast hallways that connected the foster home. I searched them for hours.

Nate never returned to his side of the mattress.

CHAPTER ONE

I delwood, Colorado. A nowhere town which held strangers that would soon be my new foster family. This process was all too familiar to me after seventeen years of being in the system. Bouncing around from home to home was just another part of my yearly routine, not that I minded all that much. I had never had any real memories of a home — the word itself felt foreign on my tongue. The uncomfortable, scratchy material of the bus seat looked as if it had never been cleaned, making the entire cabin smell of feet. The odor amplified a headache I had acquired hours ago from an older man's snores. His wheezing had been ringing in my left ear since the bus had departed from the station thirteen hours ago.

Condensation droplets dripped slowly down the outside of the bus, making the forest blur by in a foggy mist. Nothing about the town I would soon be stuck in until my eighteenth birthday screamed excitement as we traveled deeper into the never-ending line of trees. I had managed to pry one interesting fact about the town from a newbie caseworker who had been shadowing mine the week of my transfer. Every inch of skin on her body had turned a bright red shade when she realized the secret she had told me. I had to hold back my fits of laughter that threatened to explode out of my chest.

Idelwood was a strange town where the pastor's daughter had sacrificed herself within the church walls, making the entire building cursed to outsiders looking in. Now that Idelwood was rumored to be haunted by ghosts of the past, no one wanted to move into a place where such a gruesome event had occurred. Even locals had been wary of staying after the incident. Being forced to remain within the town's borders could be interesting if I managed to dig out the real story from its residents.

The bus jerked to a stop, breaking me out of

my thoughts as I flew forward into the brightly colored seat before my hands could catch my fall. Blue polyester made contact with my face, sending a sickening crunch into the otherwise silent bus. I groaned, hands tracing underneath my nose to check for any signs of blood.

The pain of the impact finally hit me when the jaded bus driver's voice spoke over the loudspeakers. "Final stop for the night, folks, the outskirts of Idelwood."

Standing from my claimed spot, I leaned back, listening to my spine let out a few satisfying pops. My eyes wandered throughout the now empty bus—the older gentleman who had sat in the spot next to mine had slipped off without me noticing. I was one of three people remaining in the cabin of the bus. A teenage boy stood tall at the front, his raven hair tousled to one side as he threw on a beat-up leather jacket over his toned arms. There was also a woman dressed too nicely to be riding the bus, her strawberry-blonde hair stuck up in different directions from a slicked-back bun sitting at the crown of her skull. She kept her face hidden, watching the boy from the corner of her eye as he walked off the vehicle with ease. I slipped past her figure, not taking a second look at her face.

Colorado's chill October air hit my skin as I stepped off the last bus step, allowing me to come face-to-face with a dark figure who leaned up against the crooked bus station sign. The beginning of a dirt road which led into town was lit only by a small lantern light. It swayed back and forth in the chilling wind, masking the figure in heavy shadows.

"I can see we have a new face in town," the figure's deep voice said over the squeal of the departing bus's wheels.

"How would you know I'm new? I could just be visiting this sleepy little town you call Idelwood." I took a step closer to the figure as I spoke. The boy from moments ago stood against the bus sign. The light of his cigarette cast a yellow glow across his face, allowing me to see his dark lashes brush against pale skin.

As he inhaled a deep drag of the cigarette, his eyes found mine before his lips parted, smoke escaping into the night air. "Because no one smart ever visits

Idelwood, love."

I was taken back by the bluntness of his statement before his powerful gaze captivated my senses. The eyes staring back towards me were the most vibrant green I had ever seen — I felt as if I could swim within their color. Each fleck of green sparkled under the continuous swing of yellow light sitting above his head. Snapping out of the sudden trance, I rolled my eyes in his direction hastily turning on the heel of my boot towards the direction of town.

"I didn't catch your name, new girl," his booming voice hollered after me.

"That's because I didn't give it," I called back in his direction, leaving him mumbling obscenities to himself.

The beauty of the square shocked me when my feet reached the edge of the cobblestone that lined the road. Each building held an eerie vibe which dated back to the Victorian era. Flickering lampposts cast a gothic glow on each structure. Idelwood's main street was one long stretch with little shops placed on either side of the road. In the middle of the square sat a large statue of a young girl, a flower crown weaved intricately through her hair while a stone cross was held down in her hand by her left side almost covered by the white marble wings bursting from her back. The figure sent goosebumps across my skin—her eyes followed my every movement when I leaned to each side, trying to catch a better look at the statue's odd beauty. Every detail of this road screamed familiarity in the back of my mind. I felt as though I had been in this exact spot once before.

Shrugging off the feeling, I pulled myself away from the statue and made my way over to a small café which sat across from the figure. The warmth of the room fell over me as I stumbled through the ringing doorway.

"Hello, dearie, take a seat anywhere you would like and I'll be with you in a moment," a woman with a kind voice said to me from across the room. She stood taking a man's order, letting out a small laugh as he cracked a joke in her direction. My feet traveled silently towards the bar top that lined the far wall, and I claimed the second chair from the end as my own. I slowly scanned a menu which was clipped by a metal ring above the condiments, trying to make myself look busy to avoid any of the wandering eyes behind me.

"So, what will it be, dearie?"

The woman leaned down towards me, placing one hand against the countertop and allowing me to get a good look at her. She looked as though she was in her late twenties with long blonde hair tied securely in an elaborate braid. Her beauty radiated off the plain walls in the restaurant.

Finding my voice, I fumbled over my words. "Um, coffee will be fine, thank you."

I quickly ducked my head down, breaking eye contact with her. She let out a melodic laugh. "Oh, you kids and your coffee nowadays. Are you sure you don't want something to eat? You could use some meat on those bones of yours. Don't worry, I'll whip you up something quick. You'll love it."

She dashed away from me, the lemon colored dress she wore floating seamlessly behind her. I swallowed down the protest that rested in my throat before sinking back further onto the bar stool in defeat. The force of my body almost made me topple over in the process. Catching myself on the lip of the counter, I managed to sneak another look at the woman. A soft light pulsed around her as she moved to each customer in the café.

"Celia's always like that. You'll get used to it, though."

Jumping back at the sudden voice, I whipped my head in its direction. A girl around my age sat on the barstool next to me, her long, jet-black hair spilling out from a glossy ponytail. She was squinting up at a water spot that had made a home on the wall in front of us.

"She seems nice." My voice was timid as I spoke. I let my eyes leave the girl to my left and travel back in Celia's direction. My gaze tracked every movement curiously as she floated on air around the counter.

"That she is. Celia owns this place. I'm Aspyn Faye, by the way. It's wonderful to meet you. We don't get new people around here often."

I looked back towards her, startled by yet another pair of vibrant green eyes staring back at me. Gathering my composure, I took the hand she stuck out in front of herself before shaking it. "I'm Liliana

Caldwell, but I go by Lily."

"Well, Lily, I personally welcome you to Idelwood, the most boring place you will ever live." Aspyn flashed me a bright smile which had formed across her face, arms moving in a dramatic ta-da motion as she gestured toward the town just outside.

"Oh, now you stop that, Aspyn." Celia arrived back in front of us, swatting rapidly at Aspyn's hands after she set a plate of fries and a steaming cup of coffee in front of me. "This town is plenty fun, darling. You just have to know where to find the mischief."

"Celia, if you would like to enlighten me where this mischief would be, then that would be wonderful for my social life. I mean, I love hanging out with you all the time but I would love to be a little bit of a rebel while I still can. Plus, it will drive Asher, my brother, up the wall which is always entertaining." Aspyn began to pick at the fries on the plate, laughing briefly before she plopped one in her mouth.

"I wish you wouldn't pick off others' plates, Aspyn! It's not polite. But just you wait—I feel as though the mischief in this town will pick up soon enough." Celia winked towards me, letting both elbows lean against the bar top, one hand resting under her chin. Her comments made me giggle into the coffee I sipped. The steaming liquid traveled down my throat, warming my insides from the biting cold of the outside.

Aspyn rolled her eyes continuing to eat the fries. "Cee, I wish you wouldn't reprimand me about my manners. I'm trying to be a rebel here."

"Well, be a rebel when we aren't making first impressions, although I think your rebel days were long ago, dear." Celia snorted, turning to walk around the diner's countertop to greet the customers who had filtered through the chiming doors. I continued to listen to Aspyn explain almost every detail about the small town, and the only exciting aspect of this place was the many parties held by the teens of Idelwood. *I guess when there's not much to do around here, you have to make your own entertainment.*

Catching sight of the watch strapped around my wrist, I gasped in horror. Aspyn looked up, giving me a strange look. "Dammit, I was supposed to be at the house an hour ago."

Bile began to rise in my throat as the panic started to set in. The only thing I had to find my new home was the scrawled address on a gum wrapper my caseworker had thrown towards me that morning. I scrambled to gather my belongings, slamming a ten-dollar bill on the countertop. Praying it would be enough to cover the tab.

"No, you keep that. Think of it as a welcome-to-town present, plus I'm sure Aspyn can take you to where you need to go." Celia smiled sweetly towards me, swiftly folding the bill back into the palm of my hand. My movements were spastic as I tried to get the strap of my duffel bag around my body without tangling it, but I was failing miserably in the process.

"Oh no, really I'm sure I can manage." I continued to wrestle with the bag, huffing at it in annoyance.

"You might get lost and, believe me, even in small towns people end up missing all the time." Aspyn grinned in my direction. "Come on, let's go."

Jumping from the stool, her feet landed softly next to me before her hand latched down on my upper arm and dragged me from the café and into the frigid night air. As we walked, Aspyn explained the people who had requested to foster me were named William and Emaline Goodwin. They had a daughter name Brinley who was in the year below both Aspyn and me, making her a junior. Both of the Goodwins were high up on the town council and Emaline was the high school's current principal.

"So I got stuck with the people in town who aren't going to bend any of the rules and are a part of the high society of Idelwood." I broke out into a fit of laughter—making it through the night with people like them was highly unlikely.

Aspyn's nose scrunched up at my comment. She turned to walk backwards, making sure she could still see me in the process. "Not quite. Brinley could commit murder and no one would bat an eye at her."

"That's their own daughter—they have to put up with her, not me." My feet found some small rocks to kick down our path. I watched each one travel across the gravel road while we walked in silence for a while. I pulled my jacket closer to my body as the night's wind picked up, thrashing around us.

Aspyn came to a halt in front of a large, two-story home surrounded by a long iron gate that was enclosing the structure from outsiders. Vines from the ground laced through each hole of the metal, and an unsettling feeling washed over me as I continued to stare. Behind the opening, the entire structure was lit from top to bottom in a glowing, white light, which cast outwards onto the trees placed on either side of the stone walkway. This would be the place I called home for a little while, although everything sitting in front of my eyes made me feel out of place. I took in every elaborate detail of the building—never had I stayed in a home this nice, or even been in a rich-enough neighborhood to catch sight of one, too afraid to be labeled a thief for just existing on the street's presence. My eyes finished taking in the last brick of the house before the slight movement coming from behind a curtain sitting next to the front door caught my attention.

"Well, here you are 28290 Saints Lane, home of the Goodwins. I have to get going or I'll have to answer to my pigheaded brother and his overprotective nature, which will make my brain hurt with all his stupid questions. Hopefully, I'll see you tomorrow at school, although I would try to get out of that for as long as possible."

A small chuckle escaped my lips as I began to think of all the possible get-out-jail-free cards I could use.

Aspyn winked in my direction before starting down the dirt path. There was a light jump in her steps as she went. "Bye, L."

CHAPTER TWO

There's this funny feeling you get when you step foot into a small town. It grows inside even the darkest corners of your heart the moment you reach the city limits. Peacefulness washes over you when the quiet of kind smiles and gentle waves surround you rather than the hustle and bustle of a big city. The warmth flooding deep in the pit of your stomach can only be described as a sense of belonging.

Even as an outsider looking in on the locals, that feeling I so desperately craved was a sensation I clung to with all the strength I could muster. Towns like these were places I wanted so badly to live longer, but being in the system those chances were out of my life. Even in those towns I loved so much, one thing always mattered more than staying in them. Finding Nate once more. Becoming attached to small towns like Idelwood was a dangerous game I was not willing to play. It would only lead me to my own heartbreak in the end when I ventured on to another place.

My gaze held tight on Aspyn while she continued down the long dirt path. The strange girl had automatically accepted the newcomer with open arms as soon as I had stepped into Celia's café. No strange looks or questions came from her tongue like so many other curious "friends" I had once known. Aspyn was beyond beautiful, which along with her vivacious personality allowed her to stand out. Her energy gave me a slight high of excitement when I was in her presence. Now that same high I had just felt moments before drained from my body as quickly as she disappeared into the darkness of the night's shadows. Dread replaced the buzz as my eyes traveled back towards the brightly lit house in front of me.

I grasped the strap that hung around my body, gulping in icy air before forcing my feet to move up the paved walkway. The only sound floating around the night air as I reached the door came from a yellowed, cushioned porch swing, its linked chain letting out a ghostly creak in the breeze. Little white dots clouded my vision as a bright light illuminated the porch when the door swung open. A young girl around my age stood tall in the doorway, straight white-blonde hair hanging all the way down her back, stopping just above her hips. A pair of striking blue eyes stared at me in a venomous glare—if looks could kill, this one surely would have knocked me dead.

"I really wish you would refrain from dragging the trash around the front of the house." She crossed her arms in front of her chest. Tension stuck in sticky globs against the doorway. Neither of us made the first move, eyes locked in an intense battle. Nothing about the girl who stood in front of me frightened me—she was the perfect example of being all bark with no bite to back it up.

"I'm Lily. Your parents are fostering me for the next few months." My wrist flicked up in her direction, wanting to cut the tension around us in half. As my fingers extended out fully, she flinched away from them like the hand was going to poison her with a simple handshake.

She composed herself back into the mean-girl disguise she wore. Her voice shook as she spoke. "Unfortunately for the rest of us. I'm Brinley. Just stay out of my sight and we won't have a problem."

A devilish smile flashed across her face before she turned on the heel of her shoes, blonde hair floating after her as she stalked into the adjacent room, leaving me awkwardly standing in the middle of the doorway. My feet stood planted against the barrier, not sure if I wanted to cross into the home. Voices floated around the banister of the staircase before a man in what looked like his late thirties descended the steps. The woman following close behind was slender with short hair that curled at the ends, the coloring identical to the girl who had passed through moments ago. The man let out a gruff laugh towards the woman, allowing me to see his perfectly chiseled cheeks and dirty blonde hair. A phone was held securely in his grasp, and his ice-blue eyes left the device's screen for a moment, catching with mine.

The woman followed his stare, locking dead on my shivering figure.

"Oh, Liliana, I didn't hear the door. I'm so glad you arrived safe and sound. We were beginning to worry you weren't going to show." The woman glided down each step with ease, landing directly in front of me seconds later. Her hands clasped in front of her face while watery eyes examined me. "You are just as beautiful as I thought you would be."

Slender arms enclosed my body as she pulled me in for a brief hug before drawing back to get a closer look at me. Her wide eyes combed over me as though I was the first person she had ever laid eyes on. The urge to squirm underneath her stare was causing every muscle in my body to tense. Most of the people who choose to foster me barely gave me a glance, let alone knew my name when I arrived in their homes. It was almost protocol for a long list of rules and their corresponding consequences to be barked toward me before sending me from their sights. That was usually one of the only times I had any contact with them. The more you blended, the better off you were in the system.

"It's nice to meet you, Mr. and Mrs. Goodwin." I forced a bright smile to flash across my face as I spoke. My caseworker would have shed a few tears of joy if she saw it.

Mr. Goodwin let out a booming laugh. "Oh please, Liliana, call us Will and Emma."

"All right, but only if you call me Lily. I despise my full name."

"I think we can manage that." Will winked at me, striding down the staircase. "You must be tired from your journey. Emma will show you up to your room, and we will all talk more in the morning."

He smiled once more before looking back down towards the phone he held in his hand. Emma began making small talk about the town's high school, explaining all the events that they would be hosting in the coming semester. I tried my best to look interested in her words, slowly nodding my head once every couple of points. My feet trailed behind her. A large wall lining the stairway was dotted with family pictures that showed off the many memories the Goodwins had enjoyed together as a family. We traveled down a long corridor before arriving in front of the last door in the hall.

Emma turned her body towards me. "No one has ever stayed in this room. It was only for guests, but we don't seem to have many of those coming to Idelwood. I want this to be your home as well, so feel free to change anything to the way you would like it."

"I'm sure it will be perfect, Emma." I played with my fingers nervously, trying to hold the woman's gaze. It was a tic I had never grown out of — Nate had always reprimanded me for it. Seconds later, though, he would end up laughing at his terrible ability to scold me. Nate could never take anything too seriously when it came to me. The jokes and games were never-ending with him.

"Well, I will let you rest. If you need anything from us, don't be afraid to ask for it, Lily." Emma began down the hall, rounding the corner only to poke her head back around the wall a moment later. "Oh, and towels are under the sink."

Then she was out of my sight once more. I gripped down on the cold metal of the door, pushing it open to reveal one of the most beautiful rooms I had ever laid eyes on. The walls were painted a light lilac color with elegant gray flowers decorating the room. A birchwood dresser sat against one side of the wall, mirroring the matching bed, which held a white comforter on it, making the piece look like a cloud. Stepping further into the room, I allowed the air conditioning to pull the door closed behind me. Turning toward the connected bathroom, I tossed my duffel onto the bedspread. A shower was exactly the thing I needed after the long bus ride.

Water tumbled from the showerhead, sending steam to fog the mirror as the liquid warmed to a reasonable temperature. I stepped into the small, stone-covered shower, letting the stream of fiery water pound against my back, the heat beginning to work out knots I had acquired from the cramped bus seat. Every trouble I'd had washed down the drain, along with the grime and dirt which coated my skin. Stepping from the shower, I wrapped myself in a fresh towel. My hand reached out, smearing the steam-coated mirror to reveal a girl peering back at me.

The girl staring at me was someone who never

truly matched the person I felt I was inside. Innocent, sea-blue eyes with pin-straight, strawberry-blonde hair mirrored the features I held. She looked like a girl who didn't know how cruel the world could be. This girl in front of me was someone who had friends and attended high school dances in hopes of winning the crown awarded at the end. Those were daydreams I could never have. I was just Lily, the new girl in every city who hid behind the crowd, careful not to be noticed by the others around her. The girl staring back at me wasn't me at all. All I wanted was to find out how to make the girl in the mirror match who I was on the inside — no town was ever going to show me that.

Daylight peeked through the window, the next morning shining straight into my eyes. I had fallen asleep with ease last night, no tossing or turning due to being in a new place. It felt like the first time in a long time I had slept well in an unfamiliar place. The clank of dishware mixed with the soft drone of music that flooded into the hallways of the home. I stepped from the warm protection of my bed, toes curling into the cool hardwood as they hit the floor.

Making my way out of the room, my body stood frozen outside the door, debating if I truly wanted to face the Goodwins. Before I could retreat back into bed, Emma rounded the corner. She jumped slightly at my odd presence in the hallway.

"Lily, I see you're an early riser." She winked at me. "Something we have in common. Would you like some breakfast?"

"Sure, thank you." My hand reached up and tucked a stray piece of hair that had fallen from the messy bun sitting on the top of my head behind my ear.

"Well, come on then or it will get cold. Also, this will be the perfect time to discuss something with you." Emma motioned for me to follow her, making my stomach drop. I tried to keep up with her as she took the stairs two at a time, reaching the kitchen shortly after. Emma gestured towards the barstools which lined the countertop. I took the seat in the first one, waiting for her to speak again.

She turned back towards the stove, beginning to prepare a plate of food. "I know you probably want to wait as long as you can before you jump straight into a new school. However, I am the principal of the high school…"

Her voice began to trail off into the silent kitchen. Placing a plate of food in front of me, her hands shook, hesitating before resting one on my shoulder. Emma's eyes held a certain fear in them. I watched them travel between her hand and my face. She looked as if there would be serious repercussions followed by touching me. Her daughter's actions from last night flashed across my memories.

"I can start today, Emma, if that's what you were hinting at. I don't mind."

Picking up the orange juice in front of me, I took a sip before continuing my thought. "Just know my transcripts are not the best, from being transferred as many times as I have been."

I dropped my eyes from her gaze as she began to chuckle, rapidly retracting her hand from my shoulder. "I am sure you are a very bright girl, Lily. All you need is to get your footing in a new school and you will excel. I can help you in any way you need."

The rest of breakfast was filled with sporadic

conversations about different aspects of mine and Emma's lives. Emma was a bubbly person who continued to go out of her way in making me feel welcomed in her home. She was leaning on the counter, talking about how much she enjoyed living in this small town, when she sucked in a sharp breath. "It's almost seven, how did I not notice? You need to go get ready."

Immediately I was pushed from the stool and up the stairs to get ready for the day. Once we had reached the top of the steps, Emma shot off in the other direction, leaving me alone in the middle of the hall. Reaching the bedroom in a matter of seconds, I dressed in a simple black T-shirt and a pair of ripped blue jeans I adored. It was plain, but more importantly, it would help me blend in as much as the new girl could on her first day. I laced up my boots before grabbing a worn jean jacket to throw on. By the time I reached the front entrance, I had tied off my hair in a side braid, watching as Emma came rushing down the steps after me, gracefully balancing an arm full of binders.

"Are you ready?" Her question came out in

breathy whisper. Taking in my nod, she turned herself towards the second floor, calling back up the staircase, "Brinley, I swear if you are not down here in five seconds, then you are grounded for the rest of eternity."

"I'm coming, Mother. There's no need for the dramatics this early in the morning," Brinley answered back to her mother, not bothering to look up from the phone she had pressed into her nose. She was dressed in the shortest cut-off jean shorts I had ever seen. I knew by just looking at them they wouldn't pass any dress code, and the navy-blue tank top was nearly painted on the top half of her body, leaving nothing to the imagination. How she was not going to freeze in the fall air was beyond me.

"Darling, I am your mother. I earned the right to be dramatic at any time of the day if I so please. Now we have to get going or—" Emma glanced down at her watch. "Well, we are already late. Let's go."

I hurried behind both of them into a car while Emma began to lecture her daughter about the tasks that they had to do later on. The entire drive, the conversation stayed directed towards Brinley, who was too absorbed in her phone to acknowledge her mother. Aspyn hadn't been lying about Brinley—she was one of a kind. The car pulled into a parking space labeled "Employee" when we arrived at the school. Barman High School was the only school even remotely close to Idelwood, which meant all the town's adolescents gathered here five days a week to stick their noses in each other's business. A comforting thought to the new girl who wanted nothing to do with the gossip ring.

The school was a large brick structure with a bell tower sitting at the top. The bell was enclosed in a marble-accented barrier, bringing a classic touch to the century-old building. Emma and Brinley filed out of the car, and I followed behind them stumbling from the seat belt I had managed to tangle myself around.

Emma turned toward me with a giant smile plastered across her face. "Now, I know that it can be intimidating going to a new school, but I promise you will love it here."

Highly doubting her promise, I only nodded in

her direction. We began up the stairs of the school and began into a front office where Emma was greeted upon arrival by her student secretary. A wooden door with her name engraved into it was hidden in the back corner of the large space. Emma shuffled through the papers that coated her desk until she found exactly what she was looking for.

"Aha, here it is. Lily, this is your schedule along with a map of the school. Since you are a senior, you will have a study period in the library the last hour of the day, which we highly recommend all students attend." Emma's lips quirked up at the corners in a faint smile before she looked at me with knowing eyes.

"Okay, I'll try to be there all the time."

"Also, here is your locker combination and the books you will need for your classes. There are supplies in your locker, but if you need anything else, please let me know." Emma continued to stack things on top of one another until my arms were full. Her eyes glanced up at the clock hanging on the wall. "You should probably run along. Class starts soon."

Starting towards the doorway, I stopped in my tracks as Emma called my name once more. "Have a wonderful day."

She sent a soft smile before going back to the work that was placed in front of her.

"Thank you, Emma. I really appreciate it

CHAPTER THREE

The journey to my locker was easy enough to navigate, allowing me to gather everything for the first class of the day slowly. I listened to the bolts of the door whine as the metal pried itself open. Inside lay a tan messenger bag filled with anything that Emma thought I might need for the school day. I tossed each book on a shelf sitting above my forehead with one hand as my eyes scanned over the printed schedule in my other. "First-period history with Professor Erickson," it read in large, bold letters. A class that I had always excelled in.

Running my fingertips along the spine of the appropriate book, I gripped it in my hand before shutting the locker. Eyeing the map, I tried to make out the miniature letters to find the correct classroom. My feet carried me forward slightly, only to be knocked back, running into what felt like a ton of bricks. Losing balance, I toppled backward onto my behind, groaning as the pain set in.

"Watch where you're going, new girl," a male's voice dripping with anger said towards me.

A smart comment I was getting ready to throw back in his direction caught in the back of my throat—one high-pitched squeak was the only thing that slipped through my lips. A boy with burnt-red hair and gorgeous blue eyes towered over my figure, tension racking his body as he stared down at me like a bug he was ready to squash. Rolling my shoulders back, as I tried to gather my composure before speaking. "I'm sorry, I didn't see you there."

His blue eyes flew into the back of his head. "Obviously or you wouldn't have run into me. Just watch it next time."

He stalked away, causing me to yank my fingers back before his stomping feet could mash them into the linoleum floor.

"You don't have to be such a jackass about it." My

voice was barely audible, making it so only I could hear my own mumbles. His head snapped back towards my direction, a dirty look covered his face. Confusion swarmed my brain, not understanding how he could have heard me. I shook my head to the side, trying to brush off any paranoia that had gathered around me. Standing from the floor, I ventured down the hallway to the correct classroom, reaching it as the warning bell rang out. In the back corner, I could see Aspyn sitting at a table, chewing on the back of her pen while she concentrated on the notebook she was writing in.

"You must be Liliana Caldwell," an older gentleman spoke through a warm smile plastered on his face. Perched on the bridge of his nose were large, round glasses which he peered over to look at me. "I'm Professor Erickson. It's wonderful to have you in my class. You can have a seat anywhere you would like."

"It's just Lily, thank you."

"Well, Lily, welcome to Idelwood." Professor Erickson turned his back towards me, returning to a desk in that curved into the side of the room. I took this opportunity to make a mad dash for the opposite corner which held Aspyn.

"Thank God you're in this class," I said, a breathy laugh slipping through my lips before I glided into the chair across from hers.

Her smiling face popped up from her writing. "Well hello, stranger. You got forced to come to school. I guess when you have the principal as your foster mom, what can you expect?"

"Yeah, you're right about that one. Although I'm just glad you're here, or I would have had to awkwardly wander around to find a seat."

"True, I mean I am the coolest person you'll meet in this town." Aspyn's green eyes twinkled with mischief as she winked at me. Before she could continue rambling, her eyes wandered towards another person who slid into the seat next to her. "Oh, Lily, this is my twin brother, Asher."

Aspyn's manicured nail pointed towards the boy next to her. Unfortunately for me, this was the same boy I had encountered at the bus stop the night before. No wonder they had the same matching vibrant green eyes.

"Why hello, love. Long time, no see." Asher's lips pulled up into a slight smirk.

Aspyn looked between us in confusion. "Am I missing something here?"

"I had the pleasure of meeting your brother last night at the bus stop just outside of town." Disgust played against my words. I allowed my gaze to hold Asher's for a moment more before I switched it to Aspyn's confused look. "He is quite the charmer, I have to say."

Aspyn turned towards her twin, taking the notebook she had been writing in previously, and smacked Asher's arm with enough force for him to cringe upon impact. "Ash, why do you always have to be such an ass to new people? I apologize for him, but I promise he isn't that bad. I have had to deal with him since birth, and he is still around for the time being. He's lucky I haven't killed him yet."

"Well, there was that one time, sister, that was a pretty close call."

Aspyn gasped in mock horror at Asher's amused face. "We were three! He is still very bitter about the time I 'accidentally' gave him a concussion when I pushed him out of a tree. Although there isn't really any proof I was the one who pushed him."

"I don't blame you, I would have pushed him out of a tree if I could have just from the first conversation we had. You had to put up with him for three years before shoving him." My eyes were trained on Asher as I spoke, turning towards Aspyn to match her wicked grin as I finished.

"You don't like me much do you, love?" Asher leaned towards me, letting his hands rest inches from mine.

My eyes flicked back to him, trying not to be hypnotized by how vibrantly green his eyes were. I matched his movements. "I haven't decided yet."

His lips curled up, ready to continue the playful banter we had going, but his words were cut off by the ring of the bell. Whatever he had to say dissolved from his tongue, causing the three of us to turn towards Professor Erickson who was writing notes on the whiteboard.

"We are diving straight into our next chapter today, which happens to be the history of our town. Idelwood has some rich history scattered throughout the centuries, and I want each one of you to write a research paper about an approved topic. Reading thirty-one of the same papers is not something I am very keen on. The research will be conducted throughout the semester within the groups you are in today. Feel free to choose a specific topic amongst your table mates, making it easier to work together."

The class let out one simultaneous groan, making him chuckle. "It's not even eight, and you are all already giving me my favorite sound of the day."

Professor Erickson continued his lecture throughout the rest of the class period, not that I could concentrate on his words with a pair of green eyes burning a hole into the back of my skull. I didn't dare look back to meet his gaze afraid that it would be impossible to look away once sucked into those green orbs.

The shrill of the bell made me jump. I gripped down on the side of the table, standing up on wobbly legs. My eyes wandered around the room, trying to find a way to sprint towards the door without being noticed by Aspyn, but her arm looped around mine and pulled me into the crowded hallway, dismissing any escape I had come up with. "What class do you have next?"

Looking down at my schedule, I said, "Um, English with Mrs. Becluse."

"She is a bore, makes me want to fall asleep every class period."

Continuing down the hallways, I turned my head back around to search for Asher, but he wasn't anywhere to be found through the sea of people. Ignoring the disappointment that settled in my stomach, I rotated back towards Aspyn, allowing her to navigate me towards my next class.

The rest of the day went by painfully slow until it was finally time for study period. The idea of sitting in a library full of seniors who had nothing better to do than gossip amongst one another about the new girl sitting just inches from them made me want to hurl. Instead, I made a sharp left towards an illuminated exit sign, pushing through the door. The sudden icy air pricked my skin, and I pulled my jean jacket closer towards my body, quickly taking the stairs leading towards a path into the forest.

Hesitation crossed my mind, reminding me that

all the great horror movies start with this stupid idea of wandering around the woods alone, but I pushed it aside and walked further into the trees. Being in school for hours as the whispers floated around my back had taken a toll on my common sense. There was nothing special about the forest as I explored, just some trees, a lot of bushes, and a rabbit or two rustling within them. I don't know how long I ended up walking the trail, but every minute that passed by allowed me to clear my head in the peace and quiet.

The path ended, opening up to a deserted clearing where a run-down church sat across a warped wooden bridge. The wood twisted down, almost hitting the bottom of a riverbank where water had once run through—now it was just a dried-up hole in the ground. The structure was beautiful with large vines and growth crawling up all sides; a place that had once been used every Sunday for worship was now long forgotten.

Crossing the connecting bridge, I made sure to follow the wooden planks that had not rotted with age. The pressure of my feet still made them creak in protest with every step, threatening to give away if they so pleased. A large, cracked bell swung back and forth within the steeple, making a slight clunk in the wind. The church's double doors hung off their hinges, making the whitewashed wood hit against itself. I started into the church, astonished by the contradiction the outside held to its inside.

Everything was in pristine condition as if the building was used weekly for multiple Sunday services. Wooden pews lined each side of the church, and not a single speck of dust clung to their shiny wooden surface. One large bowl holding what normally would be holy water cast a rainbow on the backsplash of the church's wall, the sun making the liquid swirl around in a continuous sparkle. A strange sensation of déjà vu washed over me while I weaved in and out of each pew, taking in each immaculate piece of wood. This place felt like a distant memory that made something inside of me spark alive again. The feeling felt hungry, wanting to be allowed out to play.

Stopping at the front of the church, I started towards the bowl of water in front of me, fingertips running along the rim of the bowl lightly. They grew closer to the bottom with each circle around the dish. When the liquid finally brushed up against my skin, a burning sensation flooded into my pores. I ripped my hand from the bowl, shaking the limb as the fiery pain subsided. Flipping my hand palm side up, I glanced down at it like a foreign object — there were no visible burns on my skin. My brain reeled, trying to grasp at any explanation for what had just occurred. I could hear my rapid heartbeats pounding in my ears as the feeling of being watched surrounded me.

Quickly I snapped my head towards the doorway, expecting a figure to be staring back. No one was standing in the rectangular moss-covered cutout. As I gulped back the fear, my eyes traveled around the church's perimeter, double-checking for the presence of unwanted eyes, but again I found no one staring back.

The hairs on the back of my neck stood up straight as I stared blankly towards the entrance of the church. This town had its secrets. They hid in the darkest shadows, riddles speaking softly towards the outsiders wandering through, ones that strangers should never hear. All secrets are deemed to be told sooner or later—they would spill out the cracks of any well-put town if they were ready to be heard.

"What do you think you are doing?" A rough voice echoed through the hall. My body jumped in fright as someone spoke through the thick silence surrounding us.

The pristine church which was laid out in front of me began to melt away with a blink of the eye. Everything reflected the outside. Broken pews were sprawled out around the church, and colorful graffiti painted every inch of the once-pure white walls. The bright words talked of the devil and sacrifices to their master, and each line I read sent a shiver down the base of my spine. I glanced down, realizing that where the bowl once stood was replaced by broken glass beer bottles scattered across the floor. The redheaded boy from earlier stood in the doorway of the now-ruined church. His arms were crossed against his broad chest while an inhuman grin stared back towards me.

Clearing my throat, I stood tall in the destruction. "I could ask you the same thing, couldn't I?"

He leaned against the door frame, running one hand through the red locks tousled on top of his head. "No, actually you can't."

"Oh, do you hang around abandoned churches often? Or is it that you are just so above my questioning?" I said, lacing my arms together. My mind was on a mission to find a way to get some sort of answer out of him. Did he follow me out here? Why was I being in an abandoned church any of his concern? Questions bounced around my thoughts, daring to spill from my lips. I clenched my jaw together, waiting for him to speak once more.

"I belong in a place such as this. Your very presence damages the sacred ground you stand upon." He chuckled darkly. "You are a strange little thing, aren't you? Mumbling to yourself acting as if there are imaginary pews in a church that has been abandoned for years. In the very spot, you stand is where the pastor's daughter sacrificed herself. Well, I should say above the spot you stand."

His finger traced a horizontal line above my head,

smirking as he watched my face drop in horror. I felt sick at the idea of lingering around a place where a tragedy had occurred. No matter how curious I was about the pastor's daughter's death, I wasn't that curious.

"You're an ass," I mumbled, shoving my way around the wreckage that lay haphazardly around us. The crunch of broken glass spoke volumes underneath my shoes in the eerily quiet church.

"What was that, darling?" His smirk deepened as he looked down at me. The urge to reach up to smack the grin from his face was hard to resist.

"Move."

He chuckled at my failed attempts to get around his body, standing frozen in place and making it impossible for me to get past him. "What's the magic word, darling?"

"Move the hell out of my way," I spat venom towards him through clenched teeth.

His gaze traveled down my body, scanning every piece of exposed skin he could before returning to my face seconds later. In one swift movement, he stepped out of the doorway. "Close enough."

Not giving him a chance to change his mind I made my escape towards the bridge, this time not bothering to watch where I stepped. Each board cracked under my pounding steps as I dashed across its fragile surface. The redhead's deep voice called back towards me as my feet reached the other side of the arch. The way his voice floated around the forest floor sent chilling goosebumps across my skin. "Hey, darling. My name's Finley. Finley Blackbourne."

I spun around to face the boy watching me from the front of the church, but he stood coolly against the worn building. I matched his gaze, snarling out my response—the deadly tone was one I didn't recognize as myself. "I didn't ask you for your name, and I'm no one's darling."

Then I ran into the woods, darkness encompassing the trees as the sun descended from the sky. Shadow figures played in the dark, speaking to the trees quietly through snapping branches and low rumbles. Each sound wave built on top of one another, sending a surge of fear through my body. I continued to run away from the church, not bothering to look back towards it or the strange boy it held.

CHAPTER FOUR

Shallow breathing escaped my lips as I finally staggered onto the street in front of the Goodwins' house. My thoughts raced around each other, trying to make sense of the events that had just occurred within the church's walls.

Finley's face flashed across my vision — his smug look would haunt my dreams for weeks along with the abandoned church that changed in a blink of an eye. Nothing made sense as I tried to rationalize an explanation for the sudden change the church had taken on. A feeling that was festering in the pit of my stomach felt like a warning about this town. Something was very wrong with this place, and I was going to figure it out one way or another.

I plucked out the phone that sat in my back pocket,

and the screen lit up, reading three p.m. Locking the device a couple times, I tried to get it to read the correct time. With each click of the lock button, the time stayed the same. That was impossible. I had left school hours ago, and the sun had begun to set when I had made my way back into the tree line of the forest. The sun melting down into the sky had looked like cotton candy at a carnival while shadow figures danced in the trees, making every crunch even more terrifying than the last. Still, I stared down at the device in my hand as it began to let out a shrill ring. The sudden sound sent my heart into overdrive as it slammed against my rib cage. The caller ID read unknown.

Bringing the phone up to my ear with shaky hands, I let out a whisper to the person on the other line. "Hello?"

Fear rushed through the wind as I stood in the middle of the dirt road where no one could be seen for miles.

"What are you doing right now?" A cheery tone rang out from the other side of the phone. The name which matched the voice on the other end of the phone was on the tip of my tongue.

Taking in a shaky breath, I spoke a little louder this time. "Who is this?"

"I'm offended that you don't recognize the greatest person this boring town has to offer, I me—."

"Aspyn," I said. A winded laugh broke through a smile that had formed on my face as I listened to her continue rambling off compliments about herself. Knowing that it was only Aspyn on the other end of the phone made my anxiety melt away. Her bubbly personality added a slight pep in my step as I continued to listen to her one-way conversation.

"You guessed correctly, darling L," she said. The pet name Finley had used left a bitter taste in my mouth as it found its way into my ear. "You never answered my question."

"I'm walking back towards the Goodwins' house at the moment. Why?" I answered. Aspyn's squealing voice made me pull the device away from my ear—that girl could definitely blow an eardrum if needed.

"Well, that's perfect, because I am kidnapping

you tonight. One of the famous bonfires I told you about is happening, and we are all going. I'll see you tonight, so be ready! Bye, L." The line went dead. Cutting the call short without giving me a chance to protest against her wishes was probably the best thing she could have done.

Emma's car was not in the drive, meaning that I was locked out until someone arrived back home. Rolling my eyes in annoyance, I wandered through the iron gate in front of the house. I began to rummage through the bag Emma had left in the locker earlier this morning as I sat on one of the homes front steps. Something shone in the sun at the bottom of the bag, blinding me in the process. Pushing back the books to get to the object, I brought it out to examine. In the light, it sparkled like a piece of golden glass, sending little glittering lights around the front porch.

The strange piece was broken through the middle, leaving jagged lines against the metal of a broken medallion. I dug around the bottom of the bag once more, trying to find the other half, but it was nowhere to be seen. My thumb rubbed along the uneven rim, trying to brush away the corrosion that had built up over time. Underneath all the weathering, words were etched into the remaining half:

"Mix a Demon with an Angel, you get a Night Monster, and with the child, chaos ignites in both heaven and hell. She will be the death…"

The line was cut off where the piece had been snapped in half. A shiver traveled up my back and the paranoia that had followed me from the church grounds had once again returned with a newfound vengeance. Stories which had haunted my dreams for most of my childhood flitted through my mind. I spun the strange medallion around my fingertips, and it shone with every twirl.

Remembering Nate was like ripping open a wound just to pour a continuous stream of hydrogen peroxide into the cut. The stinging reminder of how he left in the night without even considering how it would kill the adolescent sister who slept in the bed next to him. He left her to fend off the monsters in the world instead of the ones within his stories. That hurt shaped me, made me stronger even with the bad it had brought on. It taught me a lot about who I was. When I had realized Nate was gone that early morning, I had made a promise to myself that I would find him if it was the last thing I did.

Brinley's loud stomping broke me out of my trance. She shoved past me before making her way into the house, leaving the door wide open behind her. Turning to peer over my shoulder, I could see blonde hair swing around the corner of the last stair. The harsh air she brought along with her cut through me like a sharp knife. Finding my feet once more, I stalked up towards my room and threw myself on to the bed in one fluid motion as the door slammed shut behind me. Shoving the nearest pillow over my ears, I was determined to drown out Brinley's blaring rap music which rang out in harsh beats through the home.

The ring of my phone jolted me awake later on, making it feel like I was falling from a dream I couldn't remember. As I gripped the white comforter tightly, my breathing evened out before I ripped the device from my pocket to see what had scared me awake. The blinding light of Aspyn's text announcing she was waiting outside made me groan in frustration.

I climbed out of bed, looking myself up and down

in the full-length mirror. I still looked presentable even after the nap. No one would be looking at the new girl tonight when they were drowning their livers in way too much vodka. I slipped my feet into my boots, making my way towards the blonde-haired girl's room before using my knuckles to tap against the wood that separated us. Brinley's glare bored into mine when she finally swung open the door.

"What do you want?" Her poisonous voice broke through the silent hallway.

I let my eyes watch her for a moment more, the tapping of her foot signaling she was growing impatient with my silence. "Let your parents know I went out with some friends, or don't. It doesn't really matter to me."

Swiftly turning my back to the girl, I could hear a sickening laugh come from her lips, before Brinley spoke again. "Like they would even care. They don't even care about where their own daughter is half the time. Although you have always been their top priority."

Silence followed. Hoping for a response, she let

each word sink into me before the door slammed shut with a loud bang. Frozen in place, I ran my hand over my flushed skin. Every word that the locals spoke continued to baffle me. Quietly, I stumbled down the stairs and out the front door, catching sight of both twins standing just outside of the iron gate. Aspyn was practically bouncing around in a circle. Her schoolgirl getup had been replaced with a nightclub look. A short, black leather skirt laced up the front while her white shirt was ripped in all the right places, careful not to give too much away. The knee-high boots she had on made me wonder how she seemed to be balancing on the thin heel attached to the back while jumping around in excitement on the loose gravel road.

Her brother was leaning up against the column attached to the gate, not amused with his twin's antics but trying his best to look like he was entertaining them. Asher's eyes caught mine when I slipped through the small opening of the gate, his gaze tracking my every movement.

Aspyn's loud screech caused me to turn my attention in her direction, half expecting to see her toppled over in the dirt. She stood in front of me, a horrified look crossing her face as she scanned over my figure. "What are you wearing, L?"

"What do you mean?" I said. It was the same thing I had last seen her in. My eyes traveled down to my jeans and T-shirt before looking back at her.

Aspyn tightly grabbed my wrist in her hand before yanking me down the road. "You *cannot* go to your first party, or any party for that matter, looking like that, Liliana. You would be crucified by everyone if you showed up in the same outfit they saw you in at school today. You are so lucky to have me as a friend."

I threw back a glare towards the low laugh that came from Asher who was trailing close behind the two of us. He gave me an apologetic look, not wanting to get in the way of his twin sister's rampage as she continued to ramble on. Sighing at him, I couldn't blame him. Aspyn was a force of nature at the moment, one who would knock down anyone who blocked her path. Our synchronized footsteps ended up in front of the same café I had stumbled into just last night. Celia looked up from the counter she was cleaning in confusion when the door burst open, hitting the wall that sat behind it. Aspyn dragged me along through the tables and chairs while Asher followed smoothly after.

"Where's the fire, loves?" Celia was trying to hold in her laughter in as I tripped over a chair Aspyn led me into, her hand leaving my wrist in the process. The force of Aspyn's disappearance caused me to topple even farther forward, almost clipping my forehead on a table, but strong hands caught me around my hips. Asher's fiery touch burned into my bones, sending that warmth straight to a blush forming on my cheeks. I looked towards the boy behind me as our faces sat just inches apart from each other. Asher's green eyes flicked down towards my lips, and I could almost taste them as they hovered over mine.

"Thanks," I said, my voice barely above a whisper. Deciding to spare me from a smart comment about my sudden embarrassment, Asher set me back on my feet and smiled down at me. His fingers lingered for a second longer, brushing the small piece of skin that my raised shirt had exposed. Sparks danced underneath his touch causing me to choke back a gasp. I darted in the direction of Aspyn, who was speaking to Celia, to escape humiliating myself even more.

"I have to fix L up for the bonfire tonight because she thought this was acceptable." Aspyn's accusing thumb gestured in my direction.

"I'm standing right here, you know!"

Celia laughed at the commotion we were causing, waving us off. "You girls go in the back and get ready. Asher, you can keep me company. I have some questions I want to dig out of you."

Celia's knowing eyes wandered from Asher's back towards mine. Another wave of embarrassment flooded my pale skin in red splotchy patches. The discomfort was short lived with the sudden yank of Aspyn's pull. I looked back towards the two traitors with pleading eyes, but all Celia did was laugh in my direction before turning back to speak with Asher.

Aspyn navigated me to the back of a storage room, where a door sat on the far wall almost camouflaged into the white paint. Behind the door sat a large living room decorated in colorful tapestry. Each one draped down against one another, meeting on the floor in a pool of vibrant colors. A small couch sat in the middle of the room with stools sitting on either side of the armrests. The room looked like the inside of a genie's bottle in cartoon films.

"What is this place?" I asked in awe as we traveled farther into the strange, little house. Aspyn let go of my wrist once we arrived in a small bedroom that was painted pure white. It almost hurt to look at the walls against the sparkling chandelier hanging above us. There was no furniture in the room except for a large vanity that lay against the back wall while a fluffy pink rug covered the hardwood floor, making the room seem fuller than it was.

Aspyn began to rummage through the closet which sat of the right wall. "This is Cee's house. I keep extra clothes here for when Asher and I are fighting. And more often than not, I hide out here until we stop arguing."

Her hands continued to look through the different articles of hanging clothing before she found what she was looking for. Aspyn's devious grin turned in my direction. "Put this on. And there is no use in arguing with me, so I wouldn't even try."

My mouth closed quickly, silencing the protest that was about to tumble out. A silk piece of clothing was shoved in my hands before I was thrust behind a large wooden divider in the corner next to the vanity. Aspyn continued to talk while I slipped into the outfit she had picked for me. I managed to tune her out halfway through my task. The piece she wanted me to wear was a dress, it started white but slowly, as if it was dipped into the blackest of night, the colors melded together through the fabric, shades coming together beautifully at just the right time. My hands smoothed out the silk material, tugging at the bottom as I realized how short it truly was. The fabric barely reached over mid-thigh, riding up every time I stepped in any direction. My fingers wrestled with both ends of the dress, engaging in a frantic tug-of-war to make sure I wasn't giving away too much skin.

"I look ridiculous, Aspyn." I traveled around the divider, still trying to get the dress to work with me.

"Hmm, I beg to differ. I don't think Idelwood is ready for you, Liliana Caldwell," Aspyn said. She stood in front of me, smirking in a way that made me want to run straight back behind the divider to hide. Before I could even make the first move to flee, Aspyn tossed a leather jacket across the room, and it smacked me directly in the face. I guessed there really was no way of getting out of tonight.

CHAPTER FIVE

"W"ould you stop pulling at your dress and messing with your hair, Liliana?" Aspyn scolded me as we walked through the endless trees lining the outskirts of town. She began to pick at her cuticles in an attempt to cure her boredom as we continued on.

The church incident had set my senses on edge—every shadow that played silently in the night's darkness made my stomach twist with uneasiness. This was something Asher had obviously picked up on, his penetrating gaze tracking my movements once again, ready to jump into action should any of the shadows decide not to be shadows anymore. I ran my hand through the freshly curled hair, once more gripping at the roots in the process. Aspyn's glare crossed my eyesight, making me rip my hand from the pieces immediately. She had spent an hour smoking out my eyes with dark eye shadows after curling my strawberry-blonde hair into loose ringlets. Messing up her masterpiece was not going to end well for me. I felt like I had just become her own personal Barbie doll.

"I just don't wear things like this, Aspyn! None of this is me, plus I don't know whether I should be pulling this up or down. There is way too much skin showing!" I said, my voice coming out in a higher pitch than intended. I wrapped my hands around both sides of the zipper on the leather jacket, trying my best to cover myself up.

"Ugh, you look great. Stop worrying so much!" She huffed in my direction, skipping off ahead, leaving Asher and me alone in the middle of the trees. We walked in silence for a few moments, footsteps falling together easily. Nothing felt awkward as I stood just inches from a boy I had only met hours before. A boy that sent chills through my entire body just by one touch though it felt natural to be walking in sync with him.

Asher cleared his throat before speaking, "She's not wrong, you know."

"What?"

He kept his eyes forward, not looking towards me. I could see a slight shimmer play in the green orbs. "You look great, but I mean you looked great before she Aspynfied you."

Finally, I caught Asher's stare. His eyes were still vibrant—even in the dark forest they glowed. He broke away from me, looking ahead while his lip turned up in a wicked grin. "Looks like tonight's going to be a fun time."

Spinning forward, I saw where his eyes were trained. A full-out party had broken out in the middle of a typically quiet forest. Fire lit up the night sky from a bonfire, casting a bright orange glow on each of the local teens' faces. Drinks were being passed around by the dozen while music echoed off the trees in pulsing beats. I stood there, staring like a fish out of water having never seen such a spectacle before in my life.

"Is it always like this?"

"Not always, but it seems they are trying to show off for the new girl. Don't be awkward, go socialize with your newfound classmates." Asher cast me a brilliantly white smile as he quickly walked off towards the party.

"Wait, don't leave me! At least help me find Aspyn!" I yelled after him, but my voice was drowned out by the noise of the party. His figure soon disappeared into the crowd of people, leaving me standing alone watching the teens from a distance.

Why did I allow Aspyn to drag me into this?

As I headed down in the same direction as Asher, it looked like the entire teenage population of Idelwood was in attendance tonight. I guess there are only so many places to get in trouble within the walls of a small town. The middle of a deserted forest seemed the best place to partake in acts that would only be fuzzy memories the next morning. I tried to wander through the sea of people gathered around the blazing fire, trying my best to spot Aspyn, Asher, or a place to hide until one of them eventually stumbled upon me.

Everyone was packed together so tightly it

was hard to navigate through the drunken bodies without being noticed. I finally gave up, realizing they were nowhere to be seen. As I turned around to go back the way I came, my shoulder knocked into someone, spilling their drink all over the front of the both of us. The sickly sweet smell of alcohol doused both of us — we looked like cats who had accidentally slipped into a bath. I leaped back quickly, and a high-pitched shriek pierced through the commotion around us.

"What the hell! This is a custom dress, you tramp!" A tall, tan girl stood opposite of me, the front of her dress clinging to her chest as it heaved up in anger.

"I am so sorry! I wasn't watching where I was going. Here, let me help you find something to clean you up." My words tumbled out frantically, matching my body movements as I tried to search for anything that might help clean up the sopping-wet girl in front of me.

A slow clap began behind me. "Obviously you have a knack for running into people, don't you darling?"

I froze in place, the voice sending fear through

me. My neck craned behind me as only the shadow of Finley Blackbourne emerged from the darkness. Turning back towards the fuming girl, I noticed not a single person around the three of us was watching the drama occurring right in front of them. The night's darkness swallowed the teens whole, making them disappear altogether.

"Look, I didn't mean to run into you…" I searched for the girl's name, waiting for her to announce herself.

"Do you seriously not know who I am? I am the student body president." Her face was flushing red as the anger around us continued to build.

I huffed towards her in annoyance. "Sorry I didn't check out the guide to stuck-up pricks in Idelwood. Although you both would be at the top of the list."

"Come on, Tabitha. You aren't that important. You just like to think that you are. Being his favorite plaything doesn't make you special." Finley's voice was directly behind me, whispering hot air against my ear. The muscles in my back contracted in fear. I could feel his chest brush up against me as he stepped closer.

Tabitha turned on her heels, stomping away into the distance, leaving Finley and me standing in the woods alone. I took a step forward, trying to follow the direction of the fuming girl, but Finley's hand wrapped around my wrist, tugging me back against him. I turned my neck, eyes glaring up at him. "What do you want?"

"You know, Liliana, your dress is a contradiction." He spoke slowly.

I watched as his gaze gently scanned over my body, the look in his eyes making me want to squirm back, but I was held firmly in place by his strong grip. Finley's intense gaze landed back on mine after what seemed like an eternity.

"I have no idea what you are talking about, but I'm sure you will enlighten me in a few moments," I said, pulling against his hold to get away from him once again. Finley retaliated against my pull, digging his fingers into my wrist—a bright purple bruise would be left after this encounter. A blatant reminder for me that this wasn't just a bad dream.

"It starts out light and then falls into darkness. I know a few people like that, many I would have considered my best friends before their fall from power. Though I haven't decided if you will follow their actions or choose to shine in the light."

Finley's head cocked to the side, examining me further. Hot bile rose up my throat, threatening to spill all over his sneakers. I needed to get away from him and the brainwashed ideas he had conjured up for the new girl in town. My arm was starting to grow numb under his harsh grip. "Let go of me, Finley."

"Tell me, Liliana, what did you think of the gift I left for you today?" Finley continued on, ignoring my plea for him to release me.

"What gift?"

"The first half of the medallion with that verse etched into it."

His words sucked the air from my lungs. My eyes wandered around, trying to find anyone who would come to my aid. "You put that in my bag?"

My lips continued to open and close at him like a fish gasping for air on an empty shore bank. The words wouldn't form on my tongue. This whole performance felt like some sort of game I should have caught onto by this point. Nothing he was saying added up.

Finley's deep smirk confirmed all my fears. "Why, of course. It was yours once. I thought I would return it to you, Night Monster."

The air around us was stale, pulling all the moisture from my mouth. The realization that he wasn't playing some sick joke on me whirled around my mind. He believed every demented word that fell from his lips, and somehow, I had become the center of this hysterical fantasy.

Finley was silent, not flinching when I shoved my free hand against his chest, trying to remove his touch from my skin. His words made it seem as if he knew who I was before I knew who I was. Though his burnt-red hair would have been something I remembered if we had met before, even in just a passing encounter. Everywhere I turned in this nowhere town, people continued to speak about me as if I had been a resident my entire life.

"You need to let me go now, Finley." My voice hardened, sending shockwaves of emotion through the silent air. I glared into his eyes. It took all the courage I could muster not to shake against his predatory grin.

"I don't thi—" His words were cut off by the deafening crack of a twig behind me, distracting him from the sentence.

"She said let go." A deep voice spoke out. Looking over my shoulder, I could see Asher standing inches from me, arms crossed against his broad chest. Aspyn stood just outside the tree line's shadows, looking as if she didn't want to get too close to Finley if it wasn't absolutely necessary.

"You have no business here, Fin," a new voice broke from behind Finley. Through the darkness, I could only make out the silhouette of a tall girl.

Finley's laugh was low, allowing only Asher and me to hear it. "Oh, look who decided to show up. Another one of the dreaded Manson triplets. So sorry, you just missed your sister, but since you are here, I would like to inform all of you devils that this abomination is my business. The council has made her my business."

I watched him closely through my eyelashes, not wanting to make direct eye contact with him as I went to speak. I could feel the angry heat of a certain green-eyed boy radiating off his body brush up against my chilled back. Asher's presence instantly washed a sense of calmness over me. It was a strange feeling—I barely knew the boy and yet he was the one person I had subconsciously searched for as Finley tormented me. Asher was quicker than me. Speaking through clenched teeth, he took one menacing step closer to us. "I'm not going to ask you again. Take your hands off of her, Finley."

I froze in place, not comprehending what I was staring back at. Asher's normally vibrant green eyes were pitch-black. The color flooded together like ink dripping off a feathered pen. I was sure it was just a trick of the night light around us as the emotionless orbs stared back towards Finley, challenging the redhead.

"You know you can't save something that had no business being created in the first place, Asher. The world has its ways of flushing out the toxic beings," Finley hissed at him, quickly throwing me back towards the black-eyed boy. Asher caught me between his strong arms, and automatically my fingers grasped the dark T-shirt he wore. I held onto him firmly, not wanting to be ripped back into Finley's grip once again. My arm began to throb where his fingers had once dug. I glanced back at Finley, the confusion from his words finally appearing in my mind. He only smirked towards me, softly speaking. "Until next time, Liliana Caldwell."

Before I could respond to him, Finley disappeared into the shadows he had come slinking out of. His red hair shone brightly even in the darkness which encompassed the forest. I stared towards him until he was out of sight, but not without catching a final smirk he flashed towards me. Asher was looking down at me, his eyes back to the bright green orbs which mirrored his twin's. "Lily, are you okay?"

"I don't know how to respond to that. What was that all about?" I said, my eyes traveling back to where Finley had just gone. They searched for any signs that he may still be lurking in the dark. Three pairs of worried eyes watched me comb the trees.

"Finley has issues, deep-rooted ones that we can't even begin to explain. Aspyn knows that better than any of us. I'm Delaney Manson, by the way." The mystery girl stepped towards me, her mouth set in a grim line. Instinctively I stepped closer into Asher, feeling safe in his grip. His arms tightened around my shaking figure, snaking against my hip to pull me closer to his body. I knew this girl was in no way a danger to me, but after what had just occurred, being closer to Asher felt right somehow.

I looked up to find him staring at me with concern, and his gaze traveled to where Finley had held me moments before. Asher's hand dropped down toward the spot on my wrist, running a thumb over the leather jacket's material, which hid the newly forming bruises. He looked back towards the girls. "Why don't you both go ahead, and we'll follow behind you in a second."

Aspyn looked between us, hesitating. It was obvious she did not want to leave her twin's side but simply nodded in agreement. She started back towards the party, pulling Delaney along with her.

"You never answered my question, Lily," Asher said. My eyes stayed glued to the girls' backs until they were out of sight. I turned, looking back at Asher as he waited patiently for me to find my voice once again.

"Physically I may have a bruise or two but I'm fine. A little shaken but fine. Why did he call me a Night Monster and an abomination? Finley,"—I sucked in a sharp breath. His name felt toxic on my tongue— "doesn't even know me, and he keeps showing up in random places like the church this afternoon. Now he creeps out of the shadows to taunt me with names. What is going on?"

My ramblings grew frantic as the words spilled from my mouth, quicker than my brain could process them. The forest floor seemed to reverberate the words as time continued to stand still in the forest. No sounds of the nearby party traveled around us, even though I could still see the teens of Idelwood mingling amongst each other.

Asher's hands gripped either side of my shoulders, stopping me from flailing. His hold made it hard not to look into his piercing stare. "Okay, listen. Don't worry about any of it, Lil. It's not important right now."

"What do you mean it's not important, Asher? I don't even really know who you are, and I'm standing here acting like I have known you my entire life. Just moments ago, some guy was telling me I was an abomination—I think I have the right to be a little concerned about all of this."

"I promise you, it will all make sense in time, but right now I can't tell you what is going on or I won't be here next time Finley comes around. Okay?" Asher's words held a hint of urgency. I simply nodded towards his blank stare. What else could I do when this entire night had my brain reeling? "We should start walking back or Aspyn will come to kill both of us for making her wait."

So that's what we did. Asher led me past the strange bonfire with people who didn't acknowledge us or even make a sound as we maneuvered in between them. My shoulder grazed against the shoulder of a boy with a buzzcut, but he didn't even flinch at my touch, continuing to down a red Solo cup of amber liquid while his friends cheered him on. Blind screams of joy traveled around us. My feet carried me straight into town and past the café which held those who wanted a late-night bite to eat from Celia. Everything around me seemed to be moving in slow motion. I felt like I was watching myself from outside my body. The whole walk back towards the Goodwins' house, Finley's words rang in my ears. One nickname, in particular, seemed to stick out in the conversation that had just ensued: *Night Monster.*

Then something clicked in the back of my brain. The medallion he had planted in the bottom of my bag earlier this afternoon had spoken of a Night Monster. I closed my eyes, and the words were burned across my eyelids, the chilling verse screaming at me.

Mix a Demon and an Angel, you get a Night Monster.

CHAPTER SIX

I spent the rest of the weekend holed up in my room, entertaining boredom with mind-numbing sitcoms and only retreating out when Emma called for mealtime. She didn't press me about the fact that I was keeping to myself. She only spouted out generic questions, which I was grateful for. The bland answers I replied back to her were always taken with a warm smile.

My mind had never turned off since the incident at the party. Every moment which had occurred was on a constant loop. Even in sleep, nightmares of Finley's laugh and the black eyes which replaced Asher's green orbs haunted me. Exhaustion still plagued my body as I jolted awake in the early morning hours. Something about how Finley had uttered those words, saturating each of them with such hatred, made me sick to my stomach. The medallion had sat at the bottom of my bag for the better part of the weekend before I couldn't take the hole it was burning. Digging into the bottom of the book bag I found the piece lying exactly where I had last thrown it. Through squinted eyes, I examined the piece for an hour, which only brought on a headache and a useless web search.

Something about the medallion reminded me of the stories my brother once told me. This town seemed to remind me of those tales' way too often. It had been so long since I had thought about the haunting bedtime stories that they had begun to become fuzzy with age in my mind. Yet here in this town I was reminded of them daily in a new brilliant light I had never seen them before.

Nate had described the beings in his stories as beautiful creatures whose words made mortals bend to their every will. A beauty which the mortals couldn't help but be mesmerized by. Angels were rarely permitted to leave heaven's gates where

God could protect them from people who bathed in sin daily. The Elite few were God's messengers, the ones who kept their eyes and ears peeled as they walked amongst the mortals, only to report back the mortals' evils. They were the protectors of both the sinners and saints while they inhabited earth, but the Fallen—as Nate called them—were the contradiction of all things the Angels stood for. Each of the Fallen had been stripped of their wings when they had been exiled. Their only reminder of where they came from were the jagged scars etched into their backs where the once-beautiful wings had burst from underneath their shoulder blades. Eyes so vibrant in color, they rivaled all other colors mortals had seen, until they melted into the color of night as dark as a sky without the moon. Completely and utterly emotionless. That was when they were the most dangerous.

My mind retold the events which had occurred back in the woods over once again, keeping in mind the nightmarish bedtime story my brother had once told. A shiver traveled up my back as the image of Asher's vibrant green orbs melted into the terrifying image Nate once described playing across my memory.

Late Sunday afternoon I sat with my stomach pressed up against the countertop in the Goodwin's' kitchen, spinning the medallion around like it was a coin, watching the piece begin to wobble until it fell to one side. It spun in time, always falling over after a few trembles. My mind was racking for the words that could possibly complete the ending of the verse. Emma stood at the stove, cooking dinner. Blue fire licked the bottom of the large, round pot sitting on the stovetop.

Water bubbled, threating to overflow every few seconds and causing her to stir them away, leaving hot steam to coat the stainless-steel oven fan sitting just above the stove. Brinley stood off towards the fridge, which sat opposite of Emma. The girl was nagging her mother as she begged to get out of the punishment she had acquired over the weekend.

"Brinley Faith, I am finished with this conversation." Emma raised her voice, slamming down the plastic spoon she was holding onto the countertop. It clashed against the granite stone, sending a sickening crash into the silent kitchen.

Brinley crossed her arms, staring intensely at her mother. "I just don't see how this is fair. I was only like two minutes late."

"Try adding forty minutes to that, and then you'll be on the right track. Now go do something with yourself. You are giving me a headache." Emma's voice warned her daughter. I'm surprised Brinley didn't stomp her foot at her mother like a child throwing a temper tantrum. Emma shoved Brinley out of the kitchen, leaving the room to fill with only the sizzling water against the blue flames. The slam of Brinley's door caused a heavy sigh to come from Emma's mouth. She looked towards me, her eyes zeroing in on the medallion I had been spinning for the past few minutes.

"What is that you have there?"

"Oh, I found it at the bottom of my school bag. It has this strange saying on it. Have you ever seen it before?" I asked. Emma looked down at the gold piece, her hands wiping against the front of a yellow apron she had tied around her waist before picking it out of my hands. Recognition shined in Emma's gaze as she brought the piece closer.

"Not possible." Her voice was just a mumble, so quiet that I barely caught it. Emma flipped the piece around, staring at it in complete awe. The well-lit kitchen sparkled against the medallion, tiny dots of light dancing across the silver appliances.

"Did you say something?"

Emma looked up, smiling at me. Any suspicion of mine that she recognized the medallion vanished from her face. "I was just saying it was an interesting trinket. It's probably just junk. I wouldn't stress about it too much, doll."

She placed the medallion back into my palm, patting it once before she turned towards the overflowing pot. Her hands shook against the plastic spoon as she stirred, each swirl of the water tremors reverberating against the hard plastic and sending waves through the hot water.

"You're probably right," I whispered. The stool beneath me screeched as it pushed against the hardwood floor. Turning my back toward Emma, I allowed my feet to carry me up the stairs two at a time. I ripped open the bedroom door, quickly locking myself in the space that had been granted as mine. I slid down the cool wooden door, my hands knotting through my hair the entire way down. The medallion toppled towards the floor, letting out a loud clank as it bounced around.

Emma had recognized the medallion Finley had planted at the bottom of my bag. Her eyes lit up at the sight of the object, making it more than evident that it had meaning behind it. Emma's lie about having knowledge of the piece scared me even more than the recognition. I had to find out how all of this connected, or I needed to get the hell out of Idelwood.

I kept my head down as I walked towards the table in the back of the history classroom the next morning. Neither of the twins were seated when I reached my seat, which I was grateful for. I had ignored all the phone calls and texts Aspyn had bombarded my phone with while I tried to come to terms with what was going on in this town. Everything just seemed to get messier. Each time I thought I was on to something, another question pulled me ten feet back from the answers I so desperately craved. I didn't know if I had the courage to face either twin right now.

Slowly sitting down in the cold plastic seat, I pulled out a notebook, trying to give the illusion of being busy. My eyes skimmed the handwritten notes on the pages, though none of them were making their way to my brain. Every so often I flipped the page around the spiral to give the impression I was understanding the content. If they arrived, I didn't want them to sense my nerves that were knotting up in my stomach as the minutes ticked by.

The bell sounded for the final time as the chair in front of me scraped against the linoleum floor. Peering up through my eyelashes, I could see the bright green eyes of the boy who I had last spoken to in an empty forest with fear scorching through my veins.

"All right, class. As I mentioned on Friday, we will be starting our project on the history of the town for the rest of the semester, and with that, a paper was assigned. I would be kidding myself if I thought any of you went home and researched the topic of your papers, so today I'm giving you the hour to find one. It does not have to be the final topic you choose, but at least put in the effort of acting like you are researching for me." Professor Erickson motioned toward a large bookcase in the back of the room. "There are books on the shelf."

The room settled into a steady stream of conversations, allowing me to scramble from my seat before Asher had a chance to speak. Skimming through the spines of each book on the middle row, I could feel someone brush up behind me, hot breath tickling the back of my neck. I turned to see Asher standing inches away from me, his eyes trained on the shelf just above my head.

"You don't have to stand so close to me. You do realize that, right?" I twisted back towards the books, picking up the first one my hand reached out for. It was an old, leather-bound book that was worn from age. Flipping through the first few pages, I could see that it was handwritten in loopy, cursive letters that were neatly scrawled out across yellowing pages.

"You are completely correct about that, but

I thought if I stood this close, you wouldn't run away from me." Asher's eyes were burning holes in the back of my skull, making me fidget slightly. Spinning on my heels, I started around him back towards the table. He quickly followed, snatching a random book from the shelf.

I flipped through the handwritten journal—each entry was marked with dates in the top corner while the bottom was elegantly signed by someone named Claire Halloway. Asher cleared his throat, making me look from the delicate page in front of me before quickly returning back to it.

"Are you ever going to explain why you ignored Aspyn's efforts to get ahold of you all weekend?" Asher asked. My eyes left the page, nervously concentrating hard on the floor below me. The guilt of ignoring his twin started to eat its way out of my stomach, traveling into my esophagus. I looked up from the blue-stained spot on the floor into the hurt-filled eyes of Asher.

"Where is Aspyn, by the way?" I circled around the question he had asked, not wanting to admit that I thought about dropping the only friends I had gained in this town over the weekend because of what had occurred. None of what had happened was their fault, but the unsettling feeling that they were somehow involved still hung thick in the air.

"She had something that had to be taken care of this morning," Asher said, leaning in so his face was sitting directly in front of mine. I could feel the tip of his nose brush against my own. Having him this close made all of my exposed skin flush bright red as the heat of my body acknowledged his presence. Knowing I wouldn't be able to avoid his stare for the duration of the hour, I locked eyes with him. "Seriously, Lily. I can tell the wheels in your head are grinding together, and if that continues, you're going to hurt yourself."

Furrowing my brow at him, I pushed back against the table to create some distance between us. "How would you know? You don't know even know me that well, and yet you along with everyone else in this town thinks that they have me all figured out. Well, listen because I'm not going to repeat myself — Asher, you don't know the first thing about me."

Asher flinched back at my words like I had

slapped him across the face with them. A long sigh left my mouth, and I reached up to comb back my bangs a couple of times, gathering the right words to explain my cruelty, "Look, I'm sorry. I'm not particularly used to people who I just met actually caring about me or what I have to say."

The bell sounded sooner than I had anticipated, leaving the rustle of students gathering their things as background noise to our conversation. Asher stood from his desk, towering over me with his height. "Meet me in front of the school during study period."

"Are you going to explain to me what is going on then?"

A pause hung in the thick air around us before Asher nodded. He walked out of the classroom into the blur of students without allowing me to answer him about meeting up later.

"I would be careful with that one, Liliana." I turned towards Professor Erickson. He sat peering over his glasses at the papers in front of him. "That is the type of boy who make smart girls like you choose the wrong path."

Standing from the desk, I began to gather the rest of my things. "I can handle it, Professor. I have been looking out for myself for my entire life. You don't have to worry about me."

Starting out the classroom, I could hear the man mutter softly to himself, "Unfortunately we all know what you've had to endure these past years, young Lily."

I stood frozen in the classroom's doorway as students pushed past me in every direction, trying to avoid each other's touch at all costs. His words buzzed in my ears like I had a pair of headphones on. A continuous song of strange things people had said to me in this town was on an endless track in my mind. Everyone in this place seemed to know more about me than I truly did.

The sense of being an outsider had once hung thick in the air of Idelwood, but now I couldn't help but think I wasn't the outsider living in this town.

CHAPTER SEVEN

The chill of Colorado's fall air whipped around me as I stood on the front steps of the school waiting for Asher to arrive. I had debated on even showing up, wanting nothing more than to run back towards the library where I could hide behind the shelves, immersed in a world that wasn't my own until the period was over. But I knew I needed answers, and this was the only way I was going to get them.

A black mustang rolled up to the curb, letting its tinted window slide down to reveal Asher behind the wheel. Groaning, I started down the stairs of the school, annoyed at the fact that he looked like a Greek god and had the gorgeous car to match. Opening the door, I slipped into the car, leaning against the luxury seats before turning my body to face Asher. I recoiled away from his touch, tracking his fingers as they pulled the seat belt across my body and latched it into place with a loud click.

Slowly I let out a shaking breath, covering my nerves with an eye roll in his direction. "So where are you taking me?"

Asher sat back against his seat lazily. His hand flicked the gear shift into drive, pulling away from the school before answering me. "We are going to meet my sister and some other people we want you to meet. There's this place just outside of town."

We sat in silence. I didn't know what I wanted to say to him. On one hand, I trusted the twins and even the Manson girl that had been with them at the bonfire. I trusted them way too much, and that's what scared me. It felt like I had known them in another life — everything about these people seemed familiar to me, causing an automatic trust to form. But on the other hand, I felt as if this was just the calm before the storm, whether that meant with the people I found trust in or the entire town of Idelwood.

Finally, I couldn't take the thick silence that filled the inside of the car anymore. "I have a question for you."

"Okay, ask away." Asher spoke softly, keeping his eyes trained on the road, not wavering to meet mine as I spoke.

"Why did Finley Blackbourne call me a Night Monster the night of the bonfire?" I asked, leaning my head against the cool window. Pressure was beginning to build in my skull from the question that had been troubling me the most since Finley spouted off the nickname.

Asher cleared his throat, shifting side to side uncomfortably in his seat. "He has been brainwashed by the leaders of this town, Lil. Anyone new who shows up here gets the third degree by their stupid clique."

Squeezing my eyes shut, I swore underneath my breath. He was lying through his teeth, I could tell. A low chuckle escaped Asher's lips, and I could feel his eyes watching my internal struggle. "I know it's frustrating, but it'll all make sense in the end. I promise, Lily."

The humor that laced his voice was driving me insane. I peeled open my eyes, glaring at his smirk. "You're lying to me, Asher. I hate liars. Everyone I have ever been forced to interact with has lied to me. I should have known you would be no different."

"All in due time, Lil."

I closed my eyes once again, and the lack of sleep I had received recently allowed the movement of the car to rock me to sleep, but the same nightmares of shadow creatures which had recently consumed my nights played behind my eyelids. They pulled me deeper into their darkness until the sinister feeling which radiated off them consumed my soul, leaving my body feeling empty. My mind sat in between consciousness and a sleep state as we drove to the undisclosed location.

The car's engine died down to a low purr, waking me from the terrors behind my eyes. As I lifted my head from the glass, my gaze caught sight of the breathtaking scene in front of me. Everything around the car was painted green with spots of brown where the hand of Mother Nature had dotted fall's cruel chill. Large trees sprouted from the ground, standing tall against the clouds, their branches tangled together to form shade around the car. A single dirt hiking trail connected all the trees together into one large patch of forest.

I looked over towards Asher in annoyance. "I don't hike."

"Well, you do today, so just be grateful you are wearing tennis shoes." Asher chuckled at me. I peered down at my tattered Vans, then back towards where Asher had once sat. He was already outside of the car, making his way towards my door.

A groan of protest escaped my lips when the door cracked open.

"It won't kill you to get some exercise, Lil." Asher extended his hand towards me. I stared at it for a moment more before gripping onto it tightly. He pulled me from my seat, slamming the door behind me. A shock pricked against my skin, traveling through the hand grasped in his. The electrifying sensation lit up every nerve in my body like a freshly decorated Christmas tree. I ripped my hand back, holding it tightly against my chest in surprise.

"If you didn't want to hold my hand, you could

have just said so," Asher said, lips quirked up in a smirk before he started up the trail. "Well, are you coming, slowpoke?"

I clumsily dashed up the path after him, managing to catch up moments later, though his long legs made me hold a steady jog just to keep up.

"You know, you could have warned me about this little excursion." I sputtered out the words through pants, trying to catch my breath. I was not used to the altitude that plagued Colorado's air, making a simple jog feel like a mile run.

Asher looked over at me, a certain childlike gleam playing in his eyes. "Why? So you could ditch us and leave me to hike up this trail all alone?"

"Now thinking about it, that would have been a better idea than this," I admitted. My lungs felt like they were going to explode inside my chest while my feet had gone numb halfway up the trail.

"Oh, come on. You are being a tad dramatic, don't you think? We are almost there."

"I am not being dramatic, Asher! I'm not used to this elevation, plus you are walking so fast I had to practically run up this mountain." I tried to yell at the boy, but it only came out in a pathetic wheeze.

We made it over the final hill of the path, where I could see Aspyn and three other figures standing in the clearing, laughing amongst themselves. Aspyn looked like she had stepped off a photo shoot, per usual. Her dark hair whipped around her, shadowing the others' faces. The clearing was like standing in the clouds—everywhere you looked, fog held against the mountain's soil. As the figures moved, the clouds followed, forming little pockets around them. The sun danced against their skin, casting an angelic glow around each of them.

"Lily!" Aspyn shouted, her figure racing through the fog. She reached her twin and me in seconds. Her body collided into mine with a hug that knocked the little breath that my lungs still held, causing a short gasp to slip from my throat.

"Aspyn, you are suffocating the poor girl," a male's voice rang out across the clearing, followed by multiple agreeable laughs.

"Oh, you hush now, Gabe." She pulled away, smiling at me. "L loves my craziness."

"I missed you too, Aspyn, even though it was

only two days," I said. Listening to Aspyn's sugary-sweet laugh bounce off the clearing's trees caused me to add in my own hushed giggles.

"Two days in which you ignored all my calls and texts. We are going to have to teach you some manners." Aspyn's green eyes squinted playfully in my direction, only making me roll my own at her antics.

"I think after the night I had from a party you both," — my fingertips poked each twin's chest — "dragged me to, I deserved a weekend to digest all the crazy."

Asher only winked at me as Aspyn started to ramble on about my social status being in jeopardy if I hadn't gone. I could care less about social statuses in Idelwood, but it made Aspyn happy, so I stood there, enduring her outrageous lecture. The twins began to argue about who was supposed to be watching over me at the bonfire while simultaneously throwing playful insults at each other. As I continued to watch both of their animated faces, the world around them began to turn into a watercolored mess, fading away quickly. I watched the clearing slow down before spinning like a top that had been wound up one too many times. When the spinning finally came to a stop, I stood in the middle of an argument being held between a young girl and a man dressed in a black clergy outfit.

My back was against a wall, hiding me from the verbal knives they threw at each other. They stood in the middle of the church I had seen only days before. The same sparkling holy water sent rainbow rays across the wall behind where it sat.

"You don't understand. This is not the devil's work or any other biblical satire you are trying to throw at this, Father. It is not something you can sweep under the rug like everything else in this town. I have seen them in the square." The young girl was outfitted in a checkered pink dress, and a matching ribbon held her light brown hair away from her face. Her expression was full of anger as she spat the words towards her father.

"You will not speak a word about this to anyone in town, Claire. This is a childish delusion that will fade with time, but until then, I can't have you scaring the locals with these silly stories. That's all they are." Her father's tone was venomous, but he stood calmly against

his daughter's shaking figure. Turning on his heel, he tried to retreat from the room that we stood in.

Claire watched her father, crossing her arms over her chest. He didn't make it far before she straightened her spine and began to speak with confidence in the direction he had traveled. "We all know that in this town, things don't stay buried, Father. You of all people should know that. This will come out, and when it does, whose side will you stand with? The Demons that lurk in the shadows or the Angels trying to 'protect' the town? This will destroy our home if it is kept hidden. Something has to be done, and if you won't do it, I will."

The man turned on his heel, charging towards his daughter in a few long strides before a crack sounded off through the hall as her father's palm met her cheek. Claire gripped the side of her face tenderly, glaring at the man in front of her. A spark of gold dangling around Claire's neck caught my eye. Stepping closer, I recognized the medallion from the bottom of my bag hanging around her neck, fully intact.

The images flashed away as quickly as they had appeared, leaving me with a seasick feeling as the worlds changed in front of me. The images felt to real too be anything but a memory, like the destruction of the church was whispering its secrets to me. As I shook it off, everything was just how I had last seen it. Aspyn was still arguing with her other half, both laughing at each other's excuses for leaving me. Asher caught sight of me watching the interaction. He was always looking at me; I wished he would stop because I was forming an attachment to those eyes of his.

"I'm Mallory Manson," a bubbly voice spouted out of a girl with dirty blonde hair. She bounced up to me, sticking her hand in my face to shake.

I took her hand, and my voice wobbled as I replied, "Hi, I'm Lily."

"Oh, I know! You met my sister Tabitha. Laney said she looked like a cat who fell in a pool, all puffed up and angry after you spilled her drink on her. I should apologize to you on her behalf. She can be such a bi—" Aspyn cut her off, throwing a hand over her mouth.

"Okay, Mal, you're scaring her. Calm down." Aspyn giggled at the overexcited girl as Mallory practically vibrated in place. I thought Aspyn was peppy, but Mal topped Aspyn's pep any day.

"Sorry." Mal sheepishly shrank back to the group in the clearing, hiding behind the last figure.

"Mallory can get overly excited about new people in our group—don't mind her." The figure stepped forward, revealing the tall, tan girl from the night of the bonfire. She hung back from the rest of the group, not stepping any closer to me. "I'm Delaney Manson. We met the other night, though considering the facts, I wouldn't expect you to remember me."

She turned her back on me, grasping Mallory by her forearm before stalking into the woods surrounding the clearing. I watched them disappear into the trees' shadows as they began to whisper to each other.

"Well, that could have gone smoother." Asher grimaced before coming up behind me. He leaned down, whispering in my ear, "Don't worry Lil. Laney's not the touchy-feely type. That all went to Mal."

A small smile formed on my face, thinking of the bubbly girl from a moment before. Asher's hot breath hit the back of my ear, making the smile slip from my face as I fidgeted from him being so close. The temptation to step back into the boy's embrace was setting every nerve in my body on fire. The wind had picked up around us, sending his light scent of jasmine through my nose. It was throwing every one of my senses into overdrive as his musky scent overpowered my nostrils. My brain felt like mush as it short-circuited, trying to find a way to step away from him. The shaky voice that spoke was almost unrecognizable when I finally was able to find the composure. "So why did we hike all the way up this mountain? If it was for the view, I could have lived with just seeing a picture of it."

Aspyn's knowing look found mine. "Ugh, you can be such a bore sometimes. This was supposed to be fun, and we wanted you to meet everyone, so we weren't your only friends."

I nearly ran into Asher's chest when I turned around, my nose brushing up against his muscular chest. "Geez, did you want to crawl into my skin?"

He laughed at my comment, taking in every inch of my angry face. "You wish, sweetheart."

"Ugh, you're repulsive." I stomped around him.

The thought of him and me was tempting. It was actually more than tempting, as it was all my mind could think about right now. But if this town was going to be another blip on my radar in a month, then the boy with the gorgeous green eyes was definitely off limits.

"Lily, wait up." Aspyn's voice called after me, but I continued to walk down the dirt path leading to the car, desperately trying to ignore her voice. Soon after she went silent, I could hear her footsteps running up behind me. She caught up easily, falling into sync with my steps, waiting for me to say something.

"Look, Aspyn, I'm sorry for that. This is just a lot for one day. I guess I just got overwhelmed and ruined your fun." I spoke softly. My eyes could barely look at her as the shame of what had just occurred started to rapidly fill the pit of my stomach.

"It's not your fault, L. Ash even said this was going to happen. I should have listened instead of shoving this all down your throat. I guess I was just excited because I feel like I've known you my whole life. You act so much like her..." Aspyn's sentence trailed off, and her eyes glazed over, letting them wander into the distance to stare at nothing in particular.

"I act like who, Aspyn?"

"What?" Aspyn spoke quickly, her attention snapping back to me, confusion replacing the glassy look she had just worn.

Ignoring the gnawing feeling of wanting to know the answer, I continued the rest of the short and silent walk down the trail. We arrived back in front of the car before I decided to break the silence. "So, Laney hates me because of her sister Tabby, doesn't she?"

Aspyn grinned at my statement. "Laney hates Tabitha, so that's definitely not the case at all. She is just that way with everyone, not much of a people person. Asher and Gabe always call her ice queen because she's so cold to everyone. I think that nickname gets under her skin a bit."

I burst out laughing. "I think Laney and I might get along if we ever get to know each other."

"Hey, you're stuck with me, so don't even think about running off and getting another best friend." She positioned herself on the hood of Asher's car, leaning back slightly on the dazzling black paint to let the rays of sunshine peeking through the overcast sky hit her face.

"I know your butt is not sitting on the hood of my car." Asher's deep voice rang out from the tree line.

"Oh no, I'm so scared of you, Asher."

"You should be, Aspyn Jane." I jumped as Asher's voice boomed right behind me.

"Middle names really terrify me. I'm shaking in my boots." Aspyn ignored her brother's complaints, letting her elbows hit the hood, trying to make it obvious to Asher that she wasn't planning on getting up from her spot anytime soon.

"Gabe is waiting for you in the clearing so you can both find the Manson girls." Asher's voice was bored, but the comment made Aspyn jump up inhumanly fast before rushing up the trail once more.

"Bye, Aspyn." I laughed as we watched her race up the trail. My eyebrow arched at the scene in front of me. "So, her and Gabe, huh?"

Asher rolled his eyes at the comment, walking up to the car door to open it for me. "Don't even get me started with them. Get in the car."

"Okay, Mr. Demanding," I mumbled, slipping into the car easily. Asher slammed the door behind me, and my eyes watched him get into the driver's side. "Look, Asher, I'm sorry for snapping at you."

"It's fine, Lily." His monotone voice hinted that it was in fact not fine.

"Okay."

Asher began to drive before he spoke again. "Look, Lily, I don't blame you for the way you are, but you have to learn to let people in or your life is going to be lonely."

I let his words sink into me. "Aspyn said something weird when we were walking down to the car."

"What was that?"

"She said I acted like *her*. Do you know who she could have been talking about?" I watched his stare shift anxiously from the road to me. Something wasn't right with the way his fingers began to drum against the base of the steering wheel.

"Maybe you said something that reminds her of herself." Asher was trying to dance around the fact that he knew exactly what his sister had meant.

I whipped my body around to face him. The sudden movement caused the seatbelt around my shoulder to lock in place, holding me firmly against the leather. "No, she was referring to someone other than herself, Asher."

"My sister is all in her head most of the time, Lil. I couldn't tell you who she was talking about." He was lying again—I could tell by the way he wouldn't look over at me. His fingers, which had been drumming against the wheel moments before, had been replaced with a strong grip that was turning his knuckles a stark white color.

"I want to go back to the Goodwins'," I muttered before sitting back farther into the cold seat, letting my head lie back on the headrest.

"Home it is."

"I don't have a home."

CHAPTER EIGHT

The front porch lights cast a yellow glare across the front yard when we pulled up. Asher sat still, watching me gather my school bag, his hawklike eyes making sure to observe each movement I made. I reached towards the car's door handle, but it didn't budge forward.

I turned my glare towards the unlock button on the driver's side console. "Open the door, Asher."

His hand moved towards the button, barely grazing it. I watched as his finger hovered over the latch for a second as he tried to catch my eye. "Why are you so against anyone who tries to care about you?"

I didn't dare glance up at him. One look would undo the anger that I had built up in the car ride over. The pull of his eyes was torture, but I held my gaze on the lock button. "You lied to me. I told you how I felt about liars. I'm not going to ask again, Asher—open the door."

The click of the lock broke over our steady breathing, allowing me to make my escape from the vehicle. As I dashed around the front of the car, the headlights caught onto my shadow which danced across the iron as I slipped through the gate. Once in the house, I slammed the door behind me. The cool wood rested against my spine as William Goodwin rounded the corner to investigate the sudden noise. He held a glass of amber liquid in one hand that swished with every step he took while a book was held haphazardly in the other.

"Oh, Lily, it's just you. Where did you run off to this evening?" His eyes narrowed at me over a pair of reading glasses which sat perched on the bridge of his nose. It felt like I was being reprimanded with his simple question. I opened my mouth to respond to him, but no words came out.

"She was with some friends. I forgot to tell Mom after school." Brinley stood, leaning her arms lazily over the top of the banister. "Sorry, Dad."

Her eyebrows rose as I made eye contact with the patronizing gaze. She was enjoying the scene below her too much. Brinley's face melted down into an innocent look as she turned her baby blues towards her father.

"That's all right, kitten." Will's eyes crinkled into a smile at his daughter, admiration shining through his words. "Well, I suppose I will be heading back to my study for the night. Goodnight, girls." He took a sip of the amber liquid, humming a familiar tune as he traveled back down the hallway.

I met Brinley's stare. It had hardened with the absence of her father in the room. The blue that surrounded her pupils was filled with resentment, both orbs resembling the dark center of a hurricane. She looked down on me like a cobra ready to strike, cutting me off before I had the chance to thank her for covering for me. "Don't get used to this. It was a one-time thing."

He blonde hair flew around her back as she spun back towards her bedroom. The Goodwins had big hearts — that much was obvious — but they seemed to have some kind of hidden agenda for me, based on the comments Brinley had made to me days ago before the bonfire. The hairs on the back of my neck stood straight up. I didn't know who I was actually living with or what they had planned for me.

Study hall was quiet the next day. Only a few students sat in the tables lining the inside of the large bookshelves of the library. It was exactly what I needed after the chaos that had been brewing around my life recently. My schoolwork was beginning to show my lack of concentration. Leafing through a math book, I tried to finish the massive amount of homework my teacher had assigned, but the problems seemed to all mesh together. Every equation I wrote out across the lined paper had been scribbled out in frustration.

Finally giving up on the math work, I tossed the book aside and moved on to the history project that I hadn't touched since plucking the book off the shelf the day before. The journal cracked at the spine when I opened it up to the middle. Jagged pieces of paper stuck against the binding of the book, indicating that multiple sheets had been ripped out of the front, leaving a gap in time for me to somehow piece together.

Skimming through the journal, I settled on a page in the middle of the book.

February 1994

Rowen showed me what she was today. What everyone I had trusted in this town was. I knew that they weren't exactly normal, but this was nothing I could have ever imagined. None of the people in this town seemed "normal" when we arrived in Idelwood, but I just thought it was because I was the new one. The outsider. This was all most of the locals had ever known, having been born and bred in the tragic little town called Idelwood. Father was asked to serve as the pastor of the church in this town around a year ago, ripping us from our sheltered life in Oregon to this gloomy small town in Colorado.

I am absolutely terrified of the idea of living amongst these creatures. They are not the creatures that you are taught about in Sunday school. With a war brewing in the distance, my knowledge and help are the keys to Rowen and the child's survival. Xander explained this to me multiple times, though it does not cause me any more ease. I must tell Father of the creatures that live in this town, both the ones lurking in disguise and those hidden within the shadows. It is imperative that he knows.

-Claire Halloway

My skin flushed with goose bumps as I read the name inscribed at the bottom of the page. I must have reread the entry in front of me at least a hundred times until my brain was numb. The voices from the strange vision I had brushed off in the clearing were ringing back in my ears. Claire was the girl's name who had the medallion hanging from her neck, the girl who had met her tragic end within the walls of this town's church.

The pastor's daughter had died in the church, the same one I had hallucinated to be in perfect condition. Claire's argument with her father had been heated with the mention of creatures that placed them both in the middle of a war. *It was brewing right underneath her father's nose* — that's what she had told him, but he was choosing to ignore the obvious signs in front of him.

A textbook slammed down on my table, ripping me from my state of shock. "You look like you've seen a ghost, Lily." Finley's smug face stared back at me. He flipped the chair around, gently setting the back portion in line with the table. Sitting down on the cushion, Finley leaned forward against the chair, his elbows resting on the top of the table.

"Go away, Finley, I'm not in the mood for your games today." I went back to staring at the journal lying out in front of me. My eyes ran over the words again, trying to ignore the persistent stare of the boy.

"Oh, come on, Lilypad. Let's start over."

Nate's childhood nickname rang out around us, sending chills through me. "Don't call me that."

"We all know that this tough act isn't going to last very much longer. The two of us could be such great friends if you only dropped the charade."

I wanted to slap the smirk off his pale face. Determined not to allow him to get underneath my skin, I looked him right in the eye. "You don't know the first thing about me. None of you do, so why don't you get out of the chair you are sitting in, wipe that smug look off your face, and leave me the hell alone?"

Ignoring the request just handed to him, Finley stuck his bottom lip out in a condescending pout. "That was hurtful, Lilypad. I thought you would have figured this all out by now. I have given you multiple hints."

"I don't know what I would have to figure out,

Finley."

"It's all right in front of you. I thought you would figure it out on your own—you are so different from Nathaniel." My head snapped up, locking eyes with the redhead's across from me. The world around us seemed to stop as the name that haunted my dreams left his lips. I could hear my heartbeat pounding in my ears, drowning out any background noise that had once been there. The room began to heat up, sweat starting to gather at the nape of my neck, knotting my baby hairs together.

"What did you just say to me?" I forced myself to ask the question, hoping I had just misheard the name.

"I always hoped you would be the sibling that was smarter, more aware of the world around you. You might choose correctly, but I can see you are going down a path of darkness. It's consuming your soul. Then again, your brother can have his days where light outshines the dark. He just has to be put in his place. But you, Liliana, everything about you embodies wickedness. No person or thing will be able to control a Night Monster like you." Finley's words dripped with malice. Sitting straight up, he could tell that he had struck a chord in my soul. This boy who I hadn't met before stepping into the borders of this town knew a secret I kept so well hidden from everyone. "I'll leave you to mull over our conversation, Lily, but remember to choose correctly when the time comes."

Finley stood from the table, stalking away into the row of bookshelves that sat next to us. I watched him turn the corner of one before I swept all of my items laying across the table into my bag and raced out of the library.

As I entered the hall, no one was milling around in it, leaving me alone to watch my whole world shatter in front of me. My chest felt like it was going to cave in on itself while my heart hit my ribcage with such force that it was sending a sharp pain down my left arm. Tears burned my eyes, clouding my vision, as I stumbled around the hallway, the loud crash of my body hitting a locker echoing through it. Not being able to find enough air to fill my lungs, I could feel them fighting the urge to explode inside my chest.

This was what I had always feared, the thought of allowing my bottled-up feelings to fall from the shelf I had placed them upon. The shards of glass were now stabbing my every pore, making sure to cause the most damage they possibly could. Every emotion I had ever shoved aside regarding Nate was coursing through my body, making my hands rapidly shake. An illuminated exit sign blurred together with my tears, making the red glow wobble around the hallway.

"Lily?" a sweet voice questioned through the silent hall. Turning to see Mal and Delaney standing at the end of the corridor, I instantly regretted showing my face to them. Delaney looked calm and collected next to her sister's horror-stricken face.

"Go get one of the twins, Mallory, preferably Asher." Delaney pulled Mallory closer to her as she spoke evenly to her sister. "Meet us in the greenhouse."

Delaney released Mallory from her tight grasp, making her way forward in my direction. For a split second, I thought about taking off down the hall toward the exit sign without looking back, but Delaney was right next to me when the idea finally registered in my brain. "Don't even think about it—we are going this way."

Delaney pulled me in the opposite way of the sign, gripping down on my wrist to make sure I wouldn't slip from her grasp. She pushed through a door off to our right, leading me in the direction of a small glass shed connected to a cobblestone path. The sun shone through the glass, making the greenery in the building glisten against their freshly watered leaves.

My breathing was still rapid, and small sobs broke through more frequently when Delaney finally managed to unlock the door. She shoved me through the entryway, sitting my shaking figure in a chair close by. Now that I was alone with Delaney, I allowed myself to let every emotion I was feeling fall from my lips in harsh, choked-back sobs.

"Here, put your head between your legs and take some deep breaths. In through your nose, out through your mouth, Lily." Delaney's voice morphed into a softer tone, leaving the emotionless girl out in the cold. She guided me through the actions she was instructing, demonstrating the breathing until I copied her movements, though it didn't feel like it was helping at all. My brain was pounding against my eyes with what felt like an ice pick.

After what seemed to be an eternity, the door of the greenhouse slammed against the back wall, shaking the glass panels with such force I was afraid the entire structure was going to shatter around us. I peeked my head in the direction of the entrance, and Asher was the first one I could see standing in the doorway. His face dropped in disbelief when he saw the scene in front of him.

"Lily, what happened?" Aspyn pushed past her brother, making her way towards me. I couldn't find my voice to answer her worried eyes. Asher spoke in hushed whispers to both of the Manson girls, allowing Delaney to shove a key into his hand. They retreated from the greenhouse without another word.

I felt frozen in place. Aspyn's voice shook as she spoke to her twin, but her words were distorted in my ears, making it so I couldn't understand what she was actually saying. In two quick strides, Asher stood in front of me, bending at the knee to become level with my face. I avoided eye contact with him at all costs, knowing full well that catching sight of his green eyes would make everything worse in this moment.

Asher picked up my chin between his callused hands, pulling my face towards his so I was looking directly at him. "Lily, what happened?"

I let my eyes wander between the twins. Their matching gazes watched me closely, waiting for the answer to the question to slip from my tongue. They had become the only people I allowed myself to care for in such a long time. I trusted them. I knew I did, but my throat swelled shut as I tried to speak. Feeling like a fish out of water, trying to find the correct words to piece together what had happened in the library, my mouth bobbed open, but no sound came at first. Only one word could be uttered from the thousands that swirled around my head.

"Finley."

Chapter Nine

Asher's fingers curled around the lip of the table sitting to his left. I could see him trying to keep himself from trembling with rage, his feelings hanging in the bitter air. Muscles in his jaw popped inward as his teeth clenched, slowly grinding against each other. Asher's eyes squinted together, making the crease between his brows cave in. Even without him saying anything, I could almost hear his mind trying to rationalize against any violent acts he was wanting to commit against Finley. I knew that there was bad blood between the two of them, but this was something entirely different. The anger that was plastered across his face went deep—it wasn't some adolescent drama.

I sucked in a shaky breath before continuing to speak. "He brought up something he shouldn't know. I don't even understand how he found out about it."

"What did he know, Lily?" Aspyn's concerned eye's searched mine for answers. Her hand landed against Asher's back, trying to stop him from doing anything he'd soon regret.

"He said he knew my brother, Nathaniel." The name tasted like acid swishing around my mouth. I looked up at the glass ceiling, begging the tears beginning to form in my eyes not to fall. The frosted glass warped the sky above me—a deep gray shade had washed over clouds in the past few minutes, indicating a storm brewing in the distance. I looked back down to the pair in front of me, but Asher still had his eyes closed, waiting for me to continue. "Finley said I was different than Nate, something along the lines that my darkness consumes me, and I'm made of wickedness. I can't take the riddles he continues to spew at me anymore. This is the last straw, bringing up my brother."

My throat was raw from the words which came

out in one long hysterical scream. I curled down into the stool, melting back into the panic I had felt before. A loud smash of glass was followed by Aspyn yelling at her twin. He ignored her lecture, beginning to pace around the tiny shed in laps.

"Asher, you need to pull yourself together before you do something stupid. You know the rules." Aspyn's catlike eyes watched Asher, her words slicing through the thick air. Asher lapped back around in front of me, where Aspyn stopped him in his tracks, standing tall to block his path. His face met mine as he tried to retreat the other way, leaving me in shock. The black orbs that had stared back at me in the forest once before had returned, knocking the wind from my lungs. They held no emotion even though Asher's body vibrated with anger. Aspyn ran her hand down his arm. "Ash, calm down please."

"I can't calm down when that Holy bastard thinks he's untouchable. We are over here following the rules, which makes absolutely no sense considering the facts, and he is opening his mouth to her. Making her life a living hell. How does this make any of it any easier on her, Aspyn?"

The entire greenhouse began to rattle in place with every word Asher spoke. Pots of fertilizer started to fall from shelves that lined the roof. A yelp escaped my throat as I watched one plummet down towards my head. Reaching up, I covered my head with my arms and waited for an impact that never came. Peeling open my eyes, I locked them on Asher, who was standing above me, and stared up in shock at the pot in his hand.

His body relaxed slightly, making the emotionless irises melt back into the beautiful green they usually held. The breath in my lungs trapped itself in my throat as my mind began to piece together the obvious warning signs I had seen but chose to ignore since arriving in Idelwood. As I flew off the stool, the metal crashed loudly against the concrete floor of the greenhouse. Both twins' heads whipped up at the commotion I had just caused. Bedtime stories Nate used to tuck me in with continued to flood back into my memories like they were being played back on a movie reel. Aspyn went to take a step towards me, and I responded with a matching one backward.

"Don't."

"Lily." Asher's voice was soft as he watched me retreat as far as I could until the base of my spine connected with the metal table against the back wall. I hissed in pain as the sting skyrocketed from my tailbone to my skull, causing a dull pounding to form in my temples. Asher's hands reached out lightly, trying to calm me down like I was some sort of rabid animal.

"They weren't just stories, were they, Asher? The ones Nate used to tell me before bed." My voice wavered in and out as I spoke. "Every one of them was the truth. That's why Finley knows so much about me. How everyone in this town knows more about me than I do. It's because Nate was somehow mixed up with all of you."

"Whatever Nate told you, we can explain, I promise, L," Aspyn spoke softly. I could see her out of the corner of my eye standing to my right. My gaze flickered between each of the twins' faces. The hurt within Aspyn's gaze was obvious, as she stood only steps away, unsure if she wanted to close the gap between us.

"I'm living amongst monsters, and you thinking

explaining it will magically make everything ok." The fire in my voice startled me. It matched the tone Finley used against me every time I had an unfortunate run-in with him. Horror flooded my mind when the reality of the situation set in. I was trapped in a room with the things my childhood nightmares were filled with. The door was only a few feet away. If I made a quick dash for it, I could escape from the greenhouse before either of them noticed. Pushing a long table that lined the middle of the room to my right, I took my chance to escape the figures in front of me.

The metal squeaked as it slid on the cement floor, but Asher was faster than me, easily maneuvering away from the trap I had set. His body blocked the only way out, arms crossed against his chest, making me skid to a halt before I could collide with him. My skin hummed when his hand reached out to touch me — it begged me to let him trace the visible skin.

"Don't touch me," I screeched. My legs wobbled as I stepped away from his hovering hand, everything in my body protesting the movement, making it almost impossible to unglue my feet from their place.

"You don't even know half of the story, L. Please let us explain everything." Aspyn's voice was behind me now. Tripping over my feet, I stepped away from her, wanting to put distance between us. I stood with my hands stretched out on either side of me, creating an invisible barrier between the three of us.

"Explaining won't do you any good. Everything in this town always seems to come back to the same conclusion. The church. The broken medallion. Finley's taunting remarks. Hell, even the journal leads back to Nate's tales. Add a strange vision about a dead girl, and this town seems to hold way too many secrets for my comfort level." I sneered at her. My skin began to flush leaving angry, red blotches along its milky surface. Frustrated didn't even begin to cover the emotions that were bubbling deep in my chest at that moment.

Someone's callused hands began to play with the ends of my hair, making the air around me calm instantly. I knew who it was without even having to turn my head to look at him. My brain screamed at me to run, wanting nothing more than to flinch away from his touch, but I didn't. I just stood frozen, indulging myself in the light twist of his fingers tangling in my hair. Asher sent a sad smile to me when I finally allowed my gaze to meet his.

I didn't need an explanation from them to understand what was happening right in front of me. Everything I had ever known seemed to shift as I accepted the fact that I was living amongst God's creatures. Tales I had once thought to be bedtime stories stood right in front of me.

"What does this all mean?" I whispered so quietly I wasn't sure either of them had heard me.

"This town is home to things that people in this world only understand the surface of." Asher's hand found the side of my cheek, and instinctively I leaned closer into his touch. "We are all different here, even you, but I am going to explain everything to you. It just might take a little while. There is a lot of history to go over when it comes to this town."

Laughter began to bubble in my throat. It didn't seem to faze either of them that I was snickering to myself, but soon laughs slowly morphed into sobs that racked my entire body. Asher gathered my small figure against his chest, letting me grasp the edges of his shirt. His arms made me feel safe, and all I wanted to do right then was to curl up in that feeling. Aspyn stepped from the greenhouse, allowing the door to swing shut after her.

"You're actually taking this a lot better than all of us thought you would," Asher whispered into my hairline.

I let my chin rest on his chest and looked up at his grinning face. "I just called you both monsters and tried to run away."

A dark chuckle vibrated Asher's chest. "Yeah, but I was expecting more of a fight from you than just a table being thrown across the room to escape."

I buried my face back in his chest, embarrassed at my previous actions. "So, are you going to explain how this town managed to host Angels and Demons in its streets?"

Aspyn reentered the room with a newfound pep in her step. "Well, we like to call them the Holy, although they really hate that nickname. Also, there aren't Demons lurking in the shadows like all good horror films like to think. If there were, we'd be in a whole world of trouble. We are just the Angels who fell out of God's good graces."

"All right, calm down, little sister." Asher laughed as my eyes grew two sizes bigger when she finally admitted what they were. "Hey, don't give us that look. We are not evil and most definitely don't follow the orders of Lucifer. He couldn't rule over anyone if he tried, and believe me, he's tried."

Aspyn left shortly after everything calmed down, leaving Asher and me alone in the greenhouse. The sun had begun to set above us, sending dark shadows across the plants. A small lamp shone down on the papers sprawled out against the metal table. My eyes wandered down the long list of locals' names Asher had written out for me. They were either in God's favor or banished to the shadows—there was no in between. I was even living with two of the higher up Elite Council members who resided in Idelwood.

Tilting my head to the side, I noticed a name missing. "Where does Celia fit into all of this?"

"Celia is the town's Keeper. She controls all of

the records and artifacts of the town. Her family has been our Keepers since before I could remember. She is the only one left that I am aware of. Keepers never age, but that doesn't mean they're invincible," Asher explained, making sure I understood exactly what he was saying. None of this should exist, yet here it sat laid out in front of me. My pen glided across the page, making a new box to place Celia's name in. I wanted to remember each piece of this messed-up puzzle.

Positioning my body towards him, I looked over at the boy next to me and blushed deeply when he finally caught me. I quickly snapped my attention back to the pages. "I just don't understand — where do I fit into all of this, Asher?"

"You're special. To all of us, not just the Fallen. You are one of a kind." His fingertips reached over, moving a piece of rogue hair behind my ear. His touch lingered slightly before cupping the side of my face. I leaned deeply into his touch, eyes fluttering shut as his thumb began to trace the underside of my jawline.

My head shook in his grip. "I'm just Lily. There's

nothing special about me."

"That's where you are very wrong."

I opened my eyes, breathing in his musky scent, trying to enjoy the moment. Asher made me feel grounded when everything in my life had just been turned upside-down. My body didn't want to move from his warm grasp, but I needed to know how I fit into this picture. If everything I thought was true about me was going to be stripped away, the least we could do was revel in a few more moments of peace.

I peeled my eyes away from the papers to look up at Asher. He had been watching me the entire time. "Enlighten me then."

Reluctantly letting his hand drop, Asher turned to grab the pen I held. Moving some papers out of the way, he wrote down two names, one on each of the separate columns. "Rowen and Alexander are your parents. Rowen was an Angel, and your father fell years before any of us had any idea of what could happen. You are the only one of your kind. Any other time when a Fallen's and an Angel's bloodlines were mixed, the child would come into the world stillborn. It's believed it has to do with the mutation of our genes. We all have manifested ungodly abilities after the removal of our wings. But then you came along, and everyone knew even before you were born that you were to be special."

"What about Nate — is he like me too?"

"No. From what I know about your brother, he is entirely mortal. Nate was your father's first child. No one is sure who his mother is, but Rowen took him in as her own. Neither Brinley Goodwin nor him have ever shown signs of manifesting either of their parents' nature. Most of the time when both parents are Fallen or Angels, the child is mortal. They show no special abilities and age just as the locals do in the town. More or less, it appears to be a fail-safe for the Elite to ensure the population continues to grow. There are always those few exceptions that show talent, but they are very rare." I watched Asher speak about my brother, the words making my stomach twist inside out. I had never shown signs of being special in anything. Every other child growing up had been talented, excelling in the arts or school, while I had always hung back, never quite finding the right thing to excel in.

"None of this makes any sense. I have never been anything special. Truthfully I'm subpar to all the others my age." My thoughts repeated themselves out loud to Asher. I felt like my brain was turning to mush with all the information that we were shoving into it, but I kept up the appearance of being all right with everything. I needed to know every bit of information that Asher would divulge to me.

"You could never be subpar with the parents you have, but the lack of talent is most likely because you are still developing your abilities. From what you told us today, the vision you had are those fresh abilities beginning to slowly make their appearances." Asher laid a hand over the one I had resting on the table, rubbing small shapes into the skin, though it appeared that he didn't even realize he was doing it.

"So, do you have a special power?" I teased, letting myself laugh slightly at the way his eyebrows rose at my joke.

"All the Fallen I have ever met do. They are unnatural—that's why we get the reputation of being evil. Each of our abilities stems from one of the seven deadly sins. Our core group is very small, which explains why none of our abilities overlap in the sin aspect, but your father had met others who shared similar abilities from their chosen evils," he said, picking up a blank piece of paper to write all seven deadly sins out in front of us and drawing a line under each one.

"Aspyn is greed. She can show the thing you most desire and poison the fantasy while simultaneously poisoning you as well. Mallory is Envy, but we like to call her the copycat. She can replicate your ability to use against you. She doesn't get angry often, but you don't want to be on the other side of her temper when she is. Now her sister Delaney is the one who can remove all of your senses and send you into a sleep paralysis. Everything is frozen in time, but she leaves you with your thoughts. That makes her our sloth. Gabe is lust. He turns people against one another. It's like watching two rabid dogs go after each other when he uses his talent. My ability stems from wrath. I can make people's blood boil underneath their skin, burning them from the inside out." Asher hesitated when telling me his ability, like he thought I would flinch back from his grip in fright. Being around him, I didn't feel an ounce of fear pulsing through my veins. I knew that he wouldn't hurt me even if I lashed out at him.

There were two more spots left on the piece of paper, making my eyes lock on the last name scrawled out. "What about my father?"

"Xander was gluttony. He could immobilize a single person's powers as long as he needed, but he could never figure out how to expand it to more than one person at a time. That was something that drove him mad. He was so stubborn. I can see where you get it from." I was still staring at the paper, wondering about the names of my parents. These people were strangers I had no memory of, but their secrets were now my problems.

"Does that mean I could gain abilities from pride?"

"Not exactly. Like I said before, you are special. Something none of us have ever seen before, but what we do know is you're going to be more powerful than any of us. You will be able to do what both sides are capable of." I felt his eyes burning holes into the side of my head as he spoke.

"Is that why we were sent away—because I was different?" My eyes left the papers, meeting his gaze for a split second. Every pore on my body began to fill with guilt.

Asher made sure to catch my eyes before speaking again. "No. Don't ever think that. It was for your own protection that we had to hide you from the council. The plan didn't go the way we wanted it to. Your parents were banished or killed—we are still unsure of what happened to them—and you were supposed to be given to Claire Halloway. She was supposed to hide you away until we arrived at the safe house. We have been protecting you since before you were born, but once Claire lost it the night everything went to hell, we knew that we had to act fast. But we weren't fast enough. Nathaniel had already disappeared with you. Both of you just vanished into thin air, and tracking either of you down would have put you in more danger. That is why Finley and the others are trying to get into your head. They want to set off the darkest parts of you, so they have an excuse to snuff out the Night Monster, as they have so graciously nicknamed you."

Taking both hands behind my neck, I began to rub at the tension that had begun build in my muscles. My lip quivered slightly. All of this was too much for me to digest right now. The world I thought to be so normal was just shattered and mutated into a nightmare. I was nothing special. I couldn't be what they wanted me to be. None of what he explained to me answered what I wanted to know—it only added to the uncertainties gathering in my mind. Asher must have read my distressed features as he scooped up the scattered papers. "All right, that's enough for one day."

Exiting the greenhouse, we started down the long path back towards the front of the school. The parking lot was almost completely empty, leaving only a few straggling cars surrounding Asher's. A distinct female figure leaned up against the driver's side of the car, concealing her identity with the mop of hair hanging in her face until we were only a few feet away.

Tabitha Manson stood tall, flipping her ice

blonde hair away from her face. This was the first time I could actually see her properly. She was the exact replica of Mallory. Their identical features left Delaney to be the exact opposite of her sister, with her dark chocolate hair and tanned skin which differed from her sister's pale complexion. The only thing that matched all three of the triplets were the gray-blue eyes that each of them had. Tabitha's were less vibrant from her Fallen siblings, but they still stood out against her blonde locks. Her glare pierced into mine as she watched me come closer.

"Well, well, well, isn't this a surprise? Now I won't have to hunt both of you down." Tabitha moved like a lioness ready to pounce on its prey as she circled in front of Asher and me. "The council wants to see you both. It seems like some rules have been broken, and you know how much the council likes to enforce those."

Asher's body blocked my view of Tabitha as he sidestepped in front of me. "I suggest you run back to Finley and snitch to him, Tabby. Although we all know you are *his* favorite, not Fin's. I'm going to say this one more time before things get ugly — both of you stay the hell away from her."

I was propelled forward by the force of Asher's grip. He threw me into the car's opening, slamming the door shut. The metal blocked out the rest of Tabitha's words towards me. Gulping in a deep breath, I relished the moment of silence. Nothing was going to get easier going forward, and this might be the last piece of tranquility I had to myself. My life was going to turn into a rollercoaster without a safety belt that I would have to cling to with everything I had. It was either hang on tight or fall to my death.

CHAPTER TEN

The next day I lounged across Aspyn's bed, my legs tucked underneath me while I examined every inch of the raven-haired girl's room. It was everything you would picture it to be. The walls were painted a light mint green while the bedding underneath me was a soft beige color. Pillows lay sprawled out, almost covering the entire bed's surface. But what stood out the most was the wall covered from baseboard to ceiling in photographs. Some had faded from time, but the memories still bled through where they had been tacked.

"Did you take all of these pictures, Asp?" I stood from the bed, taking long strides over to the pictures. Everyone from the group was frozen in frame in at least one photo. Even Finley posed next to Aspyn in one, his white teeth standing out against his bright smile, arms loosely draped over Aspyn's laughing figure. Her nose was scrunched up as if she was snorting at a horrible joke thrown from behind the camera. Leaning in, I examined the photo closer, taking in the clearing's backdrop we had all stood in days before.

"I like to remember everything or else I forget. Time seems to be endless, but with these, I am able to keep a piece of each memory alive." Aspyn's shoulders shrugged up, not bothering to look from her toenails she was painting a bright violet color.

Scanning the wall for a few seconds more, my eyes locked on a Polaroid hidden from sight by the mass number of photos cluttering the surface. It was tucked away by a clothespin on a small, yellowing string. Pushing the other photos away, I could see that the picture held Claire Halloway leaning back in a fit of laughter, her eyes crinkled at the sides, making her look older than the girl I had witnessed fighting with her father. Two others sat next to her, laughing as well.

The first was a woman, her strawberry-blonde hair falling around her face while the crinkle at the bridge of her nose matched the one I would get in a fit of giggles. Behind her, a man sat with his arms wrapped around her petite frame. His eyes bore straight into mine, allowing me to see the exact same ones that sat on either side of my nose. The green washed into the blue surrounding his irises, a color you could only witness on the clearest days at sea. Everything else about this man was the spitting image of Nathaniel—they could have been mistaken for twins if I hadn't known any better.

"That's my favorite picture of them together." My feet wobbled underneath me at the sound of Aspyn's voice behind me. She plucked the photo from the string, handing it directly to me. I took it in my hands, greedily wanting to burn the strangers' faces into my mind. "We were so happy that day, even Delaney if you could believe it. That was right before Claire knew anything about our world, making us all just normal teenagers to her. She fit right in with everyone. I miss it."

Aspyn's eyes roamed the wall, a gleam of tears

hiding behind the green orbs. All these memories were just past lives to her, laid out to remember for better or worse. Somehow, I found it hard to believe that Aspyn forgot anything that had occurred in these stills. In the way her eyebrows began to pinch together, I could see the pain that remembering each moment caused her. Dropping my gaze, I set my view back on the photo held in my grip.

With a gentle touch, my fingertips grazed the glossy image. There was nothing more I wanted than to see this scene play out in front of me. I needed more of a taste of who my parents once were. My heart swelled as emotion pumped through my veins. The flimsy material of the old photo stiffened as the odd feeling of being sucked into the image began to consume my thoughts. The only way I could describe the sensation was like falling down a pitch-black hole.

Each tree revealed itself in glowing color around me. Birds chattered amongst each other in harmonious conversations. My hands adhered to the dew on the grass that sat underneath my hands. I inhaled deeply, taking in the scent of the dampened earth which clung to my nostrils.

"Oh, come on, Xander. Just play this one game with us." Claire's voice spoke out through the trees. I was beginning to think I would be able to recognize her voice more than my own. She had coated herself in this bizarre town's creatures and secrets, which now saturated my every thought.

"Truth or dare is a playground game for children, Claire." A man's deep voice scolded the young girl, but I could hear the playfulness that broke across his words, cutting away any tension. My feet carried me closer to the voices that hid behind the giant pines, stopping only a few yards from the figures. I stood in clear view, but none of them noticed my sudden intrusion.

In front of me sat the three people from the photo. Xander and Rowen only steps away from me in the flesh. I could see the warm blush that broke across my mother's cheeks, I was so close. They were draped across each other like magnets which held tightly together. Planting my feet in the mossy ground beneath me, I couldn't bring myself to travel any closer to them. This moment had played through my mind at least a million times. Anger mixed together with sadness in the pit of my stomach as

I watched the Angel girl lean back into the Fallen devil.

"Do you always have to take everything so seriously, Xan? Just play one round for me." Rowen's musical voice danced across the forest floor. I could listen to it forever, even if it was the same line on a constant repeat. Rowen eyed the man behind her with her caramel-colored gaze.

Xander matched her look, adoration shining through it. "I'd do anything for you, my love."

They held an intimate moment between each other, ignoring the girl next to them. Claire simply just rolled her eyes in disgust at the two. They looked like lovesick teenagers to anyone who could pass by, but I knew better. I knew the truth. Rowen broke eye contact first and then turned to look at Claire before both of the girls burst out into a fit of laughter at an unsaid joke. Xander's deep chuckle joined them moments later, mixing in with the high-pitched giggles.

A bright flash went off behind me, startling the trio out of their laughter. For a moment I thought they saw me eavesdropping on them, but tracking their stares I could feel them look straight through me. I was invisible to them. Someone they would never truly know.

Whipping my head around at the footsteps approaching,

I caught sight of the twins strolling towards the group. Asher's shoulder connected with mine. The breath caught in my throat, not daring to escape, as the boy's face strained with confusion. He looked down at the spot where I stood, still not understanding what had just happened, before Aspyn burst through me. A tingling feeling replaced her disappearance from my body. I was just a hologram in their lives for now.

"Picture-perfect." Aspyn's smiling face looked down at the small vintage Polaroid camera in her hand. The device was nothing like the ones we had, making it look foreign in her small hands.

"If you insist on taking all these pictures, at least get my good side, darling." Claire started posing from side to side, snickering at herself while she did it. The sun caught the gold hanging around her neck. My muscles burned with temptation to dive forward and snatch the unbroken medallion from the young girl's chest. I couldn't help but want to understand the incomplete verse etched into its surface. Taking a closer look, my eyes found no divots where the words were in the metal piece I had acquired. I let my eyes sink closed to soak in my mother's laugh once more.

Slowly I peeled by my eyelids open, allowing the forest to melt away and sucking me straight back into reality. Aspyn's room was distorted, causing my vision of the world to take on a slanted motion. The floor moved in waves, my body matching a boat in choppy seas. "I need to sit down."

Staggering backward, I almost toppled over in the process. Luckily Aspyn's hand shot out, catching me before my body could connect with the hardwood floor. Holding me up on my feet, she led me back towards the bed before setting me amongst the sea of pillows. My back flopped against the mattress, reveling in the cool cotton blanket resting on top.

"Lily, what's going on?" Aspyn's hands hovered over me, not sure what to do. "Your eyes glazed over just now. I thought you might just have spaced out looking at the picture, but you weren't looking at it anymore."

A clipped paint spot on the ceiling stood out against the mint-colored wall that surrounded it, allowing me to focus in on it as I waited for the world to stop spinning. Aspyn huffed at me, but my response never came. I didn't want to explain what

I had just witnessed. I wanted to hold on to it. Savor every look I had gotten from my parents; every word they uttered. I didn't want to share them, not now. Not ever.

"I'm getting Asher." The door slammed shut after her, leaving me to groan at her idea. What I needed was to be left alone with my thoughts, not bombarded with ten thousand meaningless questions by the green-eyed devil himself. This vision was different than the last. I had touched the grass, heard the birds sing, and the haunting laugh of my mother was still ringing back in my ears, but none of them had seen me. None except Asher, who had watched the spot I stood in like a hawk until the vision vanished around me.

Whatever this ability that was manifesting was, I didn't want it. The desire to be normal again was so tempting, but I would never be able to forget the things I had learned in Idelwood. The facts of this town were burned into my brain, never letting me forget them.

Aspyn's door burst open, once more hitting the back wall it was connected to. The crash of the door was followed by heavy stomping as Asher entered the room; surely his twin wasn't far behind him. I felt the bed dip on either side of me, making me sink further into the mountain of pillows. Honestly, I was just hoping that they would hide me from the onslaught of questions that were about to spill from Asher's lips.

"What happened?" Asher words sat low in his throat, making them come out in a growl. Peeking out from the arm I had thrown over my eyes, I met Asher's anxious gaze. His eyes scanned over me, checking to see if any physical damage had been inflicted.

"Calm down, killer, I'm fine," I said, though my words sounded like I had one too many drinks, wobbling out of my lips in one long, drawn-out sentence. Blocking out his intense gaze wasn't working, but I didn't budge from my position on the bed, allowing my eyes to droop closed once more. Every inch of my body felt weakened. Slowly my tense muscles unclenched from their hold on each other. As the adrenaline disappeared, so did my energy.

Aspyn snorted as I felt Asher throw himself backward in frustration, the mattress bouncing underneath him as he went. "You can be such a drama queen sometimes, Ash, it's unreal."

"This is serious, Aspyn, and you both are treating like it's some sort of game."

"Technically you're freaking out over nothing. Lily never said anything was wrong. You need to relax, or you are going to get worry lines, big brother." I cracked open one eye to watch Aspyn bop her twin on the nose, making him swat at her hand. She stood from the bed, dusting off the invisible lint from her sweater. "I have to go meet up with Laney and Mal. I promised them both we would hide out together at the safe house while you two attend the council meeting. Be sure to let me know how that goes."

Her footsteps clicked out of the room, leaving Asher and me surrounded by silence. The minutes passed slowly before I mustered up the strength to glance in his direction. The room had stopped spinning, allowing me to see every line that had formed on his face. His brows were scrunched together with eyes narrowed in concentration, trying to think of a way to fix everything that was happening around us. An airy giggle broke through the room making the features only deepen with my laughter.

"What could possibly be funny to you?" Asher's monotonous voice cut around my laughter, commanding it to stop.

"If I don't laugh at something, I'm going to lose my mind. So, I choose to laugh at the fact that you think if you stare at me long enough, I will tell you what is wrong." I smiled, looking over to where he lay. Asher turned his head towards me, his ears turning a slight shade of pink with annoyance at my actions, though he was trying to conceal his anger from me.

"This is serious, Lily! I can't protect you if you don't tell me what is happening. Aspyn burst into my room acting like you were dying. All she kept saying is that you almost passed out after standing in some trancelike state."

Sitting straight up, I towered over him. "Who says I need protecting? I am perfectly capable of handling myself. I have been doing it for ever since

Nate vanished and I was only seven then. I don't need to be saved by anyone."

Asher mirrored my position, sitting tall against my glare. He now had the height advantage, making me have to crane my neck up. Our eyes matched the same burning anger which pulsed throughout the room, making the temperature rise around us. We both wanted to be in control, neither one willing to back down to the other. He didn't scare me, even as the rage which had traveled to his bright eyes mixed together. They flashed back and forth, transforming them into a smoky green. Asher was trying to gain control of what side of him I saw.

The hunger rooted deep within his pupils disappeared altogether as his lips met mine. My thoughts jumbled together, making the anger I had felt vanish into the heated room. I sat frozen in place for a moment trying to rationalize what was happening before my lips reacted to his, both pairs moving in perfect rhythm. Asher broke away, letting his mouth roam over every inch of my exposed collarbone they could find. I sucked in a sharp breath between my teeth as he found the sensitive skin in the crook of my neck before his lips found mine again. Asher's teeth pulled down on my bottom lip, lightly nipping the swollen skin. Chills gathered on my arms, causing them to tingle against the air-conditioned room.

The electrified energy I knew both of us felt around each other was beginning to charge quickly with every touch we shared, sparking up an invisible light along my veins. He shivered under my touch as I dragged my hands up his chest and around his shoulders before knotting my fingers in the dark hair that rested at the nape of his neck. In one fluid motion, my legs swung over his hips, straddling either side of them, careful to never break from the kiss. Fire trailed up my hips where Asher's fingertips left feather-like touches against the base of my spine, pulling me closer to him with every motion.

Drawing back when my lungs finally couldn't take the lack of oxygen, I laid my forehead against his, closing my eyes to drink in every second of this moment. There was no telling how long this feeling would last amidst the chaos. Asher's kiss felt like a drug to me, leaving me with a high I never wanted to come down from. Being pulled so close to him, I could feel my eyelashes brush up against his skin as I opened my eyes to meet his brilliantly green ones. They sparkled with emotion as it swam into the color's depths.

"Lil," Asher let out a gruff whisper. "I'm sorry, I shouldn't have…"

Asher's voice trailed off from the sentence allowing me the chance to catch the corner of his lips as he turned his head away from me. Trailing my lips across his jaw, I hovered over his mouth, whispering against his lips softly, "Don't apologize. You'll ruin the moment."

I could feel a smile form on his lips as the words left mine. Pulling back, I wanted to truly look at him when he spoke. "I'm just glad you didn't run away from me."

"I could still do that if you wanted." I swung my legs off him to retreat from the bed, Asher's strong arms caught my hips, holding them firmly in place. I quirked my eyebrow in his direction, catching the smirk plastered across his face.

"Yeah, that's not going to happen anytime soon."

He leaned in slowly, his lips trailing along my bare shoulder, whispering as he went. I let my head arch back towards the ceiling, allowing his lips to roam where they pleased. Asher planted one last kiss along my jawline before pulling back, his intense gaze poring over me. I dropped my eyes away from his stare, trying my best to hide behind the bangs that had floated back into my face.

Asher caught the bottom of my chin, running a thumb across my cheek. "So, are you going to explain what happened earlier?"

Sighing at him, a mischievous grin played across my lips. "Did you kiss me thinking that I would spill all my secrets to you, Asher Faye?"

With one raised eyebrow he responded, "Liliana Caldwell, do you think so lowly of me? If we are being honest with each other now, the truth is that I wanted to do that since the second I watched you step off that bus, but I thought you'd kick my ass if I tried."

"You're not wrong about that," I sputtered through laughter as I untangled myself from his grip to sit on the bed next to him. Asher made sure to keep contact with my bare skin as he drew shapes on my thigh which poked through the dark jeans I wore. The action had become a habit he had begun since the afternoon in the greenhouse. "I had another vision, but this one was different from the last. This one had to do with a picture of my parents and Claire in the forest. Aspyn and I were looking at it before it happened."

"What do you mean this one was different?"

"It was like I was actually there, Ash. I could feel the breeze hitting my skin and the dew in the grass underneath my feet. Last time it was as if Claire and her father were playing on a screen in front of me. I was just standing against a wall watching them argue. The only thing that confused me was no one could see I was there, except for you." Asher's eyebrows shot up into his hairline at my comment. I could see the gears in his mind circling in his head. "I don't know if you actually saw me but I was standing just off to the side of Claire and the others when your shoulder plowed into mine. It shocked you because I wasn't supposed to be there, but then Aspyn just walked straight through me like I was a ghost. Your eyes didn't leave where I stood."

Asher ran his hand through his hair, making it lay perfectly messy. "With your ability manifesting this quickly, no one is truly sure what or how many abilities you will inherit from your parents. Delaney has been researching different things we know about them, hoping to find something helpful. We can talk to her about this after the meeting, but the council cannot know about any of this when we go meet them tonight. It's only going to be us attending tonight. They won't feel as threatened if we show up alone, though they have a way of being intimidating and manipulative all on their own."

The council meeting.

The perfect bubble of happiness I had just obtained burst around me as I remembered the council meeting which had haunted my dreams last night. I let out a shaky breath as the feeling of bliss was replaced with crippling anxiety. Asher placed his lips on my forehead, whispering gently into my hairline, "Everything will be fine. I won't let them hurt you."

"It's not them I'm worried about. It's *him*," I

whispered, my body automatically folding into his strong embrace. I squeezed my eyes tightly shut, hoping that I would wake up and this would all just be a horrible nightmare. My body began to shake in fear as the redheaded Angel's sinister smile burned across my eyelids. Asher's grip tightened around me, trying to calm the panic which began to surround us. His words were dark when he finally spoke again.

"He most definitely won't get anywhere near you."

Chapter Eleven

Cold air pierced my exposed collarbone on the walk to town hall. A comfortable silence hung in the air between Asher and me. Since finding out about what lived in this town, every shadow that played against the cobblestone walkway seemed to follow my every movement. My mind felt unhinged, warped by the thoughts of the council's judgment which lay only feet away. We stopped in sync, Asher's bright eyes watching me look up at the statue that stood tall in front of me. With what I'd learned, the strange Angel girl in the middle of the square held more meaning to this town than any of the locals could fathom. A squeeze on my hand broke my gaze away from her stone-cold stare right into Asher's concerned look.

"What?" I wanted to sink into my own skin under his gaze. His eyes examined every line across my face, making my left eyebrow twitch up at him.

His mop of black hair shook back and forth. "You just looked lost in your own head, *darling*."

He chuckled when I scrunched my nose as the pet name fell from his lips. The same pet name that a certain redheaded Angel liked to taunt me with.

"Don't call me that." I dropped his hand and retreated around the statute, heading up the stairs of town hall. Asher's voice called after me, making me only travel up the stairs faster. I was already tiptoeing on a tightrope in this town by falling for the angel-faced boy behind me. Just the thought was not helping me balance against the harsh winds on the thin wire. I was never supposed to stay past my birthday in this town. Even now, knowing all the answers which led back to my parents lay here, Nate's disappearance still hung heavy in my heart. No town would patch that hole.

Asher finally caught up to me, his hand landing softly on my lower back. I swatted his touch away before turning to face him. "Come on Lil. I'm sorry. I forgot that's his favorite pet name to use."

His words came through gritted teeth. The thought of Finley having any sort of pet name for me made him want to boil the blood underneath the Angel's skin. I placed my hands over my face, digging the heels of my palms into my eye sockets, "It's not your fault. It's just a name and I shouldn't let him get under my skin so much. I'm just stressed out about this meeting."

"I already told you, Lily, I'm not going to let anything happen you. I promise." Asher's hands gripped mine, removing them from my eyes. He placed them on either side of his chiseled cheeks. "You have my word, and I don't give that to many people anymore."

His eyes exposed each word he spoke was nothing but the truth. I nodded quickly towards him before we started up the stairs once more. The ill feeling gathering in my throat hadn't disappeared since Tabitha Manson delivered the requested meeting from the council. We all knew that this was no request though. Just thinking of the encounters I'd had with Finley and Tabitha, I couldn't imagine how the council would treat me. They see me as nothing more than an abomination that needs to be snuffed out. These were the times I wished Nate was around to help guide me through all the madness.

The wind whipped around my hair, making it hard to hear Asher's voice ringing through the silent whistle that it spoke. "You ready?"

"As I'll ever be."

I watched the wooden doors swing open to reveal a familiar face. Emaline Goodwin stood at the bottom of the large, marble, double-sided staircase. Her short blonde hair hung in front of her face as she looked down at a clipboard. Confusion swept over me as we approached the woman who had claimed, if only for appearances, to be my foster mother. A bright smile lit up the room when she noticed our arrival.

"Oh, good, you're here. You know how the council can get when they have to wait, Asher." Emma's gaze went back to the board in front of her, signaling us to follow her up the stairs with two pointed fingers. "Judgment is calling, and she is not known for waiting patiently."

Asher gripped my hand as he led me up the steps. A hushed whisper came from me as I leaned towards his ear. "What is she doing here? I thought this was going to be only the council."

His shoulders tensed under my words. "No. Both Emma and Will are a part of the Elite. When the council summons a meeting, everyone who is considered to be a part of the Elite is required to attend. Failure to do so is immediate removal."

The room went cold as Asher spoke of removal and I knew exactly what that meant. The Elites were the most trusted servants of God, the eyes and ears on the ground for him. Disobedience was not tolerated within his ranks.

Emma hesitated slightly when we reached two cherry-colored doors. She did not turn when she spoke. "Let's get this show on the road."

Bright lights and a chorus of voices rang out from behind the doors as Emma pushed them open. As we stepped through the entryway, the harmonious voices dwindled down to silence as they noticed my presence in the room. My eyes tracked the space, landing on a large wooden table which stretched out in the front of the room. Twelve men sat behind the counter, each one of them staring me down. I shrank behind Asher, waiting for someone to speak through the quiet air. *Speak only when addressed*—Asher's strict orders circled around in my skull.

I glued my mouth shut, not wanting to accidentally offend someone in the room. One wrong move would cause them to want me gone more than they already did. Looking through the sea of people, my eyes caught the one person I did not want to encounter. Finley's baby blues bored into mine from across the room where he stood hiding in the shadows of the corner he leaned into. The grip on my hand tightened, pulling me closer, I knew Asher had caught sight of the hidden boy as well.

"This meeting will commence." A booming voice reverberated off the walls in the hall, causing everyone's attention to shift to its owner. The hairs on the back of my neck stood up straight, and each man in front of me shared the same look of loathing. No one knew if I was dangerous, making each set of eyes staring at me feel like fire on my skin. It seemed like an eternity until another voice spoke.

"State your name for the council." The man's voice came from the other end of the table. He didn't bother to look back up from the paper he was peering down at. My throat swelled shut, making it impossible for me to answer.

I was propelled forward by Asher planting me in front of him. I whipped my head back to look at the boy, and he gave me a knowing look. I let my eyes travel back to the speaker again. "Liliana Caldwell."

My voice shook in fear, making the man look up from his paper with a glare. "State your full name."

Snickers could be heard throughout the hall. I gulped nervously, "Liliana Adrienne Caldwell."

There was a slight gasp in the room, and I knew the reason. Just like the dress Finley had told me was a beautiful contradiction, so was my full name. My first name meant pure and perfect while my given middle name meant dark one. The perfect combination of the dark and light which flowed through my veins, something I had never paid much attention to, but now it was an obvious sign of rebellion against the council, wrapped in a human package straight from my parents.

"Seems like they are still messing with our heads even from the grave," Finley sneered from across the room, his voice venomous. Chaos had erupted amongst the hall, causing obscenities to be thrown at me in every direction.

"Everyone needs to settle down. We are here for official council business. Control yourself or I urge you to leave before you are dismissed." Silence fell upon the room as his threat settled into everyone. My gaze locked on the man with the booming voice once more. "Now, back to the reason we called this meeting. We will start with some standard questions for you, Liliana."

A man on the right of him with wire glasses began the questioning storm. "Liliana, were you told in any way by anyone in Idelwood what your parents were?"

I knew they wished for me to throw the twins under the bus—they had a target on their backs as much as I did where the council was concerned. "No, I figured it out myself. Not that your little spies didn't give clues about what they thought about me."

My fiery glare landed on Finley, whose lips turned up into a smirk. "All in good fun, darling."

Everything happened so fast I didn't have time to react until Asher and Finley stood nose to nose, engaged in a heated argument. Chaos began again in the hall following their outbursts. People were yelling about the quarrel and arguing with one another that a thing like me shouldn't be in their presence. Tuning out the others, I focused in on the two boys, wanting to hear what was being said.

"You need to back off. You have no business in these matters anymore. You lost that right when you fell." Finley jabbed at Asher's chest, but Asher stood tall, not budging an inch.

"When it comes to Lily, everything is my concern now," Asher spat back at Finley. I stepped closer to the argument until I stood right behind Asher.

Rolling his eyes, Finley laughed at him. "You think something like her could care about something like you, Asher? Wait until she finds out the real reason you and Aspyn fell, then see what she thinks. Although I bet that Night Monster isn't even capable of real feelings."

Asher lunged at Finley, taking a swipe at his face before I could press myself in between both of them. "KNOCK IT OFF. The both of you."

My hands rested on both of their chests as they heaved up and down in anger. I looked towards Asher, catching sight of the black angry orbs that rested in his face.

"Oh, and what are you going to do about it, darling?" Finley's voice was laced with sadistic humor as he let the syllables of the pet name drag out. Anger shot through my body, starting at my toes before boiling up through me.

My voice hardened, cutting Asher off as he went to speak once more. "Why do you take pleasure in this, Finley? I haven't done anything to you."

Finley leaned down towards me, his nose inches from mine. "You just existing is enough for everyone in this room, except lover boy here, to want you destroyed."

Not being able to take it anymore, I allowed all the self-control that I had in me slip away. My anger had boiled over with every word he spoke. I leaped towards him, and my hand swung out, making contact with his check. A sickening crack ricocheted through the room. Asher caught me by the waist, pulling me back, but it didn't stop me from kicking and scratching at him to get out of his tight grasp. I wanted nothing more than to leave another mark on the redhead in front me, letting him know who he had decided to toy with. Asher's calm voice whispered into my ear, trying to drown out the screams. "Not here. You need to calm down, Lil."

His soothing words continued to speak until the red haze that covered my vision evaporated. I could still feel my heart pounding with anger, but the urge to kill Finley was more of a soft hum now.

An unfamiliar voice sent chills down my spine as it spoke towards us. "Come now, boys. You're ruining all my fun, dolls. Oh and, Liliana, I see you inherited both your father's eyes and that temper he always had."

Craning my neck past Finley, I looked at the woman who spoke. She wore a lace dress that cut all the way down to her bellybutton, revealing her milky skin against the black fabric. Her burgundy hair looked unnatural on her pale skin, but the eyes were what caught my attention. They were so familiar to me, but I couldn't place where I had seen those ice-blue eyes before.

"Ravana, my favorite Holy of them all." Asher's voice spoke to the woman first. She smirked in his direction. I could feel his discomfort as he watched Ravana stroll towards us.

"You are always so bitter, Asher. When are you going to get over the fact that you got caught, and I have learned how to be sinister without losing my wings?" Ravana teased, circling us like a lioness watching her prey before slowly leaning in to whisper against Asher's ear. Her lips brushed beside his neck when she retracted from our bubble.

"We all know the only person in here who is truly sinister is you, Ravana." Asher's grip on me tightened, not wanting to let go until the woman was back in his sight.

Ravana smiled slightly at his comment, then set her eyes on me. "Such a pretty girl. You look so much like your mother." I shifted uncomfortably at the mention of Rowen as she stuck her hand out in front of me. "Ravana Chadwick."

"What are you doing?" Emma's voice broke through the conversation, making Ravana retract her claw. Emma stood, watching her trying to hide the emotions on her face, hurt swimming in her blue eyes. A matching pair staring brightly towards her.

"Sister, a pleasure as always." Ravana threw her hands up and spoke in a sickly sweet voice to Emma. "I came to see if it was true. If they had really found Rowy's little girl after all these years."

"You need to leave—now."

Ravana thought about Emma's command for a second. "Hm, I don't think I will. You see, it just started to get interesting, and as you know, I do quite enjoy a good show."

Every eye in the room was watching the scene that played out in front of them. They hung on every word that the altercation was giving them.

"If you are done, we would like to continue the meeting." The man with the booming voice was watching us with a disapproving glare.

"Oh, Abel, come now. We were just having a bit of fun. Although now that I have your attention, may

I make a suggestion for you?" Ravana sauntered her way over to the wooden table, hopping up and sitting in front of Abel.

"You will even if I deny you." Abel waved his hand at her in annoyance.

"Well, it is obvious to everyone in the room that young Liliana's abilities are developing, and her birthday does land on a big day for the town. So, on her birthday when her powers are fully manifested, we should decide then what to do with her, all while having the celebration of Idelwood's Founder's Day Ball. Not only will we be able to celebrate our town but also Liliana and her abilities. The mortals will be clueless, thinking that it is just a harmless celebration like always."

I tensed at the mention of my growing abilities. My birthday was less than a month away, and that meant learning quickly how to control whatever these abilities brought on. The humans of Idelwood would be oblivious to the danger in their midst as they drank and laughed with one another. Once upon a time, I would have been just as oblivious as them.

"One condition," Asher voice sounded out. "Everyone in the town is allowed to attend the masquerade this year—that includes the Fallen."

Ravana's face held an inhuman grin. I could see how pleased with herself she was as she turned back to speak to Asher. "The more, the merrier. Now, what do you say, Abel?"

She leaned closer to the man, pleading for the plan she proposed to be accepted.

"I suppose that could work. Unless she causes a disturbance before her birthday, I don't see why the evaluation cannot be held on the night of the Founder's Ball."

"And what if I don't want the evaluation? What if I want to leave this town and live a normal life?" I didn't recognize my voice as it rang out in the silent hall. The confidence it held shocked the council members, making them mutter to each other.

Abel held his hand up towards them, silencing their words. "You will never live a normal life, Liliana, and if you try to run, just know we will always find you. Meeting dismissed."

Chapter Twelve

The words tumbled from his mouth, each one sounding off like a bomb detonating in a minefield. I stood still, staring at the man as the creatures who once hung on to his every sentence began to swirl around me. Abel stared back for only a moment more before he gave a slight nod in my direction, the final warning of his threat. Anxiety-filled rocks piled high on my chest, making it hard to breathe in the crowded room. I spun on the back of my heel, bolting between the crack of the large doors before they swung shut again. Faint shouts of my name could be heard through the thick wood. I chose to ignore them, weaving in and out of the crowd of Angels that flooded into the street.

Moments later they caught up to me, gripping onto my forearm, preventing me from traveling further into the madness.

"Let me go, Asher." My teeth ground together, making the words I spoke spit out harsher than I had intended them. Asher's grip tightened on me, afraid I would slip away from him before he could catch me.

"Lily, think for one second. Everyone is watching your every move anywhere you go now. Please don't give them a reason for them run back to the council." His voice shook with fear. One twisted word to the council, and I would disappear just as my parents had. Refusing to look up at him, I kept my gaze on a pebble next to his feet. My vision began to blur into a mess of color as the world around me started to spin, sending a nauseating feeling through my entire body. Every piece of me felt as if I was being pulled in a different direction, making it difficult to keep my balance. Closing my eyes, I gave in to the feeling, praying for the spinning to stop.

Loud footsteps next to my ear startled me awake. The old church was the first thing that came into my vision when I snapped my eyes open. I scanned over the building in front of me — it was in perfect condition. The door wasn't hanging off of its hinges and the overgrown foliage that had once crawled up the sides of the building was tended to. Claire Halloway stood shaking in the middle of the wooden bridge. Her light brown hair hung down her back, whipping around her, eyes searching for a person who wasn't there.

"ROWEN!" Claire's scream bounced around the unusually quiet forest, tears beginning to stream down her face, masking the ones that had recently dried on her cheeks. A sickening laugh echoed through the trees. Its haunting origin couldn't be pinpointed in the endless forest surrounding us. It was everywhere and nowhere at the same time, floating around through the wind.

"Come on, Claire. You know you want to play with us." The redheaded Angel's taunting voice sent chills up my spine. Finley was playing with Claire like a cat coming for its prey. She thrashed her head in different directions, trying to find the source of the voice, but it was impossible over the whistling wind. The sky was a dark purple color with quick flashes of lighting electrifying the night sky.

"What do you want from me? I have told you everything

I know – now please leave me alone." Claire stepped back on the bridge, allowing her back to hit the railing of the structure. The entire bridge wobbled back and forth in the growing storm. I could see her hands grip down tight on the bar to avoid toppling over into the rushing water which sat just below her.

"CLAIRE, stay where you are," my mother's musical voice yelled out towards the girl before Rowen came into view. Rowen mirrored my position on the other side of the bridge, her light hazel eyes burning with emotion in the darkness. Finley stepped from the tree line, making his presence known, and Rowen turned towards him. Tabitha hung against his hip while another male figure stood behind the two, concealing himself in the shadows the low-hanging branches gave off.

"Oh, come on, Rowen. We are just having some fun with our favorite mortal." Tabitha pushed herself off Finley, making her way over to the pair. She began to play with the poor girl's hair, giggling as Claire tensed underneath her touch. Every torturous trace on Claire's skin fueled the Manson girl, a wicked smirk plastered across her face.

Rowen's expression darkened at the three Angels,

keeping her eyes trained on Finley. "Leave her alone, you three. She has nothing to do with this."

The male in the shadows spoke this time. "On the contrary, Rowen, she has everything to do with this situation you have gotten yourself into. We all thought you were smarter than to get yourself pregnant by one of those foul creatures."

"Those foul creatures used to be just like you and me, Gabriel. It could very well be you one day if you keep it up." Rowen took a step closer to Claire, but Finley stood tall, blocking her path. With the slight movement of the redheaded devil, the man in the shadows could be seen. A strangled choke sob broke through my lips. Gabe stood, arms crossed, glaring at the group in front of him. The wind began to pick up, leaves and dirt that had once stuck to the ground swirling them around making it difficult to see the bridge.

A sickening crack broke through the howling wind, followed by a bloodcurdling scream. The scream matched Claire's.

I was thrown back into reality, the footing I had against the gravel road slipping away. Asher's quick reflexes caught me before I managed to hit the ground. Deep worry lines started to form across his face. My body felt drained of any energy that had once been there. I slumped against his grip, letting my eyelids drift shut for a moment before snapping them open once again. The urge to pass out was growing stronger, making it difficult to fight off the darkness that threatened to consume me whole. We stood frozen in the middle of town square, wandering eyes watching the scene as they passed by. Each pair wanted nothing more than to snitch to the council about the out-of-control Night Monster they all feared.

"Let's get out of here." Asher's voice felt distant as he helped me find my footing once more. His speech was distorted into long, drawn-out syllables, almost causing the words he spoke to be unrecognizable.

"Why? I'm fine, I promise." My words slurred together in a drunken state as I began to sway back and forth. Asher gripped down on my shoulders to steady me, but the world still swayed in wavy colors. "Ash, something's wrong."

Asher's brows furrowed deeper. He reached out a hand, touching my forehead but immediately retracted it. "Geez, Lily, you're burning up. Come on, let's get you to Laney."

The walk to the car blurred together as I tried to focus on just placing one foot in front of the other without tumbling forward. Asher had his phone pressed up against his ear, speaking in a hushed whisper to the person on the other end. Everything was vibrant, making the world around me fade into a dreamy cartoonlike state. Voices passing by were amplified, causing my head to pulse in pain. Asher slipped me into the passenger seat with ease when we finally arrived at the vehicle. The warm leather seat allowed me to slump my head to the side, letting the aches finally set in. Any slight movement sent jolts of pain through my entire body.

Asher reached over me, clicking the buckle into place. His fingertips lingered over the clasp before he gripped underneath my chin, making it so I was looking into his bright green eyes. "You can't fall asleep just yet, Lil."

All I could muster up was a moan at him in protest. Every one of my thoughts were trapped in my brain when I tried to speak. A long sigh left his lips before he shut the door and quickly slid` into his seat.

"This is going to be a long night." Asher's voice was a rough mumble under the roaring engine of the car. The sound soothed my racing heart, allowing me to give into the darkness I had been fighting.

Light hands ran up and down the sides of my arms, making me stir out of my deep sleep. The bright, yellow light burned as I peeled my eyes open, squinting in protest before finally adjusting to the light. An extravagant wood cabin stood lit from top to bottom in front of the parked car. The light wooden color stood out against the dark trim that lined the sides of the structure.

"Lily, hey." Asher's soft voice broke me out of my trance, turning my head to see his concerned face. He stood crouched at eye level with me just outside the opened car door. "How are you feeling?"

The pain from before had amplified, and it took every ounce of strength I currently had to not scream out in pain as I shifted uncomfortably against the seat. The silence was all the answer he needed before he began to help me from the car. Heavy breaths came from my lungs as burning pain ran up my spine when it extended fully. I reached out, falling forward into Asher's stronghold, who made sure I didn't drop to the stone driveway.

"Thank you," I croaked, each word grinding against both sides of my throat like sandpaper.

"Anytime. Come on, let's get you inside so Delaney can look you over." Asher's lips pressed into a sad smile when he finally caught my gaze, as he pulled me towards the door seconds later. Passing through the entryway, I could hear the others arguing amongst themselves. Our feet traveled towards the voices, making me cringe into Asher's shoulder to try and dull the yelling as it grew louder.

"If you don't figure something out quick, Ice Queen, then we are all dead." The first voice that I could make out was Gabe's. "Are you even listening to me, Delaney, or are you just going to sit there and stare at that stupid case of yours all day?"

"If it shuts you the hell up, then yes, Gabriel. I don't think you realize how this all works. One wrong move, too much of this or that, it would kill any one of us. I don't know how much her body can take or if it will kill her altogether. So please shut the hell up and let me think."

"Oh my, Lily." Aspyn's voice rang out over the other girl's mumbles. As Asher set me down on a barstool, his hands hovered over my body, making sure I wasn't going to topple over. A large granite countertop sat in front of me, allowing me to lay my feverish skin against the cool stone as the others continued to argue.

"Enough." Asher's warning tone towards the two bickering Fallen Angels caused me to jump slightly. His light touch landed on my back, stabilizing me once again before slowly starting to trace circular patterns on my exposed skin. My eyes landed on his watchful ones, his touch sending a shiver through my body, which from his upturned lips, I knew he felt too. Asher watched me lay my head back down before he spoke again, this time his tone calmer than before. "Delaney, I really hope you have something for us because I don't think she is going to last much longer. She's burning up. That fever at least needs to come down soon."

Cold fingertips landed on the back of my neck. A yelp escaped my throat from the sudden temperature change on my fiery skin. "I'll give her peppermint oil for the fever. As for the other symptoms, I have what I made for Rowen when she went through this, but I'm afraid it will be too strong for her, Ash."

"Can you dilute it or give her less of a dose?" Aspyn's quiet voice spoke out behind me.

"No. It's all or nothing. Are we all willing to risk that? The power that is flooding through Lily right now has nowhere to go because her abilities have not fully manifested. Rowen almost died because we didn't understand what was happening." There was a tremble of fear that radiated through Delaney's voice. She held it together so easily but suddenly the mask of the emotionless girl she made herself out to be to vanished. Silence was the only sound in the room as the idea of killing me traveled around everyone's thoughts.

"If we don't try, this will kill her." Asher's voice hardened at the thought. I could hear someone rummaging around in a box; vials of glass clanked together and the overwhelming smell of flowers filled the kitchen. The smell was repulsive, causing me to groan inwardly, trying to block out the scent as it traveled through my nose. It stuck in every particle of my nostrils, and I gagged at the aroma, feeling like I might vomit if I didn't get away from it. Turning to bolt from the chair, I was met with Asher's chest blocking my way, his hands landing on my hips to keep me in place.

"Take her upstairs and make her drink this, then put this on the back of her neck to help with the fever. Both will probably knock her out cold for a couple of hours," Delaney's voice commanded. Two vials were passed to Asher. One held bright purple liquid that shimmered underneath the light, while the other was clear. I craned my neck over my shoulder to see the other people in the room. Mallory stood in the corner next to the stove, trying her best not to be seen, while a fuming Gabe stood glaring at me from the other side of the counter. As I caught his stare, he narrowed his eyes at me before stomping out of the room.

"I'll check on him. See you soon, L." Aspyn placed a kiss on my fevered skin and patted her twin's shoulder before dashing in the direction of the angry boy.

"Come on Lily." Asher's grip on my hips allowed him to easily place me on my feet. He swung his arm around my midsection to support my weight as we traveled towards the stairs. After struggling for a few minutes with the steps, Asher reached under my legs and swept them up in his arms. I fought him at first, determined to travel up the steps on my own, only to give in once I realized how weak I felt. The mattress dipped under my weight as he placed me in the middle of the bed. Cuddling into the cloud-like surface, I could hear his soft chuckle. "Come on, Lil, you have to take this."

Ignoring his pleading voice, I rolled over, facing my back towards him. A squeak slipped through my lips moment later when cold liquid hit my burning neck. I craned my neck to look at Asher, my glare landing on his cheeky grin. "You're not going to win this fight tonight, so just take this and get it over with."

He held up the purple liquid, shaking the vial slightly in my direction. I stared at it for a second before snatching it out of his hand. Popping open the top, I looked at the contents of the vial – they would either kill me, or I could let this sickness drain the life out of me slowly. Deciding the chance of death was better than a definite sentence, I threw back the vial, allowing the liquid to slide down the back of my throat, burning as it went down.

"What the hell is that?" I sputtered out in between coughing at the disgusting taste that had settled on my taste buds.

"You don't want to know. Now lie back and get some rest, Lil." Asher watched me lay my head back against a pillow before starting towards the door. I reached out, catching his wrist in my hand before he traveled too far away from the bedframe. We both stopped in our tracks, staring down at my hand. I don't know what had just come over me, but the thought of him leaving was the worst possible outcome at the moment. My grip tightened when his eyes made contact with mine, causing the breath to catch in my throat.

"Don't go," I whispered, my eyes pleading with him to not leave me alone. Maybe it was all the talk of my possible death that was making me so dependent on the green-eyed boy in front of me. Asher's presence made me feel safe, and that's all I wanted, if whatever was in that vial actually killed me.

"Are you sure?" Asher watched me for any hesitation, but I simply nodded my head towards him, scooting over to make room for him on the bed. He sighed, taking off the leather jacket that had almost become his persona, and slipped out of his shoes. The mattress dipped underneath him as he lay across the bed, lifting an arm up to allow me to scoot towards his warmth. I rested my head on his chest, listening to the steady drum of his heartbeat, calming me down like my own personalized lullaby. Asher's callused hands began to play with the ends of my hair before I spoke again.

"Thank you."

"You don't need to thank me, Lily."

As I looked up at him, my words began to slur as the drowsiness of the medication took over. "But I do. You could have left me to fend for myself with the council, and you could have let this fever kill me, but you didn't. You have a much bigger heart than you allow people to see."

His eyes met my ocean-colored ones. "You will always be safe with me, Liliana. I can promise you that. I don't know what I would do if I lost you."

"You barely know me." My eyes slowly began to close from the exhaustion that was taking over.

Before sleep fully took me, I heard him whisper softly to himself, "I know you better than you think."

Even with Asher by my side, nightmares still plagued my dreams through the entire night. Every scene that played echoed Claire's scream along with my mother's beautiful voice. They would only stop for moments, allowing the suffocating darkness to hang over me. Something bad happened on that bridge to Claire – the constant taunting of the redheaded Angel paired with things that she could only grasp the surface of must have warped her brain, causing her to sacrifice herself in the middle of the church. She did it to send a message to every Angel in this town. What that message was, I may never know.

Sweat covered my entire body when I finally was

able to rip myself from the nightmares. I thrashed about as someone tried to control my flailing limbs. The person's voice was distorted under my screams, which were overpowering their words. When my sight finally adjusted to the dimly lit room, I focused on Asher's face in front of me. Aspyn stood in the doorway, her expression horrified at the scene in front of her.

Taking in a few large gulps of air, I peeled my hair off my sweat-ridden face before meeting the matching green-eyed gazes. "I'm fine. It was just a nightmare."

"L, you were screaming for ten minutes before we could wake you. You just kept mumbling their names between the screaming." Aspyn stepped forward into the room, not fully knowing if she was allowed to invade the space with her presence.

"Whose names?" I watched her eyes flick to Asher, then back to me.

"Claire's mostly, then your parents, and Nate was mixed in as well," Asher's voice answered me back.

Throwing myself back against the pillows, I let out a disgruntled moan. "I think I'm losing my mind."

"You need to speak with Emaline Goodwin. She can tell you anything you need to know about your parents' pasts." Gabe's voice spoke out from the hallway. Propping myself on my elbows, I looked at him. The vision of Claire had revealed a part of Gabe's past that I was unaware of. As I made eye contact with him, something about his remarks to me put a sour taste in my mouth, and I intended to find out what had caused his downfall.

Chapter Thirteen

The swing on the Goodwins' front porch squeaked with each gust of wind as I stood staring at the front door. Emma was waiting to speak with me about my parents' past, but I wasn't sure what I was going to say back to the woman. The people she would speak of were just images flashing across visions and Polaroids – they still didn't feel real to me. They may never feel that way. I was debating on whether or not to turn back towards the idling car Asher sat within when the door in front of me swung open, revealing a well-dressed Will. He stood tall, watching me shrink back from him quickly. Fear pulsed through my veins, as I was not sure if he had the same anger the others had against the infamous Night Monster of Idelwood.

"Emma wanted to know if you were planning on coming in to talk. If not, she asked me to give you this." My eyes trailed down towards the yellow winter coat that lay between his fingers. The air around me had started to dip as the sun departed from its place in the sky. I was so wrapped up in my own thoughts that I hadn't even noticed.

"I'm not sure what to say to her." My voice was timid as I made eye contact with the older man.

"Don't worry, she'll do most of the talking." A light chuckle left Will's mouth. He stepped aside, waiting for me to enter the home. "Emma's up on the balcony connected to our room. She made tea for the both of you."

Reluctantly, I took the jacket he held out towards me. The yellow material felt rough between my hands. Stepping through the doorway, I made my way towards the winding staircase which led to the couple's room. The door was slightly ajar, allowing me to see the chill air blowing sheer white curtains away from the balcony's doorway. They moved in sync like waves on a beach; every few seconds they gave me a glimpse of Emma's silhouette sipping from a teacup. She was dressed in a bright blue dress that stood out against the white chair she sat on. Her blonde hair was curled at the ends in perfect ringlets, not a hair out of place. I gulped in one last breath before strolling across the room towards the doorway. Emma's back still faced me when I arrived, but I knew she felt my presence instantly.

"I thought you would never show, Liliana. You've been avoiding me for the past two days since the council meeting." Emma spoke towards the woods that lined the edge of their backyard. Her eyes were trained on a doe that stood in the middle of wilting wildflowers, dying due to the harsh winter that was soon to come. The brown eyes of the creature widened as an engine of a truck backfired, the sound reverberating through the entire neighborhood. Standing still for a few more seconds, the doe wasted no more time before dashing into the safety of the trees again. Slowly, Emma turned around to face me, her bright blue eyes popping even more than usual because of the dress. "Well, don't just stand there like a fish out of water. Come sit down."

Her hand gestured to the seat across from hers, a place setting was laid out neatly waiting for me. My stomach rolled around with nerves as I sat down, facing Emma, my eyes looking just past her as I refused to make contact with the woman. Instead, my gaze rested on the side of her head.

"If you are not going to speak to me, Liliana, this conversation is going to be useless."

"I don't know what you want me to say. You're the one who knew her." Hostility filled my voice as the words scraped out against my clenched teeth, each one more painful than the last.

Emma's giggle was almost as musical as my mother's. She watched the tips of my ears flush with anger. "You do have that temper your father had. Both of your parents were William's and my best friends – we did practically everything together."

My eyes met hers finally. She was masking the pain she felt through a light and airy voice. Small flecks of sadness scattered across her bright blue orbs while her hands shook with nerves. Emma began wringing them together when she realized I had caught on to her worries, trying to distract me from the actions. Wiping sweat that had gathered on her palms down the center of her dress, she began to speak again.

"You see, your mother was special, much like yourself. Although you have differences within your abilities, we can already see those obvious abnormalities. Your father was very powerful, so it is no surprise that you will gain something from him other than those eyes of yours. Rowen's abilities manifested when she was younger, much like yours are."

"Does that mean you have some idea of how to control them?" I leaned closer to the table, watching as she sipped from the teacup once more. Terrified as I was, knowing how to control these visions was the only way to survive the council's final judgment. A wash of comfort settled around me, knowing that my mother had gone through similar trials when her abilities appeared as well.

"Not exactly. Like I said, your father's abilities will inflict some type of mutation within your visionary ability," Emma said. My face twisted in confusion at the label she had placed on the visions. Holding up her hand before I could ask more questions, she continued. "Your mother was the only visionary powerful enough to get a grip on her abilities in a long time. You see, your kind are very rare. The power only manifests around every hundred years, with the exception of you, of course. Most of those who are blessed with the visionary ability lose their minds before they understand what is truly happening. The ability warps the weak-minded individuals, butchering their brains slowly. Do you take one lump or two?"

"Excuse me?" I stuttered out the words, still trying to understand what she had just explained to me.

Emma motioned down to the teacup in front of me. As she picked it up to fill with hot liquid, it steamed against the cold air. "In your tea, sweetheart."

"Two, please."

She hummed to herself quietly, seeming to be lost in a distant memory of the past. "Sweet, just like your mom. We all went to school together, best friends all of us. We were never seen alone, seeming to all be attached at the hip. Well, before your father fell, that is. The council took notice of your mother just after he fell. They started tutoring her outside of school hours with the gifted children. Your mother hated the sessions, and the kids in them. Rowen coined the nickname the Brainiac Squad for them. She never fit in with her peers, so she decided to start practicing with her ability on her own. It worked for a while, but none of us were experienced in this, not like the Elders are. As the ability grew stronger, it was making her physically sick, and with your father falling, I thought we might lose her as well. But with Xander's help, she continued to practice even with all the obstacles that came with it. Will had isolated himself from both of them, which put a strain on my friendship with Rowen. He didn't want to be caught up in the *drama* Xander brought upon himself."

She sat back against the chair, sighing slightly. Every memory she told allowed me to understand who my parents were just a little more. But she was holding back the entire story to herself — I could tell by the glazed-over eyes that refused to look at the child of her best friends. Friends that she had no idea what their fate was. Both of us may be in the dark forever.

"How do I control this? She must have told you how she managed to do it. You were her best friend." The hope hidden in my voice made me sick. I allowed my faith to be held in this woman's hands, and she was more than likely going to drop it in a few moments. Emma's eyes wandered around the scene in front of her before she landed back against my fiery gaze. Her head shook back and forth, making it obvious that she was not willing or didn't know any more information about my mother's abilities. I was placing my bets that she was holding her tongue.

"She was very secretive about how she did it, not wanting to get any of us in trouble for knowing that she was practicing outside of the scheduled tutoring sessions. Rowen never wanted to give the council a reason to hurt any one of us. They are very set in their ways, as you saw in the meeting. After your father, she put up a wall too high for anyone to get over. She couldn't fathom the idea of losing one of us again – the pain was just too much previously."

Glaring towards the ground, I willed myself to keep calm, but the anger festering in the pit of my stomach was hard to ignore. "So pretty much what you are saying is that I'm screwed. That's just perfect."

Angry stomps hit the wooden deck as I made my way towards the doorway, wanting nothing more than to get away from a conversation that seemed to only be going in circles with a woman who refused to give up everything she knew.

"I have a box of their things that I was able to hide before the council caught up with them. I also know that your father was capable of so much more than the friends you hang around. The only one who may rival that power would be that Faye boy." Emma's voice was stronger than beforehand, confidence radiating off of every word she spoke. I turned to look at her, watching as she crossed her legs over one another. "You are going to be so much more powerful than both of your parents combined, Liliana."

My skin flushed red with anger. "You know, everyone keeps telling me what I am going to be, but so far I haven't done anything that is that extraordinary. All that seems to happen to me is being haunted by visions of the preacher's daughter your little congregation drove mad."

"Oh, Lily, you have no idea how powerful you are." Her eyes widened in awe as she clasped her hands in front of her face. A wide grin stretched from ear to ear, eyes bouncing around the porch and looking everywhere she could manage. "Just look what you did without even trying."

I traced her line of sight to see what was currently happening around the two of us. The air in my lungs vanished, leaving me speechless as I tried to grasp what was going on. Everything was frozen in place around the balcony's railing. A bird had stopped midflight, seeming to be suspended in the air by nothing but itself.

Stepping forward to get a closer look at what was going on, I came to a yellowing leaf which hung just in front of my nose, stuck in the air from the absence of the chill in the wind. My hand reached out, hovering around the leaf. This was no illusion. The shadow danced across my hand at every angle I managed to twist my arm around. I took the leaf between my fingers, listening to the familiar crunch of it breaking. One piece of the fractured leaf dropped out of my hand, causing me to reach out to catch it. The sudden motion allowed everything around us to return just as it had been moments before.

The only ones noticing the stop in time seemed to be Emma and me.

Chapter Fourteen

The soft rumble of the car's engine filled the tense silence that hung around Asher and me. My duffel bag full of all my belongings sat next to my feet while the box filled with my parents' only known items sat resting in my lap. Staying in the Goodwins' home seemed far-fetched when I couldn't trust them. They were holding back the most important details of my parents' past. What those were, I didn't have a clue.

As I gripped the edges of the thin cardboard box, it felt like the object was burning a hole into my legs. I could sense Asher's quick glances my way, waiting for me to explain what had happened on the balcony.

My talk with Emma hadn't lasted more than an

hour; he probably assumed it would last even less than that with my newfound temper which flared, even more, every day. But my mind was on a constant loop of the words Emma had sputtered out to me, trying to understand them, feel them, find anything to help me control these developing abilities. Emma had later gone on to explain that only the most powerful visionaries could manipulate real time. I had only caught bits of information after that, as her hands pulled the box from the top shelf of her closet, handing it to me with ease.

"You are going to be so much more powerful than both of your parents…"

Her words bounced off the inside of my skull like the ball in a pinball machine. The hot air of the car's heater was making me sweat under the yellow jacket Emma had insisted I place over my shivering frame before I left the comfort of her home. Its material was lined with fur, trapping a cocoon of warmth underneath.

My arms flailed back and forth as I tried to rip the jacket from my body, causing Asher to pull off to the side of the road in concern. I was finally able to remove myself from the clothing item, throwing my body out of the car door into the bitter air and greedily gulping it in. Asher was at my side seconds later. I held out my hands to keep him at arm's length. I needed some space from any human contact for a moment or I was going to crawl out of my own skin.

"What happened, Lil?" I didn't have to look at his face to know how worried he was over my outburst. My hands found my knees as I bent over them, trying to catch my breath once again. I felt like the monster that they all labeled me as.

Shaking my head towards him, I was scared of what I might admit if I opened my mouth. Nothing but the soft howl of the wind sounded between us for a few long moments. Once I had caught my breath again, I rolled my shoulders back, standing tall to make eye contact with Asher.

He stood leaning against the side of his car, arms crossed in frustration, but I could tell he wasn't going to push me into talking. Taking a small step to close the gap between us, I laid my hand on his arm, running it up and down in a soothing motion. His hand landed on my hip, gripping on like I might run if he let go.

"Nothing happened, Ash. Everything is fine." My voice was monotonous, making him scrunch his eyebrows together in confusion. I didn't wait for his response before I slipped into the open door of the car once again. Asher slammed the door behind me, and I watched him stalk angrily around the vehicle. He knew I was lying, but he stayed silent the rest of the ride back to the cabin, not wanting to pry into the private thoughts I was currently wrapped up in.

The next morning, Mallory and Aspyn walked on either side of me in the school hallway. Delaney and the boys had opted out of Mallory's offer for a ride to school, and they were nowhere to be seen through the first half of the day. I hadn't spoken much to anyone since my talk with Emma, locking myself away in my room to think.

The anticipation of the arrival of a new ability at any moment had my nerves set on overdrive. I could tell the stress was starting to take a physical toll on my body. Large circles hung underneath my eyes, even darker than usual against my paling skin.

Aspyn had tried to talk to me the night before, but I shut her out quicker than I did with her twin. Of course, I immediately felt the guilt rising up from my toes when her face dropped. She had retreated out of the room like a dog who had been scolded, leaving a glaring Gabe watching me from the shadows of the hallway as he followed after her.

"I should get to class, but I'll meet up with you for lunch next hour, okay?" Mal was practically bouncing around the hallway.

Her energy couldn't be contained in her petite frame, making me smile at the pixie-like girl. This was something I loved about her – she was so full of life even after she had fallen, making everyone in this town look at her differently. It was as if she wasn't even affected by falling from the heavens in the slightest.

The others always had a dark cloud hanging over their heads, making it known how much it had hurt them. Mallory and Delaney were polar opposites, a dark to the light. Their matching third, Tabitha, the Holy of the triplets, was the worst of the three and the one who had seemed to avoid the wrath of God, allowing her to keep her wings.

I smiled at Mallory. "Perfect. We'll see you then, Mal."

With a quick giggle, she was off bouncing down the hallway, making Aspyn and me laugh as she went.

"Bye, Mal," Aspyn called after her, waving her hand slightly. Her arm linked with mine, dragging me down the hallway after her. "So are you are ever going to talk to me again?"

"I have been talking to you." I rolled my eyes at her, hoping it covered up the fact that I was lying to her. She saw right through my façade, jolting us to a halt in the middle of the deserted hallway. There were no other students racing to class per usual, making it harder for me to worm my way out of this conversation.

"Yeah, okay sure you are, L." Aspyn's eyes glowed with frustration as she spoke. "You're going to bounce around the subject that needs to be talked about like Mallory just bounced down this hallway. We can all see you struggling with whatever Emma told you. Even Laney asked if you were all right, and she doesn't ever act concerned about anyone, even her own sister most days. Avoiding it all together isn't going to make it disappear, Lily."

My eyes trailed around the hallway, thinking for a second before answering the question everyone was wondering. "Emma gave me a box. It's full of my parent's things. I haven't opened it – the stupid thing is shoved underneath the bed and I have been pretending it's not there. Even that has proven to be difficult though."

"Like I said, avoiding it isn't going to make it disappear. I've tried that method before. It never works out in the end." Aspyn's singsong voice rang out in the hallway. "I promise you there is nothing in that box that we can't handle."

"Thanks, Asp."

"But that's not the only thing bothering you, is it?" A knowing look crossed her face as she watched me become startled by her realization. Before I could argue against her observation, a deep voice spoke towards the two of us.

"Were you two planning on gracing us with your presence in any of your classes ladies?" Professor

Erickson stood beside us, a pile of books stacked high in his arms. He peered at us over his glasses that sat perched on the end of his nose. There was a glint of humor behind his eyes, making his presence amongst us less intimidating.

"Lily isn't feeling well, Professor. We were just about to sign out at the front office for the day." Aspyn didn't miss a beat answering him. She knew how to play the system well. Being in school wasn't going to solve my problems, which meant there was no reason to be here other than for appearances. The answers were hidden away in the box that was collecting dust under the bed, not leaned up against my crumpled-up English paper in my locker.

He watched us intently for a moment more before waving us down the hall. "Just go. I never saw either of you."

My arm was nearly ripped out of its socket as Aspyn pulled me towards the front door of the school. "What about Mallory? We were supposed to meet her for lunch."

"She'll meet us at home. I mentioned to her earlier that I didn't plan on staying in this hellhole all day.

We just have to make it seem like we are playing by their stupid rules." Aspyn's devilish eyes looked towards me, a wide smirk forming on her face.

"Their? As in the council? I'm pretty sure both of their minions will notice if I just disappeared from school, but I didn't see either of them in the halls today," I said. My arm was growing numb from how hard she was pulling on it as we made it to her car. Slipping into the vehicle, I shook the limb out, allowing the tingling sensation of blood flow traveling through my veins to once again occur.

"You need to be more observant. Finley was watching you like a hawk. Most would call it stalker status the way he was looking at us." Aspyn rolled her eyes at the idea of the Angel boy watching our every move. The keys jingled slightly when she finally placed them in the ignition, turning them right to allow the car to sputter to life.

"I'm never leaving the house again," I groaned out, shifting in the seat, trying to get comfortable against the plush material. Aspyn laughed at my comment, pulling from her parking spot and starting down the road which led towards the cabin.

"That won't stop them, L. Tweedle Dee and Tweedle Dum have been ordered by their higher powers to make sure you don't run off into the night or hurt anyone." Her last words hit me like a ton of bricks.

The thought of hurting anyone had never crossed my mind until now. Possibly hurting someone I had allowed myself to grow to care about or just an innocent bystander that had no knowledge of the creatures that roamed Idelwood made me want to vomit. I wouldn't allow what had occurred with Claire or my parents to repeat itself. Their deck of cards was not my only hand to play. The driveway of the cabin came into view; it was covered in the dead leaves which had fallen from the surrounding trees' branches, signaling the arrival of winter was upon us in late October.

"You okay, L?"

My head automatically nodded towards the girl next to me. I had become so accustomed to lying about my feelings in my life that I didn't even have to think about the answer. I continued to stare forward at the home in front of us as I spoke. "I just can't let what happened to Claire happen to anyone else in this town. I won't let it happen."

"There's a lot more to that story than what you know, Lily." Aspyn's voice was just above a whisper. Her hands trembled against the base of the steering wheel. Flying out of the car before my eyes could register it, she waved me on, calling as she walked towards the front door. "Come on."

I sat against the cushioned seat for a while longer, watching her travel through the door into the entryway. Never would I have imagined that my world would be flipped upside-down like it had been. Or that I would gain so much from the chaos that had come along with it.

Information on my parents was something I had longed for all my childhood when I watched in envy at other children who seemed so lucky. Aspyn, a best friend I had always needed, and Asher, someone I didn't quite know what to label but he was special all the same. People I would have never gained in my life without going through the madness that this place brought.

This small town with the secrets I so desperately

wanted to discover at first—now as I peeled back the layers, each seemed darker than the last. Their haunting nightmares were things I could only imagine. Nate had crossed my mind more times than I cared to admit—every time I passed through this place, wanting to know if he knew all the secrets that hid in the darkest corners of Idelwood.

Reaching over to open the car door, I knew that I couldn't hide in here for much longer before someone came to check on me. I made a beeline for the stairs as soon as I stepped into the warmth of the cabin, making it to the room I'd claimed as my own for the time being.

Standing in the doorway, I stared down at the bed, my parents' box only a few steps away. It seemed to taunt me in the darkness of the bed frame like a monster does to a young child. I couldn't get myself to move towards the object though. My feet were planted on the hardwood floor, glued down in place. Nothing would get them to peel up and advance forward into the room. There were so many unanswered questions that this box could tell me, and that scared me. I didn't know if I wanted to open that can of worms, unsure of what would jump out and get me this time.

"Nothing in that box could be worse than what's in Claire's journal." Gabe's voice startled me from the trance I had been in. Turning my neck, I could see him standing behind me, leaning against the back wall. His face was masked by the shadows that covered the dimly lit hallway – he must find comfort in the darkness that he hides in. I hadn't spoken much to him since we had met. He was always brooding in the corner or glaring at me from behind Aspyn. Nothing about this Fallen Angel seemed inviting.

"Gabe," I choked out his name, testing the waters with the boy in front of me. "I didn't know you were there. Aspyn just said Asher was waiting for us."

I tried to not tremble under his intense stare, but my voice gave away the fear that I had acquired from the vision.

Gabe chuckled at me, finding amusement in my nerves. "I know you saw something the other night that has you on edge whenever you are around me. There's nothing to be nervous about. I can promise there was a good reason that I fell. It made me realize how corrupt the Elders have become."

"And that was…" I pressed on, hoping that he would give up his secrets. His face twisted with an emotion I couldn't place, and I knew that he wasn't going to reveal the story just yet.

"I would like to say it was Aspyn, but we both know that I would be lying. She was a part of the reason, but there is so much more to that tale. Come find me when you finish the journal and then we can talk, Liliana." Gabe retreated quickly down the hallway disappearing around the corner before I could argue.

Tension hung in the area where he had once been; it felt suffocating in the small corridor. Regretting having pried at something so personal, I turned back towards the room, catching sight of the monster that sat under the bed. Making my way towards it, I shut the door slowly behind me and locked it in place. I needed to face this on my own.

Lying flat on the cool floor, I reached under the bed frame, half expecting a dead hand to latch on to my wrist and pull me under. As I tugged the cardboard from its home, it scraped against the floor, making a sickening whine which sent fear pulsing through my veins.

Chapter Fifteen

In the middle of the bed sat the box. I leaned against the headboard, putting some distance between the two of us. We sat like this for a long while before I got the courage to scoot forward, invading the air that hung around the cardboard. It was larger than your average gift box with some weight to it when picked up. Carefully I took the lip of the lid in my hand, peeling it back slowly. Underneath revealed a box full of what looked like old rubbish. Nothing seemed to connect to the other—a junk drawer in a box was what this was.

A long silver chain lay out across the middle of the box. I picked up the necklace, and a simple silver locket, tarnished around the edges from age, hung at the end of the chain. The piece looked so familiar to me, but I couldn't place where I had seen it. Attached to the chain was a diamond ring which sparkled under the room's lights. Laying the piece of jewelry to the side of the bed, I rummaged around the box and came upon an overflowing, leather-bound book.

Pages spilled over the sides, having been added to the book over time. I pulled apart the leather strings that were holding it all together and listened to the worn leather crack as the spine was opened for the first time in years. A letter fluttered out from in between the pages, landing on the comforter underneath me. Scribbled in the middle of the envelope in loopy letters was my full name. My breath hitched in the back of my throat, while my hand hovered over the crinkled material. I hesitated, not wanting to dive into the note. The message would either help or hurt me in the end.

Turning away from it, I settled my attention back on the journal. It was written in another language, one that I had never seen before. Some words looked as though they were Greek, but they were mixed in with pieces of another language I couldn't quite place my finger on. The writing looked altered, making it an entirely new one. I would have to show Delaney—she seemed like the person who would know exactly where this strange dialect came from. I scanned over each page, drinking in the information that I couldn't understand. Etched in the leather on the inside flap was a name that sent chills down my spine.

Xander Caldwell.

There was something about Xander that terrified me. It wasn't him per se, being as he was my father, and somewhere deep down that made me trust the man. It was the idea that the darkest parts of myself came from him, which scared me to my core. The way my eyes could turn into emotionless black orbs when I got upset, even if Ravana was the only one to see their change during the council meeting. Just the idea of it terrified me. Along with an unknown power that stemmed from Xander. I was told he was powerful. How powerful, I could only imagine.

Tossing the journal back into the box, I continued to look through the articles that had once belonged to my parents. Scattered throughout the bottom of the cardboard were old pictures of them and the group. Some held a young Emma and Will, laughing alongside my parents. All of them looked so happy and carefree in those moments. For a few seconds, I flipped through the stack of pictures I had collected before one stood out to me.

It was a baby wrapped in a lavender blanket, the same one that lay squished in the corner of the box. The infant looked no more than a few days old. My shaky hand reached down to touch the soft fabric. As I ran my hands down the cloth, my fingers stumbled upon bumpy embroidered letters on the bottom-right corner. In a dark purple stitching, "Liliana Adrienne Caldwell" was written out in cursive. Underneath in slightly smaller font spelled out, "Littlest Bird." It was a nickname I don't remember having been called, but a strange feeling of ease settled in the depths of my abdomen as I continued to reread the purple text.

My eyes traveled down to the slightly yellowed-with-age envelope that had fallen from the journal earlier. Hesitating over it once more, I picked it up gingerly, tearing open the wax seal that held it together before pulling out its contents. A piece of thick stationary came out folded in half with a bump hidden underneath. Breathing it in, I unfolded the letter, not taking much notice of the large metal piece that toppled out and onto the bedding.

My dearest Liliana,

Hello, Littlest Bird, our very own miracle. If this letter has managed to come into your possession, one of two things could have happened, neither of which your mother or I had planned for your life, Liliana. One, you escaped with my eldest, Nathaniel. Smart beyond his years, that one is. Stay close to him, love. He will protect you from the evils of this world. He must have shared the secrets of our world with you, deciding that now is the correct time to give you this letter that William has given him. The second circumstance is Emma gave you the letter and you have been thrown into our world with the help of some of our closest friends. Trust both of the Goodwins—they are loyal to our side even though they have not fallen from God's spotlight that he shines on the two of them. Others in our circle you can trust are people such as the Faye twins. Asher is one of my closest friends; he will protect you with his life if need be. His sister Aspyn is the strongest person I have ever encountered. She will be one of your most valued allies if you choose to have her.

I wish things could have ended differently for us but the council is set on destroying everything I have worked for, Little Bird. Protecting you is the only thing that matters to me anymore. You look just like your mother, but those eyes you inherited are all mine. Devious and innocent were the chosen words people have described them as, a beautiful contradiction. Many will despise you for what you are, Liliana, but I hope you will not grow to hate who you are because of them. You are so special, and I know you will be amazingly talented. Do not allow them to push you down, Little Bird. Fly higher than any of them could ever dream.

We left you with a few treasures that should help you with your abilities that we believe will manifest rapidly. My journal—I have been writing about the ability I am known to possess since the night I fell. Ask Mallory Manson to translate. Smart girl she is, although she may not show it all the time. The other half of the medallion, I have enclosed within this letter to you. It will mend itself if you can find its missing sibling. Lastly, find Claire's journal at whatever cost. It will help guide you more than anyone knows.

I hope these tools will assist you, for I cannot be the one to help you along this journey. The idea of leaving you breaks both your mother's and my hearts. You are our miracle, Liliana. Please know we love you and will continue to love you even once we are gone.

Love,

Your Father, Alexander Caldwell

One single tear dropped down, hitting the parchment paper. Tears were streaming down my face, but I hadn't noticed them until now. Reading over the writing a few more times, I shifted my gaze down to the piece of metal that had fallen out of the note. The tarnished gold sparkled under the light of the room just as its other half had the day I first laid eyes on it. Picking it up cautiously, I inspected the object underneath the lighting. Before I got too immersed in the other half of the medallion, I leaped from the bed, scrambling to unlock the bedroom door.

Allowing the door to smack against the wall behind it, I came upon Aspyn and Asher leaning in the hall, waiting for me. The contents of the box were sprawled out across the floor. Aspyn gave me a confused look as she saw the mess on the floor, opening her mouth to speak, but I raced past them towards the stairs, taking them two at a time. I reached the hook where my bag had been hung earlier in the day, most likely by Mal. I ripped it off the hook with such force that I was surprised it didn't tear the peg off the wall with it. The twins stood, staring at the top of the stairs, watching my rampage as I began to tear through the bag for the items I was looking for.

Papers and schoolbooks flew around the front foyer as I searched frantically through the bag. It was empty—both the journal and other half of the medallion were gone, vanishing right from under my nose. My knees buckled, and I sank into the crumbled mess of papers beneath me. Tears began to well in my eyes. The only things that could have helped with these stupid abilities I never even asked for were gone.

"Lily?" Asher approached the disastrous scene in front of him with caution. I ruined it. The pain of disappointing someone I had never even met sank in, making the emotions I was currently mixing together even worse. Nate had known his whole life about this town and our parents. He filled my mind with foolish bedtime stories of this place, disappearing as soon as he could get away from me. I spent all my life searching for a boy who never wanted to be found, someone who held so many secrets about our family's past from me.

My body began to shake with emotion. First was sadness as choked sobs broke through the silent room, but as the seconds passed, all I could feel was an intense anger that set all my cells on fire. I knew only one person was capable of taking these objects. He was the only one who knew the impact that these things disappearing would have on me. The only person who could do this so undetected had done it once before to me, the first day I had met him. He was the one who had been tormenting me since day one in this hell of a town.

Finley Blackbourne.

Chapter Sixteen

Asher's and Aspyn's frantic yells broke through the quiet house as I ran from it. Neither of the twins were fast enough to see me snatch the keys to a car, allowing me to escape from their watchful eyes for once in weeks. The phone in my pocket started continuous ringing, but I answered none of the calls. I drove down a deserted two-way road that was covered by tall trees, making the already-dark sky almost pitch-black. Nothing but two white streams of light lit the road. The ringtone's noise became unbearable, causing me to jerk the car to the right into the dirt patch that shouldered the lane. I let out an angry scream, my hands hitting against the steering wheel. My brain calmed at the silence that surrounded me for only a moment before the ringing began once more. I ripped the phone from my pocket, turning the device off quickly before chucking it in the back seat, letting the darkness swallow it.

My breathing was uneven as I flipped down the sun visor to look at the mess I had become. A cry left my mouth when I stared back at the girl in the tiny mirror. My normally sea-blue eyes were completely black orbs, holding no emotions. Now I knew the reason why people became so wary of me when I became upset in the past few weeks. The eyes in front of me didn't match the ones that had once replaced Asher's at moments such as these. My eyes were completely black, no white to distinguish where the irises started and ended.

Snapping the visor mirror shut, I looked towards the shifter, ready to put it back in to drive, but something hovered in front of the car, startling me out of my action. My heart pounded in my ears, terrified to look up at the silhouette of the person standing in the car's spotlight, praying it was only one of the twins. Slowly I lifted my eyes up to meet the figure's gaze. Finley stood staring back at me just a few feet in front of the car. My initial instinct was to floor it, allowing the redhead to hit the windshield with a sickening crunch. Even if it didn't kill him, the action of it would surely bring me some joy. We continued to stare each other down, both waiting for the other to make the first move. He cocked his head in the direction of the woods before disappearing into the trees altogether.

Scrambling from the running car, I was determined to catch up to confront him about the missing items. My feet caught a random branch in the dark, causing me to trip down the path he had taken. The wind howled around us, making the air smell of rain. As I finally caught up to him, he stood at the top of a large quarry that overlooked a glimmering lake. Large rocks sat against the edge of the cliff which dropped down at least a hundred feet. Finley stood staring off into the deep water. Ice particles that had frozen over from the recent drop in temperature sloshed against each icy piece. He'd finally get the chance to push me off the cliff just like he had probably always dreamed of.

"It's not smart for you to be out by yourself at night, Liliana. Something hiding in the dark might jump out and get you." Finley's voice was even through the wind, a hint of amusement tainting his speech when he spoke of something in the dark. The only monster that was hiding in these woods was him, and he wouldn't dare defy the council's wishes.

I watched him closely, waiting for him to turn towards me before I spoke, but he stood planted, staring off into the distance. "Did you take them?"

The question made him turn to face me, a sly look shining in his light blue eyes. The same sick feeling I had once felt in the vision with Claire came over me as I realized I was the mouse and he was the cat, stalking different prey once more. "Take what, darling?"

"Don't call me that," I growled. The pet name made my skin crawl. "You know exactly what I'm talking about, Finley."

"On the contrary, darling, I don't. You'll have to spell it out for me, it seems." Finley let the name slide off the tip of his tongue, emphasizing each letter. I advanced towards him. Anger began filling my chest once more as I watched him laugh at my attempts to push him over the cliff's edge he stood inches from. Finley stood tall against my force, not allowing me to get the upper hand.

"Cut the crap, you know exactly what you took

from my bag," I spat out in anger, my hands smacking down on his broad chest one last time, trying to drive the point across to him.

He tilted his head from side to side, trying to decide what his next move would be. "Amazing. You don't even realize what you are doing."

Narrowing my eyes at him, I was done playing his games. "Where are the journal and the broken medallion?"

I was smarter than to reveal having the other half. If he knew that piece of information, I would never get back its long-lost twin. Something sparkled in the night air as he pulled out the broken medallion piece from his jean pocket. My hand shot out to snatch it, but he held it above me, dangling the prize out of my reach.

"You mean this medallion?" Finley twirled the gold piece in between his fingers, chuckling at my failed attempts to retrieve it. "If you tell me how you are managing to use that wonderful new ability of yours then you can have this. But the journal—that's going to cost you more."

My gaze traveled towards his in confusion—*I'm not*

doing anything. I could feel the wind blowing against my exposed skin, watching it swing through the bare branches of the trees. A rustle of an animal hiding in the bushes around us confirmed I wasn't using my visionary ability like I had with Emma.

"You really don't know what I am talking about, do you? A true illusionist in their purest form. Although you are tainted, so there may be something special about this new ability. The council will be pleased with your ongoing development." Finley was watching me with caution—a sliver of fear could be seen in the back of his eyes. He wasn't sure what he had just stumbled upon, and the idea of being alone with me scared him. "If you can do what I request, then you can have this back."

Scoffing at him in annoyance, I said, "I don't take requests. I'm not a circus act."

"Well, then it seems we are done here for now, doesn't it?" Finley began walking past me. His shoulder grazed against mine as he moved around me. Gripping onto his exposed forearm, I stopped him before he could get much farther. He looked down smugly at my touch. "That's more like it."

"What do you want from me?" My timid voice was barely audible over the howls of the wind.

"I want you to close your eyes and imagine you are across the quarry, watching us. Envision every piece of the picture that would appear if you were to be looking directly into a mirror." I stared at him as he spoke, a strange look plastered across my face.

Although I was curious about this ability, the thought of him standing so close to me sent the baby hairs on the back of my neck straight up in fear. Finley gripped my shoulders and turned me to face the lake he had just stared into moments before. I could feel his chest press up against my back, making me want to crawl out of my skin as his chest heaved up against my spine. Doing as I was told, I closed my eyes and envisioned myself standing across the quarry. From the laces on my shoes to the split ends that separated my strawberry-blonde hair, I imagined exactly how I looked in the mirror.

"Amazing, isn't it?"

Opening my eyes, I looked back at myself. Finley stood closely against me, but the girl in front of him had her eyes closed, listening as he spoke slowly in her left ear. I stood planted on the opposite side of the quarry, watching myself be taunted by Finley.

"You are so intriguing to me. First we get word you are a visionary who happens to be just as powerful as your own mother, if not more. And now an illusionist. The council will be rather pleased to see how far you have advanced at the Founder's Ball." Finley's voice purred as he spoke in my ear. I snapped my eyes open, finding myself once again standing in front of him, and the medallion was now in the palm of my hand. "Better run back to your gang of misfits before they find out who you have been hanging around with. Wouldn't want to mess up anything with lover boy now, would we?"

Then he was gone. Disappearing again into the darkness of the trees he had once slinked out of and leaving me standing near the quarry with one half of the medallion securely within my grip. I let out a scream, allowing myself to release all the emotions that I was feeling. With the scream came a surge of power inside me. Every fiber of me felt like it had been electrified. The feeling terrified and excited me all at once.

A snap of a stick made me whip my head to the left of me. "Hello?" I called out to the open air praying no one would reply back to me.

"Lily," a whispered voice traveled through the wind straight into my ears. It was so welcoming that before I could process what I was doing, my feet were carrying me in the direction of the voice. The whispering sound continued to call out my name as I walked deeper into the woods that surrounded the quarry. When the hushed voice came to a stop, I finally saw where it had led me to.

The abandoned church sent chills up my spine in the darkness. Last time I had seen the structure was in the vision of Claire Halloway. Now, the air surrounding the church held an eerily similar one to the actions I had witnessed before. I stared the building down, not understanding how I had traveled to this location. It was miles away from where I had last been. The walk should have taken hours to get here on foot, not mere minutes. Turning on the sole of my foot, ready to start back towards the car, I was hit with a gust of wind. The girl of my nightmares stood staring back at me.

"Hello, Liliana." The dead girl looked down at me,

brown eyes unblinking. Her hair blew in the wind, and she had a sickening grin that stretched across her face. Claire Halloway wore a cream-colored dress that flowed in the wind, feet bare against the overgrown grassy dirt that surrounded us. Her light brown hair hung curled down her back with a white ribbon tied into a headband, making a perfect bow at the top of her head. Dark brown eyes pierced into me as she watched for my reaction. Letting out a high-pitched screech, I stumbled backward, putting some distance between the supposed dead girl and myself. The very girl who had sacrificed herself in the church behind me stood in the flesh and was gazing back curiously at me.

"Please don't run, flower. I'm not here to harm you. I just had to see you for myself—the talk of the town this flower has become." Claire's eyes scanned over me, drinking in every inch as she went. I squirmed underneath her stare, not sure what to do. My mouth just opened and closed, trying to find the right words to explain what was happening, but none came to mind. Eyes squeezed shut, I pushed the heels of my hands into my sockets, trying to make her disappear, but she was still there when I reopened them.

"You're so beautiful, which I knew you would be considering who your parents were. Pretty as a flower, I would say." Claire took a step forward, and I matched hers going backward, hitting my back against a tree. "Have you figured it out yet, Liliana? Our connection? Everything seems to lead back to me, doesn't it?"

She began circling me.

I never let her out of my sight, turning with her as she went. "You're not real. You're supposed to be dead. You sacrificed yourself in that church."

Claire stopped circling me, laughing at my accusation. Her laugh carried through the trees making me shiver in fear. "Is that what they told you? Of course, they did. You are correct, flower. I am dead."

In one swift movement, she closed the gap between us, towering over me with the height she had on me. Our noses touched, making me feel her angry breath against my checks. "But I am very real, Liliana, and I can be your greatest advantage or your worst nightmare. You see, I have power over you that you can't even imagine. Considering I could get into your mind so easily from the moment you stepped into my town. Even if I was told not to mess with the flower, I just can't resist anymore."

"Do you mean all those visions weren't real? I'm not a visionary?"

"Oh no, they were your powers manifesting, but I was able to manipulate them to be what I desired them to be. If you would figure it out quicker, maybe you could put up more of a fight, just like your father did."

Stepping back, I stared right into her brightly burning eyes, trying to see if she was bluffing about my father. "He was one of your best friends, Claire. What could you possibly mean by that?"

Claire just began to giggle at me, mumbling gibberish about her flower and skipping around the small space that was in front of the church. Her mumbling became inaudible, but it continued to get louder, making my ears bleed. The warm liquid squished between my fingertips as I placed both hands on either side of my head, starting to scream to drown out the sound. Hands wrapped around my own trying to pull them off my temples, but I held them in place, refusing to let a dead girl control me. My legs kicked out, trying to fight them off. Every ounce of my being needed to get away from her.

"Hey, Lily, stop. You're fine, it's me." The familiar voice stopped my fighting, allowing me to notice Claire's mumbles had been silenced. Opening my eyes, I met Gabe's blue orbs, concern filling them as he looked down at me. Standing just behind him was Aspyn, who had her phone pressed against her ear, whispering quickly into it. Launching myself at Gabe, I threw my arms around his broad shoulders. I needed to make sure they were real. After a few moments, he wrapped his arms around my shivering frame.

"Come on, let's get you back to Ash. He's been ready to burn this town down to find you." Aspyn's voice broke me from my trance.

I nodded into Gabe's shoulder, allowing him to pick up my body from the cold ground we sat against.

"Geez, Lily, you're freezing. How long have you been out here?" Gabe's chest vibrated as he spoke, causing me to cuddle closer to his warmth. He stood up and started back up the trail. I must have dozed off, as I was jolted awake only by the sudden movement of being placed in a vehicle. I flailed about at the unexpected change, but someone's hands steadied me. The person I found on the other end of those hands was an enraged Asher. His body was tense, eyes holding all the anger he felt towards me. I cowered into the corner of the car's seat.

"What the hell were you thinking?" His words dripped with fury, a harsh contrast to the stillness of the car. "I mean seriously, Liliana. You can't just run off like that, you could have been dead for all we knew. Do you know how many people would kill to get their hands on you so they could be the one to prove the council right? I don't think you understand the severity of this."

Tears welled up in my eyes, threatening to spill over with every angry word he spewed at me. This side of Asher had never been directed towards me—it was always fixed on Finley or someone else trying to cause me harm. I guess I was the one who had tried to cause harm to myself, so I got his wrath this time. The harsh words cut me like a knife, each one growing louder as he spoke. Asher continued to lecture me, but I had blocked him out, trying my best not to break down anymore.

The slam of the car door made me jump. Aspyn sat in the front seat, not looking towards her twin. "Leave her be, Asher."

"Stay out of this, Aspyn. None of this concerns you."

Aspyn made a quick one-eighty in her seat, turning to face Asher, the rage radiating off her tiny body making her skin hum. "Get out."

"You're kidding me, right?" Asher laughed darkly at her, challenging his sister once again.

"Does it look like I'm kidding, Asher? I said get out. She doesn't need your brooding ass lecturing her right now." Aspyn's eyes locked with her twin's both green orbs, narrowing as Asher sat in his place. The green in her eyes dissolved, leaving black in its place. "Don't make me say it again, Asher."

In one fluent motion, he was out of the car, the slam of the door making me jump once again. With him out of eyesight, I broke down. Everything from Finley to Claire and now Asher was released in a mess of body-racking sobs. The backseat to my left dipped down lightly as Aspyn sat to collect me in her arms.

"He doesn't mean it, love. Ash was just worried

about you. He gets like this. I used to go missing for hours and he did the same thing. He'll come around in time, don't worry," Aspyn whispered. Her fingers made light strokes through my knotted hair, allowing me to release all my feelings into her chest.

Gabe slipped into the driver's seat, catching Aspyn's eye in the rearview mirror. She only nodded at him, signaling him to take us home. Everything that had piled up in past weeks was falling out of my lips in one continuous sob. I didn't want to hold it in anymore. I couldn't.

Chapter Seventeen

Sun peeked through the heavy curtains that sat on either side of the window, allowing the early morning sun to shine into my eyes. Gabe must have brought me up once we arrived back. The last thing I remember was burying my head into Aspyn's chest, trying to block away the rest of the world. The events of last night played on a loop behind my eyes as I tried to decode what exactly had happened. None of it made sense. My brain's gears were grinding together, making fictional smoke pour out of my ears.

Claire was dead.

That I knew for a fact, but she somehow found a way to weasel her way back into this mess she had become a part of seventeen years ago. Her taunting visions continued to muddle my thoughts as she snaked through them. The comment about my father last night sent a shudder through me. No one had a clue of what actually happened to my parents after they disappeared. Claire's insinuation confirmed everyone's worst fear.

They were dead, never coming back.

A sharp knock sounding against the wood on my door broke me from my deep thoughts. "Come in."

I didn't turn my head towards the doorway when I spoke. Instead, my eyes stared at the white wall sitting just to my right. Heavy footsteps entered the room as the door creaked before slamming tightly shut. The electrifying feeling that entered my body made me know exactly who had entered—I didn't need to look over to him.

After last night, facing him was the last thing I wanted to do, but I let him continue towards me. I had allowed him in, something I so rarely did, making his harsh words sting so much more. Even with Aspyn's constant reassurance of it being normal behavior, it wasn't an excuse. I wasn't going to give him a free pass. After what had just occurred in the woods, he was the one person I wanted to help work out the twisted puzzle with, but now as he sat inches from me, he seemed like more of a stranger than ever.

"Are you not going to look at me?" Asher's voice was defeated when it finally broke through the stale air. I could feel his stare on the side of my neck, causing it to kink as I held still, refusing to look towards the boy.

I shook my head in a firm no motion, and he sighed in frustration. I let myself close my eyes, only to be met by the image of Asher running his hand over his face, a light stubble tracing his jawline as he hadn't bothered to shave. His face was filled with annoyance as he watched me. Reopening my eyelids, I continued my battle with the wall. Maybe this new illusionist ability would come more in handy then I had anticipated.

"I'm sorry."

The words were barely audible as they floated around the room, making my stomach twist inside out. I shot off the bed in a fit of rage, turning towards him, flames dancing across my eyes as I watched his every movement. Asher didn't shrink away from my gaze, which angered me even more.

"You're sorry?" Venom caught each word as I spit them through clenched teeth. "Sorry for what? Screaming at me before you understood what just happened out there? Or was it that you are sorry for the fact that I am stuck in this one-stoplight town with creatures that shouldn't exist besides in bedtime stories?"

Asher stood tall against my tiny stature, towering over me. I stood taller, trying my best to match his demeanor, neither of us backing down to one another. "Lily, I know you are ang—"

"Angry?" A sadistic laugh escaped my throat, cutting off his rebuttal. "Oh no, I'm not angry. I'm livid about these stupid abilities. I never asked for them. They are not a 'blessing' like everyone continues to express to me. Outraged at the fact my parents would leave me in the care of a brother who would leave as soon as he got the chance. I'm furious at the fact that my own father left a handwritten letter for me telling me to trust you when all you are is an overprotective ass. I can't even begin to explain my anger towards Claire Halloway and her psychotic ghost who attacked me last night in the middle of the forest. She is supposed to be dead, but she seems to worm her way into my every thought whenever she pleases. Oh, and the fact that I have to mingle with one of the people who is partially responsible for her mind being melted down to nothing. Someone that you all consider a friend."

Each hate-filled word echoed off the four walls of the small room, making the structure tremble in time with me. Asher stood, staring with wide eyes at me, shocked at my sudden outburst.

Losing my temper was never something I was proud of. Nate used to say it was a temper only a Caldwell could have. I never understood what he meant by that but knowing he had known all the answers made me fume even more. All I wanted were answers from everyone. I was tired of being left in the dark about everything that had occurred in this town. It was my past now as well, and I deserved to know about it. Nate sure as hell didn't care about anything that had happened in our family, making me the last member willing to gather the truth.

"I want answers, Asher."

One condition allowed me to get the answers I begged for. Explain what had occurred within the woods last night. Everyone in the group sat at a long banquet table, waiting for someone to speak first. The dining room held only the table and a large china cabinet with dishes no one ever really ate from. The walls were blank, making the room seem unfinished.

"I don't know what you are all staring at. I'm waiting for someone to start explaining." Confidence filled my voice as I watched each person that lined the sides of the table. I sat at one head of the table, my eyes landing on the other end, which held Gabe. He had heard every word I had said about him, just as everyone else in the cabin had.

Delaney began to laugh darkly, shaking the mop of dark hair out of the ponytail holder it had just sat in. "Not going to happen. You're going to spill about what happened last night, and then we can get into all the juicy details you want to know."

I sank down in my chair, not wanting to speak of the events that had occurred only hours ago. Maybe if I sank straight into the cushions, I could hide forever. No matter how far I inched down, pairs of abnormally vibrant eyes stared in my direction, making me squirm in place.

"You're not going to get out of this one, L." Aspyn's voice sang out as she repositioned her legs to drape over Gabe. Aspyn was filing her nails. Looking up slightly to meet my gaze, she returned my glare with a smirk. I stuck my tongue out at her, and she began to giggle.

Asher cleared his throat and nudged Aspyn's shoulder, quickly ending our shenanigans. I prepared myself to explain what had happened in the tangled trees last night. "I don't know where you want me to start."

The words came out mumbled. Delaney sneered at me, eyes rolling to the back of her head. "The beginning would be preferred, sweetheart."

"Delaney," Asher warned. They shared a quick stare-down before Laney cowered to his intense glare. "Go on, Lily."

I looked towards him, meeting his eyes. They softened under my stare, calming down my nerves almost immediately. Even though I was still angry with him, I knew he was the one person who wouldn't call me crazy for the words that were about to tumble out of my mouth.

"After I stormed out, I just started to drive, no real destination in mind. I just wanted to get away from everything that was happening. The constant ringing of the phone was starting to drive me insane, so I pulled over to the side of the road to turn it off. When I looked back up, I saw Finley standing in the middle of the road." I tensed under his name as it came off my tongue.

Someone mumbled something about hitting him with the car, making me chuckle slightly. Aspyn winked in my direction as I continued to explain. "He motioned for me to follow him to this quarry that overlooked the lake. I had a theory he had taken the items my father had asked me to find and keep safe. I questioned him about them, but in his obvious, condescending way, he danced around the question. He called me an illusionist."

I allowed the title to sink into everyone's mind for a minute. A low voice spoke up, cutting me off. "You can create illusions to distract people. It must be different, though, due to the mix of bloodlines."

All the eyes in the room shifted towards Mallory's voice. She was smart, and they all knew this, but she kept her opinions to herself, afraid of being wrong. She was always hiding in the shadow her sisters cast.

I smiled softly at her, "Finley mentioned that as well. I did something, though I'm not really sure how I did it, but it was the price of the medallion. I was able to replicate the motion earlier in the room with Asher without really thinking about it. Finley just wanted to use my new ability for his own amusement. I need to understand how to control these abilities or the council will have no problem removing me on the spot."

I was nervous about their reactions, pleading for them to help me with my eyes. Gabe looked at me from across the table, a devilish grin pulling at the corners of his mouth. "You think after one crazy night you can get rid of us that quickly?"

"No, I guess not," I whispered, matching his

smile before I looked around at everyone else. Every single figure copied our actions, confirming that they were in it for the long haul with me.

"You mentioned Claire." Asher's voice was monotone as he spoke. Not looking towards, him I watched Gabe flinch at the preacher's daughter's name. I couldn't tell if it was guilt that passed through his hazy eyes or another reaction altogether.

Pulling my gaze away from him, I looked towards Asher. "Uh, yeah, after Finley was done toying with me, he left me in the clearing. I was ready to turn back towards the path and make my way to the car, but my name was being whispered through the trees. I know I shouldn't have followed it, but I wasn't in control of my own body. Not until the voice stopped in front of the church could I actually feel like I was back in control. I tried to turn back, but it was too late. She was standing right in front of me. Claire kept saying things that didn't make any sense." My breathing was uneven as I relived the nightmarish events, tears beginning to flood my eyes once again. "She said if I would figure it out, maybe I could put up a fight just like my father had."

Short rapid breaths made it hard to gather enough air in my lungs. All the colors in the room swirled together in a blurred mess. My vision began to fade in and out as tears started down my pale cheeks. Claire's cruel words sent me spiraling into a panic. Dragging my hands through my hair in swift motions, I tried to calm myself, but the room's air was suffocating me. The chair I sat in scraped against the wood floor, pulling me away from the restricting edge of the table.

Asher's hand reached across the table for me, but I stepped away quickly, the back of my thighs hitting the cushioned chair to escape his touch. An unfamiliar touch pulled both of my hands from my knotted hair. Through the tears, I could see the person who was sitting in from of me was not anyone I would have expected it to be, but Gabe.

Asher stood in the distance behind Gabe, arms crossed in front of his chest, watching both of us intently. I flinched at Gabe's touch—the vision of him tormenting Claire danced across my vision. I tried to scramble away from him but he held me in place as I spoke. "Stop. You're the reason why she is like this, I saw it. The night in front of the church with Rowen, you did this to Claire."

"She's messing with your mind, Liliana. Showing you only the parts she wants you to see. That night caused more than just me to fall." Gabe's voice was calm against my shrinking voice. His eyes followed my wandering ones, trying to get my attention again.

"If she's only messing with me, then why does everyone in this room seem so tense? I can feel it sticking to everyone like a disease. If you all would ever explain anything to me, maybe I would understand what happened." My eyes bounced to each person in the room watching over me, landing back on Gabe's harsh stare last.

He shook his head in anger, standing up from his crouched position in front of me. His height towered over me, and I curled into myself, not sure what he might do next. "I don't have to explain anything to a child."

Gabe's mood swings were beginning to get old, causing the same anger I felt rise up in the pit of my stomach. He had decided I was insignificant in this conversation, beginning to turn away from me. "I am not a child. I deserve to know what happened in this town so I can understand what happened to my parents. Understand why Nate would run from me. Do you see the pattern here? It's the why that I want to know, because this *child*, as you called me, is tired of being blindsided by surprises from a dead girl in the middle of the forest."

I had risen to my feet during my speech to Gabe. He was shaking when he turned towards me. I matched each stalking step of his backward until my spine was pressed up on the wall behind the two of us. Gabe trapped me against the surface, his face hovering inches from mine. I could feel the anger that radiated off him when he spoke. "You want to know what happened to all of them? What happened to all of us?"

"It's what I have been asking for from the beginning."

Gabe leaned closer to my ear, making it easy for him to feel my trembling figure underneath his hot breath. "You. That's what happened to all of us."

CHAPTER EIGHTEEN

Fire burned behind Gabe's eyes, fueled by immense hatred, all due to my existence. I sidestepped underneath his hanging arm to escape his glare. He let me go, not bothering to waste any more energy on the Night Monster. Chaos erupted in the room as I left, my feet carrying me towards the door ready to flee from this town once and for all. No matter what Abel said, I would hide in the darkest corners of the world, not allowing them to find me again. Nate had no trouble disappearing from their knowing eyes. I could hear an argument begin between Asher and Gabe, unforgiving words cutting through the air and bouncing off their thick skin. The thumping of my heart blocked out the rest of their conversation. I could only hear the steady beat and my own thoughts when my hand landed on the doorknob. None of this would be happening if it wasn't for the fact that I existed. The universe sure does know how to play a sick joke on me. Cracking open the door just enough to see the outside world before it slammed shut once more.

A petite figure stood next to me, both hands on the wood, staring forward into the surface. As I looked at Mallory Manson, her blonde hair hung in front of her vibrant gray eyes, every inch of the color was coated with an intense anger. She allowed her shoulders to slouch forward, letting her normally impeccable posture deviate from routine as the argument in the other room grew louder.

"Please don't go. He doesn't speak for everyone in the room. I made a choice a long time ago, and I wouldn't take it back even if it meant not falling. Aspyn will be able to get a handle on both of the boys. Just wait it out." Her eyes softened, pleading even more than her voice. I sighed at her, tipping my head up and down, and watched the door lock under her fingertips. I refused to retreat back into the room where screams of anger could be heard, Aspyn's voice now joining in on the argument.

Mal must have sensed my discomfort, placing a hand on my shoulder. I turned my head to look at the girl once more. "Come on, I'll make you something to eat. It always helps me when I'm upset. Plus, I make a mean box of mac and cheese."

She motioned for me to follow her down the hall towards the kitchen. I chuckled at the girl as she skipped down the corridor, seemingly ignoring the war occurring just rooms away. The kitchen was beautiful. A sink sat against a large window overlooking the backyard. Everything about this room was welcoming—it's no wonder she always came here when she was upset. Mallory ducked down, disappearing behind the giant marble countertop which separated the kitchen in half. Pots and pans began to clank together before she reappeared once more. Mallory lit the stove, setting the pot of water on the burner and waiting for it to boil.

"So, have you decided what you plan on wearing to the masquerade ball?" Mallory stood in the pantry, looking for the box she wanted. Coming out a few moments later, she set it down in front of her. I hadn't really given much thought to the dress I could possibly die in. Mostly I was trying to ignore the fact that the Founder's Ball was coming up so fast. The last week since the council meeting had seemed to melt together quickly, not giving us much time to breathe.

"No. Going isn't optional for me, so I should probably figure something out." My hand reached up to the necklace around my collarbone. I had decided to place the silver chain, which held the locket and ring, around my neck this morning. The jewelry piece made me feel closer to my parents. Twisting it between my fingertips gave me some comfort with the craziness that was flying around our heads at the moment.

"You have to go shopping with us!" Mallory let out a squeal of excitement, bouncing from one foot to the other around the kitchen. There was the Mal everyone knew and loved, never being able to control her excitement within her tiny body. "It'll be so much fun, plus it will help you get your mind off all this stressful stuff for a day. We'll have to find sometime next week."

"Okay, I don't think that even if I said no, you would let me get out of this one." I giggled at the playful glare she threw over her shoulder as she poured the box of pasta in the pot.

"That is very true, L. I am going to Aspynifiy you again. That is how Asher put it last time, wasn't it?" Aspyn's voice caught me off guard as she slid into the kitchen effortlessly. Moving closer to me, she leaned her elbows on the countertop and looked in my direction. "Sorry about Gabe back there. I don't know what has gotten into him lately."

"You have got to stop doing that, Asp. You're going to give me a heart attack one of these days," I said, holding my chest where my racing heart sat. I reached out, smacking Aspyn on the arm lightly. Dropping my voice down to a whisper to avoid the others eavesdropping, I said "Also he's not your responsibility to apologize for. Although what he said is partly true."

This time I was the one who received the smack on my upper arm. The crack of skin rang through the kitchen. Rubbing my now reddening limb, I glared at her as she said, "Oh, hush. I can't take your sour attitude as well. Everyone needs to kiss and make up or I'm going to rip my hair out. Especially you and Asher. I'm tired of him moping about. It's only been a few hours, and he is getting on my last nerve with his dramatics."

"And you're done talking, little sister." Asher's voice came from the doorway. He stood with his arms crossed over his chest, leaning against the frame, an amused look shining out towards his twin.

"I mean, she's not wrong," Mallory mumbled as she stirred the pasta, looking over her shoulder at the scene behind her. I rolled my eyes at the two girls and looked back at Asher before peeling myself from the countertop. Gripping his arm, I pulled his bicep in the direction I wanted him to go. We aimlessly wandered towards an unknown room, silently landing in a small library that sat in the front of the cabin.

"If you wanted to get me alone, you could have just asked." Asher's mouth pulled up at the corners as he looked down at me.

I raised an eyebrow in his direction, not amused by his comment. "We need to talk. Can you be serious for ten seconds?" I scolded him.

My arms found their way around my body, securely holding myself together as we both stood silently. Asher reached up, running his hand through his hair and allowing it to flop to the side in a perfect mess of black.

I was treading in new water with him, too stubborn to admit that I may have overreacted. Feelings were never something I was able to properly express to the people I cared about. It wasn't who I was. From a young age, I had been taught to bottle up every single thing I felt and put them away on a shelf, never to be thought about again. It wasn't healthy, but it was the only way I knew how to cope with everything life had thrown at me.

My eyes had found a home on the wall just behind Asher's head, not daring to make eye contact with him again. "I don't know what to say. I thought that I had it all planned out in my head, but it's all jumbled together now that I stand in front of you."

Asher's hand traced underneath my chin, pulling

my focus back to him. His green eyes looked down into mine. They were the same green orbs I had grown so accustomed to. Emotion swirled together in a dark storm cloud. I wasn't able to distinguish which emotion was directed towards me. I tried to look away from him but his hold tightened, not letting me stray away from his gaze.

"I overreacted, Lily. It's not something I am proud of. It has been eating me alive ever since I stepped out of that car door. I never wanted you to be angry with me. Blowing up at you wasn't the right thing to do. I was just so scared, Lil." Asher cupped both sides on my cheeks. I leaned into his touch as he began to make light strokes down my jawline with his thumb. "I am so scared of losing the one thing that has made me feel anything since I fell."

My arms flew up, locking around his neck in a tight hug. Immediately he gathered me in his grasp, relaxing against my touch. I could feel his heartbeat slow as we stood wrapped up in each other, neither of us wanting to break the hold we had.

"You're not the only one who feels that way," I admitted into his chest, feeling the bright red glow that was warming up my entire face start to appear. I buried myself deeper into him, inhaling his musky scent. "I just don't know what I'm doing anymore. Everything is happening so quickly, and I feel like I'm slipping further away from myself with every passing second."

Asher pulled me back from his chest, looking down at me in concern. "You never have to worry about losing yourself. I'll always be here to remind you who you are, no matter how dark it gets. Deal?"

I stared at the pinkie he had held out in front of me, laughing at the childish gesture. "Really? We are going to pinkie swear on this?"

"It's the only way to make sure I never break that promise. Pinkie swears are the real deal," Asher joked, pushing the finger towards me again. I took his pinkie in mine, and we shook on it.

No matter how childish it may have seemed, it made the worry in my chest untangle itself more than it had in weeks. Throwing my head back with laughter, I drank in the moment with the Fallen Angel with the heavenly green eyes. I never wanted to come down from the high he ignited in my soul.

CHAPTER NINETEEN

Florescent lights danced off the crystals clinging on the beaded dresses within the only dress shop in Idelwood. Each garment on the rack looked like it was made for a princess straight out of a fairy tale.

But I'm no princess and this is no fairy tale.

Idelwood's annual Founder's Day Masquerade Ball was this Saturday—an invitation for each member of our small group had shown up in the mailbox. The extravagant paper had felt rough against my skin and sharp enough to cut the throat of any Night Monster who stepped a toe out of line. My invitation had been personally signed by Abel. A silent threat of my impending evaluation marked in bright red ink on stark white paper. Aspyn, Mallory, and Delaney stood on the opposite ends of the shop, chatting amongst themselves as they searched through the mountain of dresses that hung upon the racks. I stood back a few feet, my right hand running across the silk material. None of these dresses were ones that I could imagine myself in. They were all such frilly things.

"L, come here. I have some ideas for you," Aspyn's voice called out from the direction of the dressing rooms. I started towards where she stood on a pedestal surrounded by paneled mirrors. She was dressed in a deep-blue silk dress, the material pooled around her feet and cutting up the side of her leg in one long slit. The dress shimmered against her pale skin as she moved around the light to slowly admire herself in each mirror. "There are a few dresses in that room for you to try on."

Walking towards the dressing room she motioned to, I saw more than a few dresses that she wanted me to try on. The colors ranged from bright orange to midnight black, each a different cut and style. I would play along with the game to please Mal and

Aspyn for a few hours, but the likelihood any of these would work was slim to none. Every dress they threw me in was pretty but just not me. I felt like a fish out of water, parading around the store for their amusement. I walked out in the last dress they had hanging in the room; it was a velvet purple material that dipped down in a deep V, landing just above my belly button. It lay nicely on the ground as I walked to the pedestal to once more look into the four-way mirror. The three girls sat lounging on a couch sitting just behind the mirrors, their eyes criticizing the ensemble they had dressed me in. Smoothing my hands down the dress, I watched the fabric unwrinkled in the mirror before catching Aspyn's eye.

"This is no use. None of these dresses are me." I would have all eyes on me when it came to this party as it was—I didn't want to make any more of a fool of myself than I already would. The whole town would be judging my every move, not just the council.

"I think that one looks gorgeous on you," Mallory said, gushing over the dress, hands clasped in front of her mouth like a proud mother watching her daughter try on wedding gowns.

"You said that about the last six I tried on."

"I don't have all day, you know." Delaney picked at the fuzz that had gathered on her gray sweater, eyeing me every so often. "Why don't you just get the one from Celia? She would look great in it. Rowen sure did."

The chain around my neck felt heavier as Delaney spoke my mother's name. I had found myself playing with the trinkets on the end of the necklace more these past few days—it had become a nervous tic. The cool metal of the ring danced across my palm, sending a rainbow of shimmers across the room underneath the glowing lights. Aspyn eyed Delaney curiously, not catching on to what the bored girl was speaking of. "What dress?"

"The one in the white box. It's emerald green. Celia kept it in the Crypt for safekeeping so none of those Holy bastards could get their grimy hands on it." Aspyn still stared wide-eyed at Delaney, making her sigh loudly and quickly sit up in annoyance. "Oh, come on, Asp. The green lace dress in the white box with the long train and beaded belt. I am not going to spell it out any further for you."

I could see that the idea had clicked behind Aspyn's eyes, making her squeal in glee. "How could I have forgotten about that! Oh, it will be perfect. Come on, let's go see Cee."

Aspyn began to drag me from the step towards the front entrance of the store. I stopped her short of the exit. "Um, Asp, I might want to go change. Don't want another shoplifting count added to my record."

The girls' laughter filled the store. I turned on my heels, walking back into the changing room. The dress slipped off my body smoothly, allowing the itchy material to be hung back on the hanger. Lacing my shoes after I had dressed fully, I sat on the bench in the room, feeling the familiar pull of being sucked into a vision begin to swirl around the small space.

Lights of the night stars twinkled over a large garden party that was occurring around me. Couples spun in sync as a formal waltz began, leaving me stranded in the middle of the dance floor, staring at the formations they began to shape. Glasses of champagne clinked together as a toast was given while others mingled amongst themselves. Masks decorated each guest's face; I could feel each one turn to stare in my direction. A cold hand curled around my shoulder, sending an icy shock through my entire body. I turned to see a man who stood behind me. His face sucked the wind out of my lungs, leaving me gasping for air.

"Oh, come now, Liliana. Don't act as if you aren't happy to see your big brother." Nathaniel stood, flesh and bone, in front of me with a flushed look as the cool air hit his skin. A sinister grin was painted across his face while his eyes scanned over me hungrily. He watched me blubber for moments more before chuckling at my shock. "Better watch your back, flower. You're wilting under their stares."

A cold bead of sweat trailed down from my hairline. My knuckles had begun to turn white from gripping the bench so tightly. One shaky breath slipped out from my lips—I had been holding my breath from the second my sight fell upon Nathaniel's face and my lungs were beginning to burn from the lack of oxygen flowing through them. Gathering up my purse, I tumbled from the curtains that blocked me from the store. Aspyn was the only one left, standing at the entrance and staring down at her phone.

She gave me a puzzled look when I arrived in front of her. "You okay?"

Trying to keep my breathing even, I nodded at her. The hammering of my heart was in my ears, making it hard to hear her, but I tossed my bangs to the side and smiled. "Yeah, let's get going."

We walked down the short path towards the café, the vision playing in drumming repetition with every step I took. Nate was gone, I knew that. He had been gone for years and never came back to check up on me. It didn't make sense for him to show up in this mess. He escaped all of this long ago, and if I were him I would have stayed as far away from it as I could. Claire had told me she was messing around in my mind, and as much as I hated to think about her worming her way through my brain, it was possible she was playing with my weaknesses in a vision. The bell above the café door rang as we passed through the entryway.

The normal hustle and bustle of the shop was

silenced today — only the clank of dishware being washed in the back could be heard. A quiet hum from the only guest in the place was hidden behind a newspaper in the back corner booth. Tan kitten heels stuck out from underneath the table they sat in.

"Cee?" Aspyn called out for the woman who was nowhere to be seen.

There was a crash followed by muffled words that trailed behind Celia when she appeared around the counter seconds later. Her appearance was startling; she didn't look like the Southern housewife as she normally did. Instead, her blonde hair was dull, sticking out in every which way from the bun sitting on top of her head. The lack of life traveled down into her eyes, which were sunk into her head. Dark purple circles hung underneath each of them. Celia had a sour look plastered on her face, but it seemed to melt away when she realized it was only us. Who could have made Celia this unhappy?

"Oh, thank god it's only you two." A sigh of relief left her lips as she rounded the countertop, coming towards us.

"Who else would it have been?" I questioned her, not sure of who would be harassing poor Celia into this sort of state.

Celia looked over towards the lone patron, motioning us to follow her into the back hall that led to her connecting home. Quickly we followed her, trying our best to keep up with her quick pace. "That stuck-up Manson triplet—what's her name again?"

"That would be Tabby." Aspyn's words were laced with disgust. "What was she after this time?"

"The same old thing, saying she had orders from the council to look through the archives of the town in the Crypts. I told her to bring me back some paperwork or a council member, and then I would let her grubby hands tear through my rooms." Cee laughed at herself. I joined in, knowing full well how red in the face Tabitha Manson got when she was told no. "She thought that if she brought that redheaded kid to me that it would persuade me into cracking open the door."

"Finley," I whispered to no one in particular. What was so important about the archives that the council wanted to get in there so badly? From the way

Asher had explained it the day in the greenhouse, it was just a room full of dusty old books and papers. Nothing special.

"You can't let them in, Celia. They would find everything we have been hiding from them since the beginning of this mess they created." Aspyn strained to keep her voice down, trying her best to not let me hear her words.

Celia tensed under Aspyn's reaction. "You know if they bring me the papers or a council member shows up, I have to let them in. I took an oath long ago and I have to honor it, no matter how much I don't particularly want to."

Both of them turned towards me. They seemed to be debating with one another whether they wanted to divulge any further information about this mysterious Crypt they keep mentioning. Idelwood's secrets continued to spill over like a cup under a running faucet each day I spent here.

"Lily, if we show you this, no one but us can know about it." Celia watched me, her eyes serious as they traveled between me and the double doors to her left. When Aspyn had first dragged me through this hallway, I hadn't even noticed their presence. It was as if only those who were worthy were granted a glimpse of them.

"You both know that I won't be able to keep a secret from Asher; he can see straight through my lies. I don't really feel like getting into another argument with him. There's too much going on right now." I ran my hand down my face, as a thin sheen of sweat had collected against my skin.

"Well, it's a good thing my sister knows how to keep the peace," Asher's voice whispered into my ear. I jumped back, hitting him in the chest and making him chuckle at the fear that was coursing through my veins.

"What did I tell you about sneaking up on me?" I spun around and pushed against his shoulder, but he didn't budge an inch. The attempt to move him only made him chuckle louder.

"Hm, I don't remember. Care to remind me?" Asher wrapped his arms around my squirming figure, pulling me close to him. He leaned down towards me, his lips hovering over mine. I could almost taste them they were so close. Being near

Asher made me forget about the two people watching our interaction.

"You two are disgustingly cute. It makes me sick." Aspyn looked at us, annoyed, earning a pointed look from the older woman next to her.

"Stop being bitter, Aspyn. It's not becoming of a lady," Celia spoke towards Aspyn, who only stuck her tongue out at the woman's comment. "Now let's show Lily what I have been hiding."

CHAPTER TWENTY

Celia turned her back towards us, facing the pair of double doors that she had been eyeing moments before. Both doors were a deep brown color with intricate carvings that covered every inch of the panels. The designs swirled together, making circles as they went and leaving space around a pair of large angel wings. Wrapped around the middle of the wings was a saying that appeared to be in Latin.

In principio erat Verbum et Verbum erat apud Deum et Deus erat Verbum.

"What does that mean?" I reread the line over again. The words flowed together like a song, each one fitting together perfectly with each other. Asher still had his arms wrapped around my shoulders, watching me closely as I examined the door.

Celia smiled proudly, running her hand down each carved word. "It's the Keeper's creed. It translates to, 'In the beginning was the Word, and the Word was with God, and the Word was God.' It is the most sacred saying to the Keepers. We vow to keep what is inside this room safe, even it means giving our lives to protect it."

She reached towards the bronze handle on the door, pulling it down. Celia turned to look at me, silently asking me if I was ready to enter the dark corridor. Turning back towards Asher, I unwrapped myself from his grip, letting my hand trail down his arm and into his hand. I began to walk towards the room, but he pulled me back towards him.

"Have fun with Celia. We will be waiting for you when you're finished." Asher unlaced his fingers from mine and gave me a little push towards the door.

I looked between the twins in confusion, not understanding why they were not coming along. "You're not coming in?"

"We aren't allowed. You have to be a Keeper or

in the good graces of God himself to be invited in. Fallen might mess with things they're not supposed to." A glint of mischief played in Aspyn's eyes as she spoke.

"What happens if you try to cross into the Crypts?"

"The wrath of God is thrust upon you, and that is something none of us want to endure again." This time Aspyn's voice was so quiet I almost didn't catch her words. She shrank back against the wall, slumping down onto the ground lost in thought. Her hands trailed up her back reaching for nothing. I could only imagine losing something like your wings was a lot like losing a limb. It might not be there, but without even realizing it, you forget it's gone. A ghost of what once was left in its place. Eyeing the door again, I thought about what they must have gone through when they fell. One day I hope to be privileged enough to know their full story. None of the group seemed to deserve the fate they had been handed.

Realization hit me like a truck. I assumed by the way the council had treated me thus far, their higher-up wasn't the biggest fan of whatever I was. Panic began to sink in as I looked back towards the twins. "How do you know that won't happen to me if I try to enter?"

"We don't," Aspyn stated simply before beginning to pick invisible fuzz off her T-shirt, acting as if she didn't just tell me I had a fifty-fifty chance of having God's wrath rained down on me if I crossed over the threshold of the Crypts.

"It'll be fine, Lil. Don't mind Aspyn. I'm almost positive he has a soft spot for you even if he won't admit it to anyone else." Asher laughed at the expression I plastered across my face as he spoke of God's feelings towards me. I highly doubt given the recent encounters with his disciples that he had any feeling other than hate for me.

Celia rushed forwards, latching on to my right arm and pulling me towards the doors. "Oh you two, shush. Stop scaring the poor girl. Lily, you'll be fine, I promise. I wouldn't allow this if I thought harm would come to you."

With that, she pulled open both doors and pushed both of us through a narrow hallway. The paneled walls were painted with different stories from history shining against each one. I recognized many—the Titanic sinking into the Atlantic Ocean, tipped vertically in the air as it went down, along with the famous painting of the Battle of Bunker Hill smeared in vibrant color against the pure white paneling. There were even ancient Egyptian hieroglyphics hanging. The stone they were originally painted on sat right in front of my eyes.

Each piece of art I passed went deeper into the beginning of time until we reached the end of the long stretch. The room opened up into a circular chamber closely resembling a globe. Every so often you would see the bookshelves that lined the walls shift against one another. Every other shelf moved in the opposite direction of the other before quickly clicking into place once more. The movement made the room move in a clockwise motion. In the middle of the room was a long table that stretched from end to end, mismatched chairs lining either side of it. More books were piled high on the table, reaching up towards the ceiling. Celia had walked ahead of me, allowing me to take in the amazing room she had led me into. I had never seen anything so magical in my life. There was so much information to consume in this room. I could live here forever, visiting different worlds in a matter of seconds.

"I did that once. It gets stuffy in the summer months," Celia said, smiling at me. My hand slapped against my mouth, not realizing that I had spoken aloud. "Welcome to the Crypts, Liliana—my pride and joy."

The love that radiated from Celia in this room was evident in every move she made around the space. She almost floated around, even more than I had ever seen her do in her café. Who could blame the woman, though? This place was enchanting. To think Celia had all of this information at the tips of her fingers at any time of the day or night was amazing.

"Wow." That was all I could muster. "Have you read all of these books, Cee?"

"Well, when you have stopped aging long ago, you have a lot of time on your hands. These books are like my antiaging cream. Plus, it's kind of my job to be a know-it-all." Her hands skimmed over the spines on a shelf to her right. The books seemed to purr under her gentle touch. "Now, to get to what we are really here for."

Celia turned to a blackened door that sat in the back of the room. She swung open the doors to revealed another decently sized room with boxes piled high. Each one was labeled in alphabetical order, tiny letter signs hanging down to indicate the rows. I trailed behind her slowly, watching as she filtered through the letters, her feet stopping in front of the R's. My breathing halted for a moment, my hand reaching up to touch the silver heart once again. I knew she was going to pull a box out with something of my mother's inside it.

"There wasn't much left after your parents disappeared. The council cleared out most of their belongings from the Crypts, but I was able to hide away a few items for safe keeping. It's tradition, you see, anytime one of our own, fallen or not, is killed, the Keeper at the time performs a send-off ceremony for them, allowing them to be laid to rest. If this doesn't happen, the souls of those who have perished will be stuck in a middle-ground purgatory. It's a part of our job description to make sure all souls are peaceful when they are laid to rest in the end." Celia plucked a white rectangular box off the top shelf. "This was your mother's. You're lucky Delaney remembered that I still had this in here."

Handing down the box to me, Celia stepped from the ladder she had to used to get to the shelf. I ran my hand over the top, feeling the divots in the lid. It was worn from the time it had spent in the room, but none of that mattered to me because I knew my mother had once worn this piece. Celia's hand reached out, picking up the necklace from my chest to examine it closer. Her eyes glazed over as she came across the ring, taking it between her grip carefully.

"This was your mother's wedding ring. I remember when your father gave it to her. He was so nervous that she wouldn't like it, kept going on and on about how she might think it was too gaudy. But I knew she would love it, and she did." Celia smiled sadly at the memory, laying the jewelry back down against my chest carefully. A gasp escaped from Celia. "I almost forgot, your father gave her this too before he fell. Rowen never went to any event without it after."

The smile in her words lit up the room. Celia turned from her spot and bent down towards another section of the piled-high boxes. Remembering my parents was something that I didn't have the luxury of being a part of. It hurt to think about the uncertainty of my parents' fates. Everyone's mixed opinions were starting to weigh heavy on my mind as the masquerade ball approached. Another unanswered question to sort out in my mind — those were starting to add up quite a lot lately. Hopefully, some will be solved sooner rather than later.

"Here it is." Celia jumped from her crouching position, sprinting over towards me. "It could use some shining up, but the gold always looked so good in her strawberry-blonde hair. You look so much like her."

A nurturing hand stroked the side of my face before Celia handed me a gold hair comb. The comb was jeweled around the base with crystal flowers that weaved beautifully throughout the hairpiece.

Even being dulled with time, the comb shone around the room.

Rubbing my finger over the piece, I looked up to Celia with grateful eyes. "I don't know how to thank you, Cee. For everything."

She gathered me in her arms, holding me close. "You don't have to thank me, dear. Anytime you need somewhere to think or my help, the Crypts are always open for you. Just promise me one thing, Lily."

"Anything."

Releasing me from her hug, she gathered the box into her hands and set it in my arms. "Just promise me you will try to stay safe for me."

"Of course, Cee. I'll try my best." I smiled at her. The woman in front of me had given me more motherly love in this hour than I'd had in my entire lifetime. The least I could do was make a promise to her to try and keep myself out of trouble until judgment day. I turned to walk back towards the twins who sat in the hallway, drinking in the amazing room one last time before departing the Crypts.

Chapter Twenty-One

One long continuous groan slipped from my mouth as I slammed against the blue mat that lay underneath me. After the adventure deep in the Crypt's archives I managed to slip the box underneath my bed, securing the hairpiece under the lid without glancing at the material hidden within it. Aspyn was insistent that I wait until Saturday to see the dress for the first time. She knew I would love the piece no matter what. The dress could have been the worst one seen by anyone, and I would still love it for the sheer fact that my mother had once stood in my place wearing it.

Now I lay sprawled out on the hard surface of an exercise mat, eyes closed in pain. Every muscle in my body was throbbing against each other. I could almost feel the pulsing sensation as I ran a hand under my neck, trying my best to undo the constant knots that were beginning to form. The group had been trying to help me train for the past two days, building up my endurance against the less harmful abilities that they were gifted when they fell.

I was making no progress, which was starting to wear on me mentally and physically. Everyone standing around in the small gym seemed to notice as well. I could feel the disappointment they were feeling with each blow of a new ability that was thrown my way. I rubbed my fingertips around my temples in a circular motion in hopes to decrease a forming headache as I tried ignoring their constant chatter.

Mallory was on the opposite end of the mat, preparing to use the copycat nature she gained from Envy once she lost her wings. The taunting illusions she was able to conjure from my ability were growing stronger with each round we partook in. First, she had started out small, only showing me small illusions of pleasant images such as kittens and butterflies. Now, she had gotten a grasp on the illusionist ability, seeing each intricate detail of its power. Mallory was able to create multiple versions of herself, taunting me with soft whispers and giggles until she had confused me enough to take the legs right out from under me.

I could feel she was holding back on the full power the illusions could create until I could get a grip on the surface of what she was using. Lifting my head off the mat slightly, I could see Mallory's smiling face. She was enjoying this game way too much.

"Again," Asher's bored voice called out from the stool he sat on. He had been watching every move of mine with hawklike vision, becoming a drill sergeant the second we entered the gym.

"No." I groaned inwardly, throwing my head back onto the matt again. The stinging of the hard material hitting my skull made me hiss in pain, and I regretted the decision almost immediately.

"Come on, Lily. You have to work with us, or you are never going to get a handle on these abilities. You're not even fighting Mallory back. That's the whole point of these training sessions." Asher's voice hovered over me. Squinting through one eye at him, I could see the dissatisfaction in his eyes. My hand reached out towards him, which he gladly took to help me to my feet.

"One more time, then I need at least a five-minute break, Ash. Everything in my body is going to fall apart if I push myself anymore." He nodded in agreement of my terms before taking his seat back on the stool and motioning towards Mallory to begin. She stared me down, eyes flickering dark as she did.

The room fell eerily quiet as she began to conjure up her illusion. Allowing the others to fade away, I stood in the middle of the gym as one single swinging light shone down on me, masking Mallory in the shadows. I could see the outline of her, my gaze tracking every move she made so I wouldn't lose the true girl once she began to multiply. The door to the gym swung open to reveal a carbon copy version of Aspyn. She had a hungry look on her face as she watched me.

The illusion of Aspyn rushed forward in my direction, arms outstretched, ready to take me down before I had even begun to put up a fight.

Sidestepping her attack, I focused my attention back on Mallory. I could feel the ability gnawing at my insides, begging to be let loose from its cage to play for once. Although I couldn't see features, I imagined them exactly how they were when I stared at the Manson girl. Cloudy gray eyes sitting next to a petite button nose, her blonde hair shining in the light even on a cloudy day. Having the perfect picture version of Mallory conjured in my head, I meddled with her features, allowing them to melt down her face. Eyes dropping low as they mixed with pale, softening skin that dripped down, a large drop splashing off the tip of her nose.

My hair was yanked down, distracting me from the melting girl. Head thrown back by the force of the pull, I could see the vicious grin of Aspyn smiling down at me. Her hands were knotted in my hair, tightening with each tug. She was trying to bring me to the ground. Her grip loosened only for a second, wanting to get one last tug in before she broke me. This allowed me to throw my head up, forehead connecting with her hovering face. A sickening crack of the illusion's nose rang out, blood spraying from each nostril as it clutched the broken bone.

A snarl ripped through my throat, focusing in on Mallory once more, who still stood stoically in the dark. The power within me sputtered to life as I envisioned the melting face once more, this time with more force than before. Holes began to form along Mallory's body as the skin dripped down, leaving only white bones underneath. Her ear-piercing scream started up, allowing the gym she had created in her mind to slide away.

We both stood back in the original gym, Mallory scratching at her skin, screaming as she went. I just continued to stare. Delaney rushed over to her sister's side, trying to get her attention. She yelled out to Aspyn, who was positioned sitting next to Gabe. Horror painted their faces as they watched the scene happening in front of them.

Asher's face landed in front of my vision, making me crane my neck towards Mallory again. I was stuck in some sort of trance. He took my chin under his thumb and forefinger, pulling my face close towards his. "Lily, you have to stop. You're torturing Mallory now."

I was looking into his green eyes, but I could still see Mallory behind my vision. She had become a puddle of liquefied skin. The only thing left standing in her place was an off-white skeleton. The power within me hummed—I didn't want to let go of it. The warming sensation that was filling my body made me feel superior to any of the Fallen Angels that stood around me. A voice in my head kept whispering that none of them were powerful enough to take me down.

Without hesitation, Asher threw his body against mine. We hit the mat with a loud bang. The wind had been knocked out of my lungs, causing me to cough against Asher's shoulder to get oxygen back into my body. Mallory's screams had stopped, leaving the air around us sour.

"What the hell was that? She could have killed her." Delaney's furious voice reverberated off the hardwood floor. She started towards the pair of us, eyes fully black and emotionless. Aspyn reached out for the girl, trying to stop her from coming near us. One flick of Delaney's wrist sent Aspyn crumpling to the ground in a sleep-paralysis state. The fever within Delaney's eyes amplified as she got closer, the heat of her stare burning holes into my skull. I tried to scramble backward away from the angry girl, but Asher's iron grip held me underneath his body.

Mallory was calling to her sister, begging for this to stop. Her hands clung to the fabric of Gabe's T-shirt. He was debating on whether or not to intervene, watching as Aspyn's eyes moved in rapid movements. Her mind was still intact, but she was unable to move under Delaney's spell.

Asher turned towards Delaney, blocking me with his back from her rampage. "Delaney, you need to get a handle on yourself. This isn't you talking, you, know this. You're allowing the darkest parts of you to overthrow your rational side."

"Oh, this is the best part of me, Asher." She smirked down at him. "Now move so I can stomp out the little twit."

"I can't let you do that." Asher's voice hardened, sending chills down my body. "Don't make me do this to you, Laney. I don't want to have to hurt you."

"You couldn't hurt me if you tried," Delaney snarled out. Stepping forward, she gripped onto my ankle that rested just behind Asher's hip, ripping me from his protection. I screamed, not sure what to do. Flailing about, she threw me down on the mat beside her, hovering over my figure menacingly. "You're mine now, Night Monster."

I rolled away from her swinging fist, it came down just inches from my face, connecting with the mat. Asher roared in anger, coming towards us in long strides. Delaney paid no attention to him, zeroing back in on me. I pushed my hands down on the gym floor's surface, scrambling back towards Gabe and Mallory. Delaney's hungry eyes watched me in amusement as she followed my trail. My back hit the concrete wall of the gym, trapping me in the corner of the room. She knew she had caught me. Fear scorched my veins as I closed my eyes, waiting for the blow to come.

Delaney let out an inhuman scream. I snapped

my eyes open to see her back arched in a U shape, cracking on its way down. Her body fell forward, hands catching her weight underneath them as she hit the gym floor. I watched her skin crawl, blowing up in small bubbles in random spaces along her arms. My eyes looked up towards Asher's—they were pitch-black and fixated on Delaney. He was making her blood boil underneath her skin. After a few seconds, Delaney collapsed in a heap of herself, allowing Aspyn to be free from the grasp she had been held under.

A choked sob escaped my mouth, staring at the motionless girl in front of me. Hands landed on my shoulder, making me rush away from their touch. Asher's eyes had returned to their vibrant green. "She'll be fine, just passed out from the pain."

Curling into his embrace, I buried my head into his chest. I had caused this. Without even knowing it, I had continued on with the illusion, torturing Mallory in the process. The worst part about it was that the power I had felt in those moments felt good. I had never wanted to come off the power high I had been riding on. Now, looking at the destruction one little illusion had caused, I knew why they had chosen to give me the nickname of Night Monster. My body was shaking against Asher's touch, but I could see from the small crack of vision I gave myself that Aspyn was standing, leaning on Gabe for support. Mallory sat staring at me, a mix of shock and fear shining under her tears. I never wanted people to fear me. It hurt knowing what I had just done. Asher laid a single kiss on my hairline, breathing my scent in deeply. If he was afraid of me, he wasn't showing it. Even I was afraid of me at this moment.

I was a monster. One that should have never existed.

CHAPTER TWENTY-TWO

We had been attending school sporadically the past month. The idea of dropping out completely had been wiped off the table. I needed to keep up appearances, which a certain green-eyed devil had lectured me about when he ripped my body from the nice, warm bed I was cuddled up in this morning. Not one of us spoke of the incident that occurred in the gym days before. Delaney had locked herself away in her room soon after we arrived back at the cabin, bumping past me with just enough force to send me stumbling forward. Although she must not have noticed it was me—regret shone in her eyes when she turned to apologize.

I didn't want to discuss what I was capable of.

In my mind, everyone's idea of my power was just speculation. A fable of the monster I was to become. Torturing Mallory, who was still itching at her skin even today, showed me just how much worse the story they made up really was.

My feet carried me to history in a zombielike state, the shoes I wore never picking up from the tile floor as they dragged underneath me. I had only slept around two hours last night. The darkness that had consumed me was filled with haunting laughs and twirling couples. I was alone for once in the past month, shoved ahead by the twins as Gabe pulled them aside, speaking in an urgent hushed whisper. I didn't mind though. Not having someone hovering over my shoulder every second of the day gave me time to think.

"Hello, Lily." Professor Erickson stood at the front of the classroom, writing in loopy letters on the chalkboard. "I sent everyone to the library to work on their semester project, but you would have known that if you had arrived to class on time—or at all, for that matter."

A red flush crept up my cheeks, though I could

hear the playfulness in his voice. "I'm sorry, I had some family things going on."

That was the understatement of the century.

"There's no need to explain. I am well aware of the secrets this town holds." Professor Erickson turned towards where I stood in the doorway with a smile plastered on his face. "You have been the talk amongst these creatures lurking in the shadows a great deal as of late."

My mouth bobbled open, not understanding how he would know anything regarding the Angels of this town. Bending down to the desk that sat to his left, he shuffled around some papers. A familiar brown, leather-bound book hid underneath the mess of the desk.

"You really shouldn't leave things lying around, Liliana. They might fall into the wrong hands." The book came flying across the classroom towards me. I caught it with ease, running my hand over the cool leather. "Now run along, Lily. Wouldn't want to keep that Demon boy waiting, would you?"

Giving him one final look, I turned towards the door, trying to wrap my head around what he meant by Demon boy. Rotating back towards the man once more, I opened my mouth to comment back to him but closed it immediately. I needed to find Mallory.

Mal sat at a back table of the library thumbing through some mind-numbing tabloid magazine. Cautiously I walked towards her. "Mal?"

She looked up, eyes widening when she saw me. I held my hands up in surrender hoping she wouldn't run from me. "I'm sorry. I don't know what happened the other day. This ability got the best of me, and I'll never do something like that again to you. Please don't be afraid of me. I don't think I could live myself if you hated me, Mallory."

My voice died down to a timid whisper at the end, scared of how she would take my apology. I knew what I had done, and I deserved the punishments that came along with it. Mallory sighed, closing the magazine before she motioned for me to sit across from her. Leaping into the chair, I waited quietly for her to speak.

"I'm not afraid of you, Liliana, not in the slightest. None of us knew you wouldn't be able to stop once you started. It takes practice to hone your abilities. All of us know that." Mal reached across the table, grasping my hand in hers. "I should be the one apologizing for my sister's behavior. She is way too pigheaded to admit when she is wrong. Delaney is just really protective of me ever since we fell. Though I don't need her to protect me, I know it comes from a good place. We both lost a sister that day, and she can't imagine losing me as well."

"It's okay. I kind of deserved it," I whispered. Lifting open my bag, I looked down to where I had safely tucked Claire's journal next to Xander's. I had slipped my father's journal into my bag this morning, silently praying that Mallory would be willing to help. Setting both books out, I pushed my father's over towards her. "I need your help. That was Xander's journal. It's written in some other language, but he said you would be able to translate it for me."

Mallory reached out, taking the overflowing book in her hands. "I always told him he wrote everything down."

She cracked open the spine, looking over the foreign words. Her gray eyes sparkled with excitement, recognizing the strange text as she read.

"Can you read that thing?"

"Of course, this is an old Angelic language. It's rarely used anymore, but that must be the reason Xander chose to write in it. This might take some time to dissect fully though."

"Take as much time as you need. I have to get through this," I said, holding up Claire's journal.

"Is that Claire's?" Her eyes widened at the sight of the familiar diary.

"Yeah, Professor Erickson was keeping it safe for me. Gabe told me to read the whole thing and he would explain the rest." I thumbed through the delicate pages, watching as the words melted together. Mallory had already begun to read Xander's notes. A pen hung from her ear while a notebook sat to her left, and large scribbles of notes were scrawled across the pages. Smiling towards the girl, I left her to her reading as I dove straight into the first entry in the journal.

February 1993

I unpacked my first box today in this gloomy town Father has moved us to. I know, I know, he got an amazing job offer. It doesn't make me any less upset about him ripping up my entire life and moving me into a one-stoplight town. Everyone in this place is strange. They all walk amongst each other like gods gracing the earth. Also, that awful statue in the middle of town does this place no favors. School was uneventful, just like I thought it would be. But I did make a friend. Her name is Rowen, and she is the nicest person I have ever met. Not the fake kind of nice either, genuinely nice. She invited me to eat lunch with her friends as well. They seem nice enough for now. Emma Chadwick hung all over her boyfriend William way too much. I might have a cavity from how sugary-sweet they were. The other boy Xander was quiet most of the lunch period, not speaking unless Rowen spoke to him. Dark circles hung around his eyes, making his stare chilling.

Father is calling me now for supper. I will document more about my boring experiences as they come along. Maybe this will be my memoir they read at my funeral.

-Claire Halloway

Most of the entries that came after that consisted of Claire's mundane activities in Idelwood. I had gotten to December of 1993 just as the bell rang. The sound startled both Mal and me out of our work. Gathering up everything around us we made our way towards the exit. Mallory was gossiping my ear off about the latest celebrity scandal she had read in the trashy magazine earlier. I was laughing at the drama she was spewing my way, her arms acting out the dramatic scene for the entire library as we walked through the rows of books. Watching the girl's animated expressions distracted me from the person entering the doorway I was trying to exit. My body collided with them, sending me tumbling a few steps back into the library.

"Well, well, well, look who it is, Fin," Tabitha Manson's squeaky voice spoke out. "Hello, sister."

Tabitha smirked in Mallory's direction, making the bubbly girl's eyes grow cold. Mallory's body stood rigid as she intently watched the sister that had kept her wings. "Tabitha, don't you have someone else to bother? I'm sure he would love to have you in his company—he always used to."

Stepping back again, I noticed they weren't alone this time. Hanging on Finley's other hip was Brinley Goodwin. Her arms were crossed over her chest, and fiery eyes lit up an otherwise emotionless face. Finley pushed Brinley aside, making his way towards me. My back hit a random shelf that lined the room, causing some of the books to topple onto the ground and lay open like a tiny tent. He leaned one hand above my head while the other made lines up my arm, toying with me. Each line he created made me sick.

"Liliana, we have to stop meeting this way."

"I'm not playing your games today, Finley." I tried to walk away from him, but both of his hands hit the shelf next to my face, the loud bang making me flinch back into place. Finley's face drifted in front of mine—the famous smirk he always wore pulled at the corner of his mouth.

"Aw, the poor little abomination is scared, isn't she, Brinley?" I could see both of the girls snickering at me under Finley's arms. My eyes caught Brinley's as she laughed, though the laugh didn't meet her sad eyes. This wasn't her. It was just a cry for attention to her parents. The animosity she held towards them was my fault. If they could only see what their daughter had gotten herself into.

"As she should be," Finley hissed, reaching down to stroke my cheek. I shuddered under his touch, making his smirk widen. He could see the fear he had placed in my heart, which brought him immense joy.

Closing my eyes, I tried to concentrate on ignoring his movements. Their snide comments stopped. I peeked out of my right eye to see all of them were frozen in place, not moving an inch. Finley's blue eyes wandered around in confusion, realizing quickly that he could no longer move.

"I find it hilarious you think you can toy with me like you used to, Finley. I have learned a lot more about what I am capable since the last time we spoke in the quarry." I tapped into my illusions, causing every word I spoke to echo around him and his minions. The slight tweak in my voice made it so I was everywhere and nowhere all at once. A chilling feeling filled the area we stood. "I mean, you were the one who showed me what I could do now, weren't you?"

I dipped under his frozen arm, starting to circle around the two Angels in front of me and leaving Brinley for later. Continuing my speech, I let my voice carry from ear to ear. "Tabby is just the sidekick for Fin. Trailing around him like a lost puppy, but you are just too much bark and not enough bite for my taste."

I turned my attention towards the mortal girl, twisting around in front of her. When I reached Brinley,

I could see her eyes burning with tears that were unable to fall. "And Brinley is just trying to prove something to the both of you, but all this time you just want to defy Mommy and Daddy. Am I wrong? You're going to end up getting yourself stuck in the middle of a war that has no concern for you."

Brinley's face looked as though she wanted to scream at me in a fit of rage. The thought made me laugh darkly at her. I was tapping into the same energy as I had felt only days before. The same energy I vowed never to use because it turned me into this soulless monster. Today it felt so much stronger, buzzing around me like fireflies in the night sky.

A hand landed on my shoulder, making me jump. "That's quite enough, Liliana."

Professor Erickson stood behind me, staring in amazement at the three frozen people in front of him. I sneered at him in disgust as he told me to stop, the little voice in my head angry that someone like him, a mortal, would demand such a thing from someone as powerful as me. I'd held so much anger against Finley and Tabitha for weeks, the least he could do was let me with play with the pests I had trapped. Throwing his hand off my shoulder, I spun around to face him fully. I was tired of people controlling my every move in this town. Before I could open my mouth to speak, my body was pulled back by my waist, the sudden movement making me flail in panic.

"Hey, Lily, chill out," the voice whispered into my exposed ear. I fought against them until they dropped me out of their grasp. "What has gotten into you the past couple days?"

Facing the voice, I found both of the twins staring at everything around them with dread. Their faces snapped me back into reality, making the dark cloud which hung over my brain clear away as I realized what I had just done. The Night Monster inside my brain laughed sadistically at the chaos it was causing. It loved being let out of its cage to play. My breathing became panicked, and I stepped closer to Asher, who stood just inches from my trembling figure. Unclenching my hold on the three frozen statues, I allowed them to move once more.

Finley turned around slowly before charging towards me. Aspyn stepped in front of him, blocking his path. He stopped immediately, watching the girl challenge him. "Back off, Fin. You brought this on yourself, antagonizing Lily like that."

"Oh, now the sister speaks. Aspyn Faye, it has been a long time since I have heard that voice. Not following your brother's first move this time." Finley placed his fingers underneath her chin, tipping it up to examine every inch of her beauty, "My, my, what has gotten into my little devil?"

Aspyn reached up towards Finley, gripping onto his wrist before harshly pulling it away from her chin. "Don't touch me. You don't know anything about me anymore, Finley."

Her voice shook with emotion, eyes narrowing towards the redheaded boy in front of her. As they spoke, the energy in the room electrified much like the way it did when I was around Asher. But their electrifying sensation was hot and angry, causing the room to pulse with tension.

"On the contrary, Aspyn, I still know exactly what makes you tick. I know you better than Gabriel ever will, and that still scares the hell out of you. Be sure to tell him hello for me next time you snake your way back into his bed." I watched his eyes roam over her body, coming up short of her vibrant green orbs in the end. "If you had not followed Asher to the depths of the earth, just think of what you could have been. He was destined to fall. We all knew it with the loyalty he had to that Night Monster's parents, but you had a choice. Just think of your potential, what we could have been if you had thought about your decisions before plummeting down after him."

Aspyn's eyes were wet with tears, one lone droplet falling down her face. She rolled her shoulders back, biting her lip, where I could see she had drawn blood with her front canines. She did not want to give Finley the satisfaction of getting under her skin. "Just stay away from us, Finley, but especially stay as far as you can from me."

She raced from the library's exit, Mallory quickly trailing behind her. Asher stood planted in his place, worried eyes following his sister's figure out. My gaze traveled back towards the Angel, locking on Finley, who stood standing in a state of shock. I could see the heartbreak in his eyes setting in as the dark-haired girl vanished from his view. He wasn't as stone-cold as he let on to be. Seeing this part of him made me realize his deep-rooted hate towards me started and ended with the loss of Aspyn.

"Come on, Lil." I felt my eyes wander back to Asher. He cocked his head towards the direction Aspyn had gone, leading me towards the exit. I wrapped my arms around my torso, the regret of what had just happened sinking in with every step we took. Asher steered me towards the parking lot of the school, but Mallory was nowhere to be seen, leaving us alone. Aspyn sat in the back seat of the Mustang with her head buried in her hands. Violent sobs racked her entire body, not noticing us as we slipped in the car. We all sat there for a while listening to Aspyn's cries.

"Asp," Asher whispered to his twin, eyes looking at her through the rearview mirror.

Aspyn looked up, meeting his matching eyes. "Don't. Just leave it alone, Ash. It's not worth worrying about. Just let's not mention it to Gabe."

Asher nodded once at his twin, both of them having a silent conversation with their eyes before he turned his attention back towards the car's ignition. The drive was silent the whole way back to the home. I could feel the tension radiating off both of the siblings. One held a heated anger while the other held immense sadness—they both mixed together in a swimming motion around the small cabin space of the car. As we pulled in towards the cabin, it was dark, and relief washed over me, knowing no one was here. As soon as the car came to a stop, Aspyn jumped over me and out of the vehicle, racing into the pitch-black home.

Asher looked over towards me, taking in my concerned face. He reached over and placed his hand on my thigh, starting to rub small, calming circles against my jeans, one of his many habits that I would never get tired of. "She'll be fine."

"Do you really believe that?" I watched the front door, left open when Aspyn had rush through it. Shifting my weight to one hip, I looked over towards him. You could see that it hurt him to see his sister in pain.

"No, but I have to hope that one day it will all be okay. I thought that with Gabe things were getting better, but you can tell she never let go of Finley. Never stopped loving him, not that she really has a choice in that matter. She says she doesn't blame me for everything that happened, but you can tell deep down she does some days. I think both she and Gabe use each other just to numb the pain. Both lost so much more than all of us when they fell."

The pain that he held in his eyes hurt me to the core. I wanted to take all of it away. Reaching up, I turned his head to look at me. "You know you can tell me anything when it comes to your past, right?"

Asher leaned into my touch, closing his eyes. He softly hummed a yes towards me. "I know, Lil. I just can't bear the thought of you hating me yet."

"That'll never happen, I promise you."

Chapter Twenty-Three

We sat in the car's warmth for a while longer before I made the decision to go check on Aspyn. I wanted to make sure she was okay and not going to do anything stupid behind our backs. Walking up the stairs, I headed towards the room she and Gabe had been sharing for the past few weeks. My hand knocked on the door before entering the room. This space was nothing like her beloved picture-filled room. Here the walls were painted a light yellow color, and since the large bed took up most of the room, there was no other furniture. She was lying across the bed, staring up the ceiling with glassy eyes. Making my way towards the mattress, I lay next to her, our bodies aligned together. Both of us continued to stare at the ceiling, not speaking for a long time.

"Did Ash send you to check on me?" Her voice was hoarse from the crying.

As I turned to face her, she kept her eyes trained on the stark white ceiling. "No, I came to see if the one person who always checks on me is okay."

"I'm fine, Lily, really." Aspyn's eyes continued to wander along the different spots of the ceiling above her. She had transferred some of her pictures that had hung on the wall in her room to the cabin — they lined the wooden beams in jagged patterns.

"You don't have to put up a front with me, Asp. You can tell me anything. Whatever is bothering you, I'm here to listen." I watched her head turn towards mine. She was trying to tell if I was going to take back what I had just offered. "I'm serious, anything you tell me won't make me run away. You're in too deep with me now."

"Great, now how am I supposed to get rid of you?"

"You won't. You're stuck with me forever." I wiggled my eyebrows slightly, making her choke out a rough laugh. Once the laughter died down, the morbid feeling in the room returned around us.

Aspyn sat up slowly, sitting cross-legged on the bed in front of me. I propped myself up on my elbows as she struggled to find the right words to speak. "Before I fell, I wasn't much different than how I am now, but Asher and I had a best friend. Finley had been at our sides for as long as I can remember. We were all so close, but as we got older, Fin and I grew a lot closer. We dated for years before I fell. He was my best friend, first love, and he always knew that Asher would fall after Xander went. Your father was like an older brother to the two of us, and it was like ripping a family member out of the picture when he fell."

She took in a shaky breath, "Even if he was still right next door in this town, it was never going to be the same as before. I grew distant after that. There was a giant hole in my heart even Fin couldn't fill. He used to be sweet—the Fin that he is now wasn't the same one that I grew up with. He's grown cold and detached from everything that has happened in his life since all of this began. I think it's a defense mechanism since I broke his heart. Our hearts. That's mostly my fault. I fell because I followed Asher, knowing the consequences of my actions. It broke all of us. I don't think either of us fully recovered from it. Even now that I'm with Gabe, I can't help but always be in love with Finley. He was the one I was destined to be with, and I ruined us."

Aspyn spoke in a watery voice, and I gathered her into my arms as she sobbed against my shoulder. We sat there for a while in silence after the cries had stopped. When she spoke again, her voice wobbled with regret. "It's not even that I fell that keeps us apart—it's me."

"What do you mean, Asp?" I pulled back to look at her.

"He once told me that even if I fell, it wouldn't matter. Destiny doesn't lie, and even if it's a heavy price to pay, he was willing to pay it. I was the one that walked away from him. I didn't want him to be hurt by decisions that I ended up making. The council would have torn him to shreds after that if we kept what we had going. Fin is too smart to not be in the position he is in, and he's worked his whole life to be there. I couldn't take that away. Even if it tears me apart being anywhere near him, I'm willing to hurt for him."

"What about Gabe? Doesn't he make you happy?" Everything was silent in the room while Aspyn thought about the questions that hung in the air.

"He takes away the pain for a while, but it's nothing like what I feel with Fin. Unfortunately, it never will be, but without Gabe, I would just be numb. I think he feels the same way about me."

"Don't be ridiculous, Aspyn. That boy loves you. Anyone with eyes can see that." I tried to reason with her, but all she did was shake her head at me. Aspyn broke her gaze with me leaning back against the pillows to stare at the ceiling once again.

"Not like he loved Claire Halloway."

I left Aspyn's room later that night once she had fallen asleep. As I walked down the stairs of the cabin, everything was still as silent as it had been when we arrived back here. The only light lit up was the one leading into the dining room. Asher sat at the long table, pen in between his teeth as he read a book.

His eyebrows scrunched together, leaving deep furrows as he concentrated on whatever he was reading. I rested my shoulder on the archway, content to watch him. A small smile played against my lips as I stood there. Asher ran his hand through the mop of black hair on the top of his head. His eyes caught mine as he looked up from the book.

"Are you watching me?"

"No, not at all." I let the lie slip through the mischievous smile playing against my lips. "But even if I was, what are you going to do about it?"

One of his eyebrows quirked up at my challenge. Standing from the table, Asher started around it, his fingers trailing the edge of the wood slowly as he made his way in my direction. "Was that a challenge, Ms. Caldwell?"

"No, because I know you won't do anything about it." I giggled at his words, but the corners of my mouth fell as he rounded the table, coming closer to me. I turned on my heels, making a mad dash for the staircase. My feet never landed on the bottom step as my body was hoisted off away from it and into Asher's arms.

"Asher, put me down!" I screeched at him, secretly loving being so close to him.

"Hm, I don't think I will," Asher mumbled into my neck, peppering my collarbone with feather-light kisses. His hot breath against my skin made me giggle. Asher landed one more kiss on my shoulder before setting me down back onto my feet.

"I wish it was always just this simple," I whispered, turning into Asher. I could live in this moment of pure bliss forever. Where there was no impending doom hanging over our heads, no "dead" parents, nothing. Just a boy and a girl living in their own story.

Asher rested his forehead against mine. "You have no idea how long I have waited to love you, Liliana."

Capturing his lips on my own, I savored the moment, knowing it could all come crashing down at any second. If the council caught wind of my little stunt this afternoon, nothing would stop them from killing me the second they found me. I was hoping Finley would keep his mouth shut for Aspyn's sake.

The kiss deepened, Asher's hungry lips capturing mine. My feet left the ground as he lifted me up from their place on the floor. I followed the motion by wrapping each leg around his torso. He backed us up against the table, laying me down on the piece of furniture. I kept my legs locked around him, making him pull closer to me as his lips left mine, trailing down my face and quickly continuing towards my neck and kissing any exposed skin he managed to get to. Pulling his face back, I placed his lips against mine, sitting up to meet him halfway. Asher's hands traced the outline of my hips, sending chills down my spine. Reaching down towards the hem of his shirt, I tugged at the material, tired of it being in my way.

Breaking the kiss slightly, he lifted the shirt off his body, connecting back to me seconds later. My hands roamed on the new skin, taking my time to run my fingertips down his exposed stomach. I could feel him shiver under my touch as my fingers grazed his abs, making me smile into the kiss.

Reaching back up, I twisted my arms around his neck before letting the hands venture over his broad shoulders. The muscles tensed as my fingertips trailed over the scars which lined his shoulder blades. Where there were once wings, now jagged scars remained. I continued to trace the lines, wanting to know every inch of him.

Pulling apart from my lips, Asher continued to kiss the delicate skin next to my ear, whispering softly to me, "I love you."

Freezing under his words, I turned to look at him, my eyes lingering just below his gaze before he spoke again. "Please look at me."

I shook my head at his request, refusing to meet his eyes. Deep down I felt the same way, but hearing those words leave his mouth for the first time caused my brain to scream for me to run and never look back. I heard him let out a frustrated sigh as he got eye level with me.

"Don't hide from me. Tell me what's wrong." He took my shaking hands in his, clasping both to his chest. Tears began to fill my eyes, embarrassed that I was pulling away from him once again. Everything in me wanted to be with the green-eyed boy, but one strand of doubt sang out louder than all other thoughts. I didn't want to be this way anymore, not with Asher. He brought his hands to either side of my jaw cradling my head in them.

"Nothing, that's the problem. You're perfect, but with everything that has happened, everyone always ends up leaving. I'm afraid if I let myself admit how I feel, everything will come crashing down around me, just like it always does." I looked into his eyes, not hiding from their stare this time.

"There is nothing wrong with pulling away from me, Lil. You have been through so much. I would have been worried if you didn't pull away. You wouldn't be my Lily then." Asher's mouth curved into a smile.

I let out a watery laugh. "So you knew I would do this?"

"I had my suspicions."

Laughing once more at him, I leaned further into his touch and closed my eyes. "How do you always know what to say at exactly the right time?"

"I've been around the block a time or two," he joked. Snapping open my eyes, I pushed my hands against his chest. Asher raised his hands out in surrender. "Hey, I'm just kidding!"

"You better be." My lips pursed into a deep pout, watching him laugh at his own stupid comment.

"Hm, I like this side of you. The jealous side. It's hot." His hands pulled against my hips once more, making me roll my eyes at him. I maneuvered my way off the table, leaving him behind.

"I'm going to bed. You can come with or stay down here with your book. It seemed way more fascinating than me earlier," I called back towards him, placing my first foot on the bottom step of the staircase. Quickly, heavy footsteps trailed after mine. Asher's fingers caught in mine as we continued.

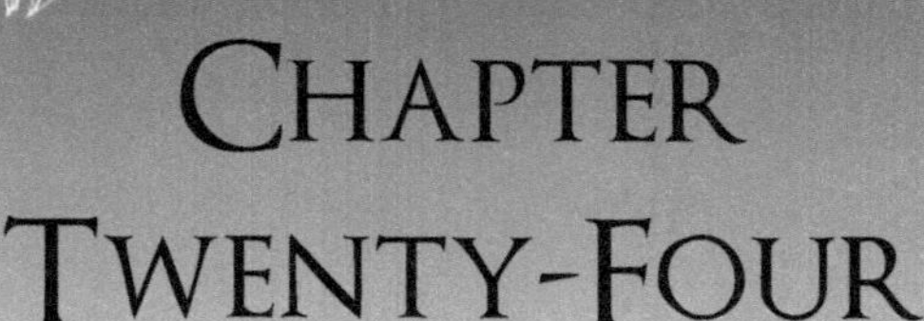

Chapter Twenty-Four

The morning of the masquerade ball, Asher and I stood in the middle of the gym. Being back in this place where I had lost control once before sent a chill up my spine. Asher had explained to me that he wanted to run through any tests that the council could ask me to perform for them tonight. I felt drained from trying to conjure up every illusion that Asher thought up. Lying back on the cool mat, I closed my eyes.

"You can't fall asleep, Lil. We have to finish this." Asher's voice hovered over my body. I tried to ignore him the best I could, hoping he might just disappear altogether. "You're not getting out of this, Liliana Adrienne."

Letting my eyes fly open to meet his stern gaze, I matched it with my own glare. "Did you just use my full name against me, Asher?"

I raised an eyebrow at the boy in front of me. His mouth turned up into an evil smile. "What? Does it bother you when I do that?"

"Maybe."

"Noted."

His hand reached down towards me, waiting for me to grab onto it. I snatched it in my grip, feeling myself being pulled up to my feet. "Come on, let's get this over with."

My grip on his hand tightened as I waited silently until he turned to look at me. "I don't know if I can do this, Asher. I got somewhat of a hold on this illusionist ability and whatever that was in the library."

"I think I have an idea of what it was." Asher pushed a stray piece of hair behind my ear. I stood waiting for him to continue explaining. He cleared his throat before speaking. "Your father was only able to immobilize one person at a time. You seem to be able to expand that to as many people as you want or need. The fact that you can do what he couldn't—it would have driven him mad."

I smiled towards Asher, thinking of the man in my visions. My heart ached, wishing I could have grown up with him, learning everything there was to know from him. "I'm worried about the visionary ability. It's tricky to control, and I haven't been able to figure out what triggers each one. They just come at random. I had another the other day."

"When was this?" Asher's mouth dropped into a deep frown, waiting for me to continue explaining.

"Before Aspyn and I left the dress shop. It was weird this time—I don't think it was from the past, but I'm not sure if it was the future either. Something about it was just so strange. It didn't feel the same as the other visions I have had." I mumbled out my words, chewing on my bottom lip nervously. The hand that wasn't latched in Asher's reached up to play with the necklace still hanging around my neck. The piece had never left its place since I had put it on. I ran through the vision once more in my mind, still not coming up with an answer to my question.

"Just walk me through it. We can figure out what

it means together." Asher watched me toy with the trinket, still trying to understand what I was supposed to say to him.

"I was standing in the middle of a ball. I was almost positive it was the ball that is being hosted tonight, but then someone came up behind me. It was Nate. He told me I wasn't happy to see him, which would be the furthest thing from the truth if the vision was real. You know I would be elated to see him, even if he did keep all these secrets from me. I know there must be an explanation for all of what he has done. But what has had me reeling since I saw him was what he said to me. Nate told me to watch my back. I keep thinking that it is some kind of riddle for me to figure out, but I have no idea what it could possibly mean."

Asher stayed silent, the gears behind his eyes working double time as he processed the vision over and over again. "Do you think it could possibly have something to do with Claire? She said she was able to manipulate your visions."

"I'm not sure. I already thought of that, but why would she show me that, of all things? She has only revealed things to me that have to do with the past, mostly pertaining to her." I bit into my lip, a metal taste beginning to fill my mouth as I drew blood with my teeth.

Asher snorted loudly. "She always was full of herself. Now that she's a ghost, it must be amplified."

"So you're saying I have a self-centered teenage girl's ghost haunting my visions." I watched him nod his head in amusement, "I guess I've been told weirder things in the past month. I want to try something."

He met my eyes, waiting for me to continue with my idea. "I want to try to immobilize someone's powers one more time."

"That's not happening. You saw what my ability did to Laney. I refuse to put you through that just for sport." Asher crossed his arms over his body, squaring off with me. His chest rose and fell with angry breaths.

Blowing the bangs out of my face, I rolled my eyes towards him. He wanted me to practice so badly just two minutes ago—now my suggestion was out of the question. "You're joking, right? I'll be fine."

"Does it look like I'm joking in the slightest? I make people's blood boil under their skin. I refuse to cause you any harm. The risk of you not being able to stop me before I start is too high. I wouldn't be able to live with myself if you felt the pain my ability brings to others."

Letting out a huff of anger, I concentrated on Asher, willing myself to make him freeze in place. I had done it to Finley and his gang with such ease. I needed to know if I could do it on command. No moving, no speaking, nothing at all. I wanted him to silently breathe in place, allowing his mind to wonder as to why he was stuck.

"Lily, it's for your own goo—" Asher's words caught in his throat as he stood frozen in place. After the initial shock had run through my body, I stood staring at Asher with wide eyes. I could see his mind trying to figure out what was happening as he watched me eye him. He knew full well what had just happened.

I giggled to myself, proud that I had actually accomplished what I had set out in doing. "I quite enjoy this one, it stops the never-ending lectures that come out of your mouth. Aspyn will get a kick out of it too, I am sure."

I could almost see Asher narrowing his eyes at me if he wasn't frozen in place, silently telling me to knock it off. Breathing out once, I released the tight embrace I could feel myself holding on him, it was like untying a knot. As the knot loosened, so did Asher's body, allowing him to regain control of himself again.

"—d." The end of Asher's words tumbled out of his mouth. "That's not funny."

Smirking at him, I brushed my hands together, letting them rest on my hips once I was done. "I thought it was a pretty good way to shut you up. I was testing to see if I was able to do it on command. All I have to do is concentrate, choose a single person or a group, and focus in on them. Immobilizing their movements until I decide to allow them to regain control. Then I just release them like I'm untying a knotted shoelace," I said, explaining my process to him.

Asher looked at me smugly. "Your father could barely immobilize one person at a time. It drained him to hold on for very long. You could immobilize the entire school with just a bat of an eyelash."

"Is that supposed to make me feel better about how I turn in to a psychotic bitch with these abilities when I'm angry? I'm just your modern-day Carrie White over here—just add pig's blood."

"We will work on that later." He brushed past me. "Come here. I have another theory."

Asher walked over to his bag, digging through the pocket until he pulled out a shiny red apple. Bringing the fruit towards me, he held it in the palm of his hands. "I have only heard that the most powerful visionaries can control time. I want you to take this apple and speed up its life span. Think about it like it has an internal clock you are adjusting. Then just let it rot."

Nodding towards him, I picked up the apple and held it in between my fingertips. I began to stare at the fruit, examining it in the light. The red of the apple shone even under the bad gym lighting, allowing me to see every bruise the fruit had on its surface. Thinking about what Asher had explained, I allowed a clock to appear behind my eyes, twisting the knob around and around again until I was able to perform the motion without thinking about it. My eyelids fluttered shut, allowing me to concentrate all my energy on the apple.

The lights flickered around us as I felt the piece of fruit fight back against my ability, not wanting to give into the change. I opened them once more, but this time I stood slightly back, watching myself rot the apple until it turned into mush in my hand. I could feel the squish of the browning fruit, its juice leaking down and my arm spilling onto my long-sleeve shirt. Like a timer went off in my head, I knew the fruit was fully rotten. Gasping back into my body, I opened my eyes and stared at the rotten apple that was fresh in between my fingertips just moments earlier.

"That is disgusting." I set the fruit on the table next to us, trying to shake the rotten juices off my hand. I could smell the sickeningly sweet smell on me still, making me nauseous.

"No, that is amazing. I have never seen anything like that." Asher's look dumbfounded eyes still looked at the apple.

"I don't get it. Why would anyone want to rot their fruit in seconds?" My nose twisted up in disgust. Anyone who enjoyed that was sick.

"It's more of a defensive tool since you can control the eternal clock of anything. In theory, you could use it against someone who was trying to cause harm to you."

"You mean kill them?" I couldn't imagine killing someone, no matter the circumstances. After what had happened here last time, I already felt like the monster everyone expected me to be. The outburst in the library really didn't help deny my feelings either. There was something dark inside me, and I liked how it felt when I tapped into it. My mind couldn't even wrap itself around the idea of what the monster that lived deep in me would do if it took someone's life. I don't think that it would be as easy to shove away after that.

Asher took two long strides towards me, closing the space between our bodies. "Nothing will ever come to the point that you will have to use it."

"I don't want to be the monster everyone thinks I am." My voice was just above a whisper. Even if I hadn't said the words aloud before, I had a feeling Asher knew my fears firsthand—the dark could so easily win over if I let it. I watched Delaney snap in a split second. Now she barely comes out of her room. The intense regret in her eyes spoke louder than words.

"You won't be. I won't let you lose yourself, remember?" He held his pinky up in remembrance, "I stand by my promises, Lil."

"I know." My words squealed off as Asher thrust me into his arms.

He spun us in a circle around the mat. "I still think what you did there was amazing, no matter how much you hate it."

Throwing my head back and laughing at his outburst, I found myself happier than I had been in months. I wished tonight didn't have to come, but as the hours ticked by, I knew that the time to run had long passed. I looked up towards him, staring at his face. Even with the slight gleam of sweat that coated his face, Asher was still the most beautiful creature I had ever met. Noticing I was staring, Asher leaned down, grazing my swollen lips against his.

The kiss deepened, holding me in like I was going to slip away from him at any moment. I pulled away to catch my breath, still watching him. Asher was everything I had grown to love about this town. His humor bounced off the walls, radiating to the others in the group constantly. The protective nature he held onto always came from the good in his heart. Oh, and those eyes. I could swim in those green eyes for hours.

"You're staring again." Asher chuckled at my blushing cheeks, running his thumb over one.

"Sorry, I was just thinking." I tucked my head in the crook of his neck, fitting to him like a puzzle piece.

"What about, love?" he asked. My mouth curved up into a hidden smile at the word. Every time he said it, I could feel my insides warm. Pulling back to get another good look at him, I took in every line that formed on his face when he was thinking.

"I was just thinking how much I am in love with you," I whispered. My body stilled in place, but it took everything in me to not hide back in his neck.

A wide grin grew on Asher's face, his eye winking

towards me. "I am pretty great, aren't I?"

Rolling my eyes at his comment, I let out a light chuckle. "I pour my heart out to you, and you become a narcissist."

"Hm, I mean you already know how much I love you. It is pretty obvious." Asher grabbed both sides of my face, peppering it with kisses. The force of the sudden movement made me slip, taking Asher tumbling to the mat with me. Laughing in between kisses, we stayed there in our happy little bubble, ignoring the outside world.

Chapter Twenty-Five

Later that night I stood in front of a mirror in Aspyn's bathroom. She and Mal had sat me down in a chair the moment I walked through the door. They poked, messed with, and practically ripped out my hair as their delicate hands weaved my strawberry-blonde locks into an intricate braid.

The style lay across my left shoulder, curls softly framing my face. Aspyn had carefully placed Rowen's hair comb at the crown of my braid, making the piece sit securely against my head, a constant reminder of her that would be with me the entire night. Mallory painted a light layer of makeup on my face, lining my eyes with black to make the blue that swam around against my pupils stand out.

The hours spent between the three of us were fun. They helped me forget the knots that were forming in the pit of my stomach, replacing them with plenty of laughter and smiles.

It was judgment day. Tonight would decide my entire future. One misstep in front of the council, and the family I had built for myself in Idelwood would come tumbling down around us. The nerves I felt were beyond words could fathom. I could see them manifesting on the outside as I tightened the back of my earring.

Don't let them see you sweat.

I had to put on my brave face now. They wouldn't get the best of me. Not tonight. My hands latched onto the lip of the bathroom's countertop, gripping it to steady myself. The white box laying in the chair behind me, burned through the cloth material it sat upon. This was my mother's, the woman who I resembled in uncanny ways. I didn't want to be the one to tarnish her name. Rowen was obviously very loved by both the council and the creatures who roamed this town, but I was not my mother's daughter. Hell, I wasn't even my father's daughter.

I only knew the things that others told me about them. Both sides giving me more mixed reviews than a chick flick in theaters. They left a mess for me to clean up—that was the only thing I knew for certain about them.

My fingers floated over the white ribbon that held the box together, pulling at the delicate fabric as it unfolded with ease. I lifted the box, folding back the lining paper to reveal a dress placed neatly inside. The deep emerald-green color stood out against the white box. I ran my fingers over the lace before carefully lifting it up to examine closer. The top had thin spaghetti straps that connected to lace and crossed in a single X on the lower back. The bodice held the billowing skirt that pooled against the floor with a crystal beaded belt. It was the most gorgeous gown I had ever seen. A light scent of lavender perfume held on to the fabric from the last person who had worn it.

"I told you that you would love it." Aspyn stood, watching me in the doorway. She was wearing a long-sleeve, black lace dress. It cut up both sides of her legs, leaving a panel in the middle. Her hair sat in a sleek bun on the side of her head. She looked angelic just like always.

"Dressed to impress, I can see." I nodded in her direction, taking in her appearance one more time. She scoffed, at me not amused by my insinuation.

"I don't know what you are talking about." Aspyn rolled her eyes as she walked towards me. "Now, let's get you dressed. We have to leave soon, and Asher will lose his mind if we are late."

Taking the dress from my arms, she stepped towards the large walk-in closet, hanging the piece on the rack. It shone underneath the chandelier that lit up the space. I trailed behind her slowly, not ready for tonight to start. Dropping the robe I was currently wearing, she held open the dress for me to step into, allowing me to shimmy the straps over my shoulders. She turned my body towards a full-length mirror that hung on the back wall.

Aspyn leaned her chin against my shoulder, watching me examine myself in the mirror. "You look amazing, L."

Smoothing out the material around my body, I stared in the mirror. This girl looking back at me wasn't the same one who had come into the small town of Idelwood. I stood taller than ever before, even with the concealed dark circles from the lack of sleep. I felt more powerful than I had ever thought possible. That girl from before didn't want to stay in one place for too long, never letting herself grow close to anyone. This girl in the mirror was strong and passionate about the people in her life.

She had learned to love with every fiber of her being, throwing herself blindly into feelings she had once stored far away from her heart. This girl didn't care if she got hurt as long as those around her were out of harm's way. I never understood what had been missing in my life, always feeling this void that could never be filled. Now that I filled that piece of my heart, I never wanted to be the girl from before. Idelwood had given me more than I returned. To think I had wanted to bolt from this town just a few weeks ago seemed so far away now that I stared at myself.

This girl in the mirror, she was the one I had always dreamed about being.

"I almost forgot." Aspyn bolted from the closet,

coming back seconds later with a gold object shining in her hand. "I picked this up for you. It matches the hairpiece perfectly."

She reached out, handing me a gold mask. The metal swirled together, making soft details all over the front ending in a fleur-de-lis, which sat in the middle of the eye. Smiling up at the girl, I threw my arms around her. "This is stunning Asp. You didn't have to do this."

"Of course I did, you would have forgotten." Aspyn laughed, pulling out of the hug. She pinned the mask into place, making sure it wouldn't fall from my face during the night. "Now, come on. Asher is waiting for us, and we both know how impatient he can be."

Quickly slipping into my heels, I rushed from the closet after Aspyn. She had started down the stairs, meeting Asher at the bottom. Aspyn stood smiling at her twin as she fiddled with his black tie to make sure it was straight. I stopped at the top of the stairs, taking in his appearance. A bright smile complemented the glowing green eyes which were shadowed by a simple black mask. The dark tux he wore made him look even hotter than he did normally. There was just something about a guy in a suit that made any reasonable girl swoon.

My heels clicked down against the wood of the first step, sending both twins' heads snapping up. Asher went slacked-jawed as he met my gaze, the action causing my cheeks to warm with a blush. I started down the stairs, feeling his gaze on me every step of the way.

Aspyn's smirk could have been seen from miles away as she patted her brother's shoulder, leaning in to whisper loudly to him, "Close your mouth, big brother, you'll catch flies. Then you'll never get the pretty girl to kiss you again."

Aspyn winked at me before heading out the door, most likely to meet Gabe. I made my way to the bottom step, careful not to trip over myself in the process. As I came face-to-face with Asher, he still towered over me, even with added height from the step.

"Wow," Asher breathed out. His eyes scanned down my body taking in every inch. "Just wow."

"My eyes are up here, Ash." I caught his chin

under one finger, lifting it to meet my gaze. His green eyes sparkled with wonder, making the redness that splotched across my milky white skin amplify.

"Hmm, and they are almost as beautiful as you." Asher leaned in, each word grazing across my lips. My breath halted with him this close. I could feel the smirk that played across his plump lips.

"You're so cheesy, you know that, right? You're more of the girl in this relationship than I am most of the time." I giggled out my words, making them barely audible.

Pulling back only an inch, he rolled his eyes at me. "Wow, this time it wasn't me ruining the moment."

"Come on, let's just get this over with." I pecked his lips, snaking my way around him. My fingers laced with his, pulling him with me towards the door, but we didn't budge an inch. His grip pulled me back towards him, and my back landed against his chest.

"Happy birthday, Liliana," Asher's hot breath whispered in my ear, making the hairs on the back of my neck stand up.

With everything going on, my birthday had

slipped from my mind. I had been so focused on the Founder's Ball that my eighteenth birthday was the last thing on the list of things to worry about. Only weeks ago it was the one thing that I longed to come faster, allowing me to be free from the system and all the nowhere towns I had traveled to. The looming fear of the council's judgment had shadowed my idea of becoming another year older. Smiling, I shook my head at him before peeking over my shoulder to see his face matching mine. "Thank you, Asher."

His lips met mine, blocking out Aspyn's nagging voice in the front telling us to hurry up.

"Come on, your sister is going to have an aneurysm if we don't go." I tried to turn once again towards the door, but he kept his grip around my waist, locking me in place.

"She can wait." Asher loosened his grip on me. Reaching into his pocket, he extracted a gold chain necklace. "This is for you."

Pulling his hands around my neck, Asher placed the necklace on. I looked down at his gift. It was a simple gold chain that hung in the middle of my collarbone. A bright green jewel fell at the end, glistening as it sat against my skin. The piece of jewelry sat in the middle of the longer necklace I had gotten from my parent's box. It was hidden underneath my dress, allowing Asher's present to stand out.

"Asher, it's beautiful," I whispered, my hand grazing against the jewel. I looked up

"I'm glad you like it, love." Asher smiled against the kiss he planted on my lips. Butterflies spouted over the anxiety I had been feeling. Just being around him always melted away any worries that clouded over us. He made me stronger. Something I could never repay him for. The kiss deepened, my lips desperate to be on his. A low growl came from Asher's throat, confirming that he felt the same way.

Aspyn's voice rang out again, breaking us out of the kiss. I shook my head, laughing at the raven-haired girl's screams.

"Come on. Aspyn's waiting."

Chapter Twenty-Six

The town hall was lit up, casting a white light on the normally gloomy street. People swarmed the area as Asher's callused hand found mine, helping me step from the car. Most of the people around us were locals who had no knowledge of the Angelic creatures that they walked side by side with. Stepping closer into Asher's protective bubble, I looked up towards the building, knowing what waited behind those wooden doors.

"You'll be fine, I promise," Asher's voice whispered into my ear. A shiver went up my exposed spine, feeling the familiar calming sensation travel around me as he spoke. "I won't let them hurt you."

"None of us will." Aspyn stepped up next to her

brother while the rest of the group stood just behind her. Mallory wore a floor-length purple gown, the silk flapping in the harsh wind that swirled around us. Delaney stood farther back in a midnight-blue, off-the-shoulder dress, which slit all the way up her leg, landing just above the middle of her thigh. She hadn't spoken to me since the training room incident, but a curt nod in my direction signaled she would have my back no matter what. Both girls were on edge, eyes traveling around the crowd looking for the other girl who completed their trio.

"I know. We all will be fine." My voice was confident as I spoke to each member. Placing one foot in front of the other, I traveled towards the large double doors. They were propped open, allowing guests to flood into them from every different direction.

Music invaded my senses as we stepped inside the building. The room that had once been barren was now decorated in white and gold decorations. Champagne glasses sat on top of silver trays floating around the room under the weight of a server. People easily accepted the drinks, drowning their minds in alcohol.

"Best not drink the Kool-Aid. Knowing these Holy bastards, they mixed in some kind of hallucinatory syrup to keep the locals from asking questions." Delaney watched the gold chalices travel around the room.

"Could make things interesting." Gabe smirked into Aspyn's hairline. Peeling my eyes away from the cups, I looked towards Asher. A glass door on the black wall was wide open, revealing a garden surrounded by woods just outside the large dance floor. Couples spun in rhythm with each other, just barely missing one another as they weaved into a new formation.

"Come on, let's try to hide from everyone's stares for as long as we can," Asher said to me, watching me stare at the floating skirts of the woman dancing. He grasped my hand, squeezing it in his. I smiled at him, breaking him from his serious demeanor. We traveled through the massive amounts of people in the room, making it out into the night air of the garden.

Fairy lights strung up twinkled against the

flowers of the garden, illuminating it in a romantic light. A small pond pooled around a large pad of stone in the center of the land. Tiny ducks waded against the stream of water—soon they would migrate out of the cold and into a warmer climate. The chill night sent a slight breeze around us, and I could see a light layer of ice freezing against the ground. Remnants of music floated through the air. Most everyone inside was enjoying the festivities. They talked amongst neighbors, leaving the room feeling stuffy and claustrophobic. Being outside felt like I was able to breathe again.

"When do you think they will come for me?" My warm breath made a cloud of smoke against the cold air. Asher led me into the middle of the garden, claiming the stone surface as our own.

"Let's not think about that for now." He pulled me closer to him, his warmth washing over my body. "Dance with me."

"I don't dance, Asher." I eyed him, turning from his grasp, ready to venture farther into the garden. Hopefully, I would come upon a rabbit hole to get lost in. At this point, an evil queen sounded better than twelve threatening Angelic council members.

"Well, today you do." Asher held me in my place in his iron grip, not letting me go. I looked back at his grinning face.

Rolling my eyes at him, I turned back into him, placing my hands around his neck. "Happy now?"

"Very," he mused, hands latching around my waist and pulling me closer to him. "Stop being so tense, you're fine."

His hands massaged patterns into my lower back, trying to unknot the tension within my muscles. I leaned my head against his chest, breathing him in. The outlines of his hands on my bare back left my skin on fire, burning against the cold wind.

"I'll relax once this is all over with." I motioned towards the party happening behind us. "It's all way too extravagant for my taste."

I looked over my shoulder at the party, all of the people in this town just pawns in the game these creatures liked to play. Just like a game of chess, each piece was strategically moved from spot to spot, and if you didn't fit in the game anymore, checkmate.

Our bodies began to sway in sync with each other.

Asher turned my head back towards his.

"You're doing it again," I said.

"I don't know what you're talking about." Asher cocked his head to the side in fake confusion.

"You're watching me." I gave him a knowing look.

"Well, considering I have something beautiful to stare at, it helps." I buried my head in his shoulder, trying my best to hide my blush. I could feel the vibrations of his laughter rumble against my cheek, but the sound cut off abruptly, making me peek up at him. His face hardened, eyes staring above my head. Turning to look in the direction of his gaze, my eyes focused in on Finley, who had his hands clasped in front of him. Finley wasn't watching us though. His blue eyes stared up at a large balcony on the second floor. Tracing his line of sight, I found Aspyn holding his gaze. She stared back down, returning the same intense look as his.

"Lily." Asher kissed my forehead, mumbling the words into my hairline. "Only speak when spoken to directly. Your ability to control your temper in their presence is imperative. I know you can do this."

Nodding numbly, I let go of Asher, my fingertips lingering on his before I turned towards Finley. The redhead walked towards the building swiftly as I followed. Looking up to the ledge, I noticed Aspyn had since left her spot, leaving nothing but darkness. I maneuvered through people as Finley led me to the double staircase where the last meeting had occurred. I picked up my skirt so I wouldn't trip going up the marble stairs. Finley was holding the door open for me when I arrived at the top. He turned towards me, glancing down at the party. I met Asher's intense gaze. Asher and Finley shared a silent conversation between each other. A nod for Fin ended the exchange.

"From what I have seen you do, the council won't touch something as powerful as you," Finley's voice spoke to me from behind. "Just remember everything that Asher has told you."

"You forget so quickly who my father was, and what you called me the first night we met," I whispered, still holding my stare with Asher.

"Did you mend the medallion?" I was surprised by his question. It made me whip around to look at him.

"The medallion?"

"Mend it—explains why we like to call you a Night Monster." Finley turned into the doorway, strolling into the room.

Chapter Twenty-Seven

I took a deep breath, composing myself as the air filled my lungs. The council couldn't see the fear that had settled deep within my stomach before walking into the room. Just as before, twelve men sat behind the table. Each set of eyes watched as I entered the room. Two additional people were added to the space as well. Ravana leaned back on the desk next to Abel, examining each detail of her nails. She looked bored as she went from one cuticle to the next, her bright white dress billowing around her leg which was hanging over the desk through a large slit. In white, she looked less intimidating than before. I could see the resemblance between her and Emma as she looked up towards me. If it wasn't for the pin-straight burgundy locks that fell down her back, they would be identical. Another woman sat in the corner, her large velvet cloak was placed over her head, hiding all of her facial features. The only things I could see under the heavy cloth was a pair of tan kitten heels.

"Liliana, it's so wonderful to see you again." Ravana's high-pitched shrill rang out around the room. She leaped from the table, circling around me like a predator hunting her prey. "Such a pretty girl, just like your mother."

A single red nail trailed along my skin, connecting my shoulders to one another before she let out a giggle like she had made a joke only she knew the punchline to.

"That's enough of that, Ravana," Abel's voice warned the mischievous Angel. Ravana pouted, crossing her arms over her chest before she stalked over to the table to assume her position back on top of the piece of furniture once again. "Now on to the real reason we are here, young Lily. I did hear about the incident in the school from the Manson girl."

Finley swore in the corner. I looked at him,

feeling the annoyance radiating from him. Tabitha would hear an earful later on, I was sure of it. My eyes flickered away from him, landing on the floor as I realized the inevitable fate that was coming my way. The council wouldn't let something like me walk out of here alive.

"But Brinley Goodwin has since come forward, informing us that you were provoked into using your newly developing abilities. What she has described to us is very intriguing." The council members mumbled in agreeance with their leader. "Now, we wouldn't want to ruin a perfectly good occasion with an accident, so I would like to propose a compromise to you."

"Whatever you think is the best, sir." I kept my voice low, still staring at the floor. My vision turned towards Fin. He only nodded at me. I took a deep breath and met Abel's eyes.

Clasping his hands together in front of his body, his voice boomed throughout the empty chamber. "Excellent. We are going to use one of our best visionaries to look into your mind. They will look into your past memories, creating their own vision to find out what your abilities are capable of. You seem to be developing very well, but we just want to see everything. Since you are the first of your kind, we will be taking every necessary precaution."

My body was pulled down. I yelled out in surprise at the sudden movement. Finley held my arm in his hand, dragging me down into a chair, leather ties strapping my wrists down on the armrests. They tightened together, cutting off the circulation that flowed through my arms. I could feel them growing numb by the second. Finley stood in front of me, repeating the process to my legs. I began to fight him before meeting his gaze. The fear that wrapped around his blue eyes stopped me in my tracks. Something about them told me to comply with the council's wishes.

"Don't struggle. They will use you fighting this against you if you let them." Finley's voice came in a low hiss. He let his fingers linger against my ankles for a moment, waiting for me to confirm I would stop. I nodded slowly, and the fear in my stomach crawled through my veins. The urgency in his voice sent shock waves of emotions through me. He was doing what he had to do to survive in this world. Finley wanted to keep himself as the council's go-to man, only to ensure no harm would come to Aspyn.

"Now, on with the show." Ravana sent a wicked smirk my way. "You are going to be so surprised."

She purred out her words, watching me squirm under her gaze. Abel turned his attention towards the cloaked woman. "Now, all is settled. Rowen, if you will."

My stomach dropped a hundred feet down when he spoke her name. I felt like I was going to vomit watching the woman stand from her seat. Thinking my mind was playing tricks on me, I tried to rationalize another explanation. He must have said another name—it wasn't possible. Closing my burning eyes, I waited for the tears to drop out of them. Light clicks of heels came across the tile floor. Peeking out from my eyelashes, I watched the woman remove the heavy velvet mask.

Rowen stood tall next to Ravana, her long strawberry-blonde hair framing her piercing hazel eyes. She was even more stunning than the visions did her justice, standing with her head held high.

Her sharp eyes met mine—they weren't innocent like the ones I had witnessed before. The brown in her eyes glinted off the lights, showing off their vile nature. I tried my best to ignore the terror creeping up my neck as she eyed me.

"My darling Liliana." Her voice was musical, drawing me in with every word. Rowen glided towards me, reaching out a hand to stroke my face. I flinched away from her touch, afraid it might burn me if left there too long. Rowen was taken back by my sudden movement. Not the reaction she wanted from me, it seemed. "Hm, it does appear that you have inherited your father's flair for dramatics."

She sneered down at me, taking my chin into her talon-like fingers. Rowen squeezed the skin under her grip, making me cry out in pain. She turned my head to each side, taking in every part of my face into her memory. "Well, I don't have all night. There is a party to attend."

Abel waved his hand towards her, motioning for her to begin. Everyone seemed to step back a few feet from the two of us. I turned my stare towards Finley—his face was just as shocked as mine. Rowen ripped her fingers away from my chin, making sure she scratched the underneath on both sides. I could feel warm liquid begin to run down my neck. Replacing her hands on the top of my temples, she looked down upon me. "This may hurt a tad, sweetheart, nothing personal. After all, you are mine."

A burning pain began near my temples, traveling quickly behind my eyelids. I shut my eyes in hopes to numb the agony, but the sting turned into pulsing pain which was not letting up. The longer Rowen sat her hands on my head, the worse the pain became. It felt like I was burning from the inside out. As I reopened my eyes, my vision wavered in and out of focus. Screams echoed throughout the room, bouncing off the walls and causing my throat to become raw. Rowen began slicing through my brain. I could feel every memory she extracted like a tooth being ripped from my gums. It felt like she was digging around my brain with a spoon, scooping any valuable information out of my brain and leaving giant gaping holes behind.

Flashes of Asher danced across the memories.

She wasn't just digging for just memories from the past month—she dug deeper, watching a young version of myself. Young Lily had a toothy grin, and two pigtails sat high on her head as she happily listening to her older brother tell stories in the corner of a darkly lit room. Rowen wanted to know every piece of me so she could use it against me. I let out a choked sob as Nate's animated hands told me one of his famous bedtime stories. My bright eyes drank in every word he was saying. He held the stars and the moon in my eyes—no one could compare to a brother's love. That was the last memory she seemed to want to see, removing her hands from my temples. Every nerve in my body hurt, feeling exposed to the harsh air of the room.

"I have what I need, but I need some time to decipher everything." Rowen laid a hand on my forearm, digging her nails in. She turned towards Abel, who wore a proud smile.

"You may go, Rowen. Once you are done, we will make the final decision." Abel peered over his glasses at her.

Rowen swiveled back to me. My breathing was

hard from the recent torture she had put me through. "Till next time, my beautiful Lily."

She laid a single kiss on my sizzling forehead. As she did this, she caught sight of the locket and brought it up to her face. "Hm, your father never did have the best taste in jewelry."

Laying it back down between my breasts, she turned to leave the room in long, drawn-out strides.

"Finley, escort Liliana back to her friends. I want her to enjoy the rest of the party. Also, clean the blood off of her. We don't want the locals to question anything." Finley bobbed his head down in the direction of Abel. The redhead waited until every Angel exited the room before dashing over towards me.

Bending down at the knee in front me, Fin began to rip the arm straps open, allowing the blood flow to tingle back into place. "Are you okay?"

I let out a watery laugh, rubbing the red marks the leather had left. "My mother was just resurrected from the dead in front of my eyes. Instead of acting like she had any sort of love in her heart for me, she tortured me for the council's gain."

A cold rag hit my chin. "Look up for me."

I did as I was told, letting Finley dab at the blood, whispering once more to no one in particular, "I thought she was dead."

"I promise you I didn't know she was alive, Lily. If I had known they were going to put you through that, I would have warned Asher…" Finley trailed, off pulling the rag away from my skin. I looked down at him, seeing the regret in his eyes. "You don't know what the council is capable of. Just watch your back, Lily.

Chapter Twenty-Eight

Finley stood tall, leaving my body shaking from the pain that had come once the adrenaline drained from me. The only noise in the room being my harsh breath, I was still taking in what had just happened. Placing my feet on the tile floor, I braced myself against the chair. Standing on my legs, I wobbled back and forth on their jellylike state. The council wanted to see how fast they could break me down. I had come way too far for Rowen to tear me apart in only the few seconds she decided to be in my life.

I couldn't feel my legs underneath me as I staggered from the room. My hands tightly gripped the banister of the stairs, making my knuckles turn white as I slowly made my way down towards the large crowd of people who filled the room. I needed to find Asher or Aspyn. They had to know about Rowen's untimely return from the dead. Anyone she came in contact with was in immediate danger. Her powers felt amplified from the years of hiding. Along with her working so closely with the council, it wouldn't sit well with any Fallen in the group. They stuck their necks out for her years ago, and Rowen just stabbed them all in the back. Whipping my head in every direction, I was hoping to catch sight of at least one familiar face.

I felt a light tap on my shoulder and spun around, coming face-to-face with a man dressed in a half-face mask smiling at me. "Care to dance?"

"I'm sorry, I really can't. My friends are waiting for me." I tried to keep my voice as even as possible. "Sorry again."

I turned to retreat from the stranger, but his voice called back to me before I could get too far away.

"Just one dance, Lily, then you'll be free to go about your night. I promise." The man held out a hand which rested next to my shoulder. I stared at it from the corner of my eye before looking back at him. My eyes wandered the room, trying to see if I could catch sight of someone before lacing my fingers in between his. Being pulled so close to this stranger made the air tense near us. He left no time for me to change my mind as we started to move with the beat of the light violin playing around us. There was a familiarity to the man in front of me that set me on edge. That smile that was staring down warmed my stomach like a child on Christmas Day. It wasn't something I was able to push away—the uneasy presence of this man was consuming me.

"Do I know you from somewhere?" I leaned in, trying to get a closer look at him under the mask. It was hard to make out any noticeable indicators of where I had seen him before.

Letting out a gruff laugh, he shook his head. "Oh, once upon a time you knew me, Liliana. Very well, I would say."

I was taken back by the bluntness of his answer. He never faltered in tone as he continued to twirl me around the dance floor. "Would you like to enlighten me on how and where we have met before?"

"Oh, well, you could say I have known you since birth, Liliana." He smirked down at me. There was a slyness hidden in his voice as we swayed in between the other couples. The comment was meant to set me more on edge, but I had come to accept that most people in Idelwood had known me since before I could even remember who I was.

"You and half of this town." I laughed along with him. "Did you know my parents?"

"I was very close to your father. Some may say he was a father to me." Every word that came from this man's lips seemed to be a riddle.

"Are you always this mysterious?" I was growing annoyed with the game we were playing. "You keep answering all my questions with a riddle. It is getting quite annoying."

His face twisted into a puzzled look underneath the mask. "You used to love my puzzles as a child, but you truly loved my stories, little sister."

I almost stumbled over my own two feet as the words tumbled out of his mouth. As I stared at the man in front of me, tears began to fill my eyes. The sudden emotions I was feeling made me reach into the middle of the room, freezing everyone around the two of us. Stopping the movement around me allowed me to process what was happening without others' prying eyes digging into our conversation. My heartbeat drummed in my ears, matching my accelerated breathing. Tearing myself from his grasp, I gripped onto the edge of my skirt to keep me aware that this was actually happening.

"Nate?"

My timid voice questioned the man in front of me. He slowly reached up and undid the back of his mask, allowing it to fall forward to reveal his face. The man in front of me was different than the boy I had once known. Nate's face had matured over the years, strong cheekbones holding up matching sea-blue eyes that stared back at me. He was watching my every move with such precision that it sent a terrifying chill across my body. Goosebumps quickly began to scatter across my pale skin. I wouldn't have recognized him on the street if he had passed me by. The brother from before was just a ghost of the man who stood in front of me. Nate's mouth turned up in a sinister smirk as he clapped his hands slowly. His eyes wandered around our surroundings.

"Well done, Lilypad. My, this little trick is very impressive I must say. I knew you would be powerful, but this—" His hands moved around us, indicating the frozen locals surrounding us. "This is something entirely different, darling sister."

My voice was caught in the back of my throat. I had so many questions tumbling around my brain it felt like they were set in the dryer on the highest setting, but none of them moved to my tongue. The shock of seeing someone I had searched my entire life for and who was now was just inches from my grasp left me speechless. Making matters worse, he was making light of my pain.

Nate didn't know about the years of searching, always remembering that nowhere would be home without him. Idelwood was the only place in the past few years that I had opened myself up to, but the thought of Nate not being here always hung heavy in my heart. He was a constant reminder that people always leave in end, even family. Reaching up, my hand cracked against his cheek, slapping away the smirk which rested on his face.

Nate hissed in pain, touching the large red spot blooming against his cheek, "I can see you're not happy to see your big brother. Well, I was hoping this wouldn't be the case, but hope does always disappoint in the end."

I began to walk away, only to be ripped back towards him. Nate held a firm grip on my wrist, squeezing it tightly while I struggled to get free from his grasp.

"You're hurting me. Let go." I continued to struggle against his hold on me.

Nate watched my failed attempt to get away, letting a dark laugh slip from his mouth. "You've grown fiery through the years. I'm not done speaking with you, little sister. You'll do best to remember who the older sibling is now, won't you?"

"I don't see what you could possibly want Nathaniel. You left me alone, knowing what I was capable of, who our parents were. If you wanted something to do with me, you shouldn't have left that night. You would have stayed and fought all of this madness by my side. You're a coward, and you ran from the one person who adored you no matter what." I spat the words in his face. My face was glowing red as my temper rose. I was grateful that the people around us stood still, not wanting to explain the scene that I was causing to a room full of people who would snitch right back to the council.

Nate's voice was emotionless when he spoke, the calmness scaring me. "I left because my job with you was done. The council ordered me to stay with you until you were eight. Feeding your mind with all the stories I could about this world until then. They wanted you to grow into your abilities without me always being there. They knew if I stayed, you would depend on your big brother and, in turn, become underdeveloped in their eyes. Being underdeveloped is something they don't accept. You would have been dead the second they found us. I left to protect you, Lily."

"Oh, so you're just one of their pawns. Like our mother, Rowen? You didn't leave to protect me. You left to get a pat on the head for following orders from twelve old men who control everyone in this town." I hissed back venom at him, watching his face flick to hurt if only for a moment.

"Such disdain for me, darling. I'll have to make sure you are taught to have more respect for me." Nate's grip twisted as we heard the clack of heels ring in our ears. I turned to see Rowen striding towards us. "That's quite enough, Nathaniel. Let your sister go. Isn't it nice to have both my children together at last? Although it does seem our little Lily has become resentful towards her family. Nonetheless, we are a family once more."

"I would rather rot in hell than call either of you my family." Poison dripped off over my tongue. I could feel Nate flinch back as he dropped my wrist. Rowen, on the other hand, didn't even bat an eyelash at my outburst. She just continued to stare at me quietly.

"Watch it with the threats. She can have that arranged." Nate's hushed warning spoke into my ear. Reaching down, I yanked off the necklace that had belonged to her, breaking the chain from my neck. I threw the necklace across the room in her direction. The piece flew in the air, hitting her square in the face and making her snarl towards me.

"Seems like someone needs to learn how to

respect her elders." Rowen lunged forward towards me, ready to strike like a cobra. Nate pulled me back, standing protectively in between the two of us. Rowen sneered at him, annoyed that he had gotten in the way of her rage.

"Leave her be, Mother," Nate challenged Rowen, eyes burning with emotion as he stared in her dark ones. "You know what Abel will do if you cause any harm to her."

Rowen shrank back into her spot, the reminder setting fear in her. "Very well, let her go. You're not going to get any more out of her. Goodbye, flower."

The nickname took me back to the church where Claire had taunted me. She had used that exact name to torture me around the forest until I curled up in hysteria on the grassy floor. That night quickly flashed across my mind, putting the pieces together. "It was you, wasn't it? In the woods that night after Finley left me in the quarry. You were hiding behind Claire's face trying to get inside my head."

Rowen smirked in my direction. "You're smarter than you look, Lily flower. I'm impressed you put everything together so quickly."

Without another word, she pranced away from us. I released a long breath, letting everything around Nate and me go back to how it was before. Chatter and the clank of glasses fell back into place within the room. Couples continued to spin like someone had rewound them up on a music box.

I felt Nate's hand brush up against my arm slowly as he leaned down to whisper in my ear. I continued to watch the party as he spoke softly, "Better watch your back, flower. You're wilting under their stares."

Chapter
Twenty-Nine

Nate disappeared into the crowd after Rowen. I stood planted in my spot, staring at where he had just been moments before, remembering the whispers he had made in the vision just days before. Feeling so many pairs of eyes burning holes in my head, I dashed to the back of the building where the garden was located, frantically searching for Asher. Delaney stood in the corner, turned away from me. She was sipping a glass of champagne. The same one she had warned us not to drink earlier in the night.

"Laney," I shouted over the music, quickly running in her direction. My body dodged through the crowded room full of people, finally making my way behind her.

She turned in the direction of my scream, her face horrified as she looked at me. "Lily, what happened? Are you okay?"

I could feel the light stick of sweat sitting on top of my face. The air in the room became too thick to breathe. All the people around us made me feel like I was being squished into a tiny box. "Mal, go find Asher."

I hadn't noticed Mallory standing next to her sister until she dashed off to find the raven-haired boy in the crowds of people. Looking back towards Delaney, I tried to speak, "I-I ca-an-n't br-ea-at-he."

My words stuttered out as the world began to spin around me. I could feel myself starting to sway back and forth, ready to catch my fall when it came. A pair of strong arms gripped my shoulders, holding them steady. I didn't bother looking to see who it was. Nothing around me was recognizable as the room began to meld together in pastel colors.

With the spinning beginning to grow faster, the person holding on to me must have felt like I was going to fall flat on my face, as their grip tightened. A deep voice spoke in a hushed tone, urging us to move away from the crowd of Angels watching our every move. The strong arms started to guide me away from the corner we stood in, taking on most of my weight as my feet were deemed to be useless.

Cool air hit my face the second we stepped into the garden, and a sense of relief wrapped around me as my vision returned. I could see Asher rushing out of the same door we had just exited with Aspyn and Mallory following closely in tow.

"What is going on?" Aspyn's voice was the first to question the situation in front of her eyes. "Get away from her."

I was ripped sideways out of the strong hands which had once held on tight, swiftly landing into Asher's protective grip. The quick motion caused me to groan from the dizziness that it brought along with it. I laid my head against Asher's puffed-up chest, trying to focus on my breathing. Just praying I wouldn't vomit from the motion sickness.

An argument had broken out between everyone in the group. No one's word made any sense as each person demanded to be heard, only causing them to talk over one another. I peeked out from my hiding space to see who had come to Delaney's aid when she was in need. My lips released a silent gasp, surprised to see a familiar redheaded Angel standing tall against the fiery glare of his former lover. Pieces of Aspyn's once-perfect bun had fallen out, allowing her ink-colored hair to fly rapidly around the bickering group.

Finley spoke softly against the angry voices, "The council is talking over what was found in Lily's mind. I was only able to hear bits of what was being said, but from what I did hear it's not a good sign. We have to get her out here now, Asher, if you want any sort of a chance at running."

"There is no *we* in this situation, not unless you are willing to be labeled a traitor for the rest of eternity, Finley. That would cost you your wings if they caught up to you. Are you willing to risk all that for us?" Aspyn's voice was cold. I could tell she was putting up a wall against him, trying to reason him away from the decision she had fought so hard for him to avoid. Even though the thought of having Finley back was one she dreamed of daily, Aspyn wasn't willing to give up all he had achieved for her selfish fantasies.

My hands gripped tightly onto Asher's suit jacket, scrunching the material in between my fingers. "They're back."

Heads whipped to meet my soft voice, almost silent against the whistling wind which had picked up suddenly. "Rowen isn't dead. She has been the one messing with my mind, not Claire. The council had her pick through my brain with a fine-toothed comb to see what I could do. She went deeper than she needed to just for her own gain."

I winced into Asher at the memory, a lingering headache still residing in my brain. His grip tightened around my trembling form, concerned eyes sweeping over me to check the injuries that had been left behind. One finger brushed up against the remnant of dried blood that sat underneath my chin where Rowen's sharp nails had left their mark. "You said they are back, Lil. Who else is here? Xander?"

Pausing, I looked at all the faces that stood around me. They would be devastated by the news of Xander not showing himself if he was still alive. That would hurt even more than the pain they were feeling from Rowen keeping herself hidden while they all assumed she had been killed. She hid from the people who had done nothing but try to protect her child. Now Rowen was a robot, only following the commands she was given. She had no real emotions when it came to me. Rowen was not the same girl from the vision. Her mind had been dipped in a slow bath of the council's poison.

She held no remorse for hurting her daughter or the people who cared for her. The way she held herself was almost more sinister than Ravana, if that was even possible. Rowen hurt whoever was in her way, even her own family, if it meant she gained something from it. She didn't care what the outcome was tonight—she would side with the council as soon as she was given the chance. I may look like her, but I was nothing like the woman she had become.

"Nate is back. He has been following orders from the council for years now. Right next to Mommy dearest, they are both just rag dolls to the council. He left when I was eight because they told him it had to be done. They purposely had him plant the stories in my mind to twist my view of the Fallen.

The council wanted me to be afraid of all of you so it would be easy for them to mold me into what they wanted, but the only creatures I'm afraid of are the ones under their control." My voice cut through the night air like a knife, never wavering with the fear that swirled around my mind.

Footsteps running towards the group rang out in the silence, causing us all to turn to the sound. Tabitha Manson arrived in front of us, her wild eyes landing on Asher before slowly traveling down to mine. "They have made their decision. I didn't hear what it was, but the council has been dismissed for the night. If you are going to run, you need to go now."

Both of Tabby's sisters stared at her with wide eyes, not knowing what to think of their sister's sudden betrayal to the council. With Finley now trading sides, either because he knew what was happening was wrong or because of Aspyn, it made sense that Tabitha would follow his lead just as she always had.

For the second time that night, the ring of someone's slow clapping came from behind Asher.

I couldn't bring myself to look to see which person whom I shared blood with had come out from the trees, ready to taunt the people around them, so I buried my head deep in Asher's chest, wanting to block out the garden altogether. Asher's arms gripped my body tightly, making me feel slightly safer for the time being. I knew who it was the second they stepped on the cobblestone pathway — the small clicks against the stone spoke loud and clear.

"I am impressed you lot have stuck together for this long. With Xander gone, I thought you would all go your separate ways. Though it does seem like you found yourselves a new leader to look to." Rowen's voice taunted her old friends, not shying away from the same confidence she had when she spoke in front of the council. "Are you surprised to see me in the flesh again?"

"We thought you were dead." Aspyn's voice sounded broken. I turned my head to the side, watching as she stepped back to where Finley stood behind her. Rowen had been one of her closest friends and allies at one point in her life. I knew the pain that Aspyn felt. It was the same pain that had coursed through my body since Nate's betrayal was announced to me in the middle of the ballroom.

"Quite the opposite, lovebug, I have never been more alive in my life." Rowen's face held a large smile on it, snickering at the thought of being dead. "You should have known, silly girl. The council loved me too much to let me go. Only a few privileged souls knew the truth. Let's see, there was my good friends the Goodwins. Both Emma and Will know how to keep a secret rather well. Also, there was— "

"WE THOUGHT YOU WERE DEAD!" Rowen's rambling was cut off by Aspyn's screams. She lunged forward to the girl she once knew, wanting to leave as much damage as she could across the Angel's face. Finley caught Aspyn around her waist before she could inflict any harm on Rowen. I could see him whispering soothing words in her ear, trying to calm down the girl he loved. Aspyn's eyes flashed between green and black as she listened to the boy's reasoning words. That was one thing no one could deny at this moment—anyone with a pair of eyes could see the obvious fact in front of them. Finley held so much love in his heart for Aspyn.

"You always did have a temper on you Aspyn." Rowen eyed the sobbing girl, not caring about the pain she had just caused. "The council has come to a decision like your little messenger told you. That will be your wings, my dear Tabitha."

Tabby's face paled at Rowen's threat, stepping back towards the glass door which had been closed sometime during our conversation. "I don't want them if that is the cost of all of this. Nothing is worth the wicked things that all of you do to the innocent people in this town. I'm done following blindly after people who only choose to look after themselves."

Rowen watched Tabitha look towards Aspyn, who allowed her body to slouch against Finley's arm, silent tears still pooling around her vibrant green eyes. Rowen pursed her lips at the blonde girl. "Only the strong deserve to wear the crown, Tabitha. He is going to very disappointed another one of his favorites has fallen."

Tabby let out a soft scream as she watched two men emerge from the shadows of the garden, making their way towards her. She scrambled sideways in the direction of Asher and me, losing her balance in the process. Rowen shouldered her way around us, standing over the quivering Angel. "You really should have thought about this decision longer, Tabitha."

Both men stood on either side of the Manson girl, yanking her arms roughly to her sides. They held them up, making the girl's shoulder blades curve into each other. Tabby struggled against their hold, pleading for Rowen's forgiveness. Rowen only laughed at the girl, taking Tabby's throat in her hands and squeezing until she could barely breathe. "You of all people should know we do not give out second chances."

Mallory was curled into Delaney, sobbing at the scene in front of them. They both knew nothing could be done as Rowen squeezed their sister's throat tighter in her hands, leaving red marks as they bloomed around her talons. Tabby gasped for air. I could see her back resisting the urge to spout the wings I knew lay beneath her shoulder blades. With one last squeeze, large off-white wings burst into the night sky. They fluttered in the air, making a ruffling sound that was almost like a hummingbird hovering over a flower in the dead of spring. I had never seen anything more beautiful than the two wings that hummed with joy as the wind passed through them. The feathers lay flat against each other, looking soft to the touch. Rowen reached out, grazing her hand against them like she was petting an animal. They shimmered in iridescent colors under her touch, purring with every stroke she gave. They had no idea what would happen in the moments to come.

Asher's hand turned my face away from the girl, locking eyes with me. I could see the fear that coursed through them as he gazed down at me. "Try your best to bury your head into me. You're not going to want to see this."

Tears pricked my eyes, knowing that what was coming next was anything but pleasant. I tucked my head into the crook of his arm, trying my best to block out the horror happening just behind me. Asher pulled me even tighter against him, anchoring both of us to each other. The first tear of skin was sickening; it was mixed with Tabitha's painful screaming which rang out against the trees. Each strangled shriek was more painful than the last. I tried to conform myself into Asher, he held tight, not letting me move from my hiding place. One of his hands caressed my hair as I let out my first sob.

Tabitha had risked her wings to warn us; now she was paying the ultimate price. Stripped of her wings and cast out of the gates of Heaven. I couldn't imagine the pain that seared her back with each tug. The mix of tearing and screams seemed to go on for hours. Rowen was taking her sweet time plucking each feather from Tabby's skin like she was a chicken. Then the night air went silent, and all any of us could hear was Tabitha's light sobs that shook the bricks that we stood upon.

Asher's tight grip loosened, allowing me to lift my head from my hiding spot. My face was wet with tears as I looked over towards Tabby. The men had dropped her arms, allowing her to grip the gravel in front of her, stabilizing herself as her shoulders shook from the immense pain they were feeling. A mess of bright red blood pooled down her back, seeping into the beaded pink dress she wore. The soon-to-be scars were deep wounds underneath her shoulder blades, which pulsed lightly as they tried to find the missing feathers. The worst part of all of it was her wings lying directly in front of her, now splattered with blood as they died. Each piece of the wings twitched like a bug that had just been squished but was not completely dead yet.

"Now that we have taken care of that, I can relay the council's decision to my lovely Lily flower." Rowen stood behind the broken girl, smearing Tabitha's dark blood against a white rag that had appeared out of nowhere.

"Why did you do it? Fake your own death. Why not just let your true colors show when it came to the council? Wouldn't that have just been easier for everyone involved?" Gabe stood off in the shadows, barely visible to Rowen. I could see his arms crossed in front of his chest, a slight tremble radiating from his body.

"Because it was the council's wishes. You know about those a little too well, don't you, Gabriel?" Rowen made her way over to Gabe in long drawn-out strides before she met his figure, hovering inches from his face. "But you couldn't kill her, the poor mortal girl who fell in love with the Angel. You were given an order and you didn't have the strength to follow through with it. You let her go, trying to give her a head start against the monster coming after her. Too bad that monster was me, and she couldn't hide from me. Not when she ran straight into my arms without knowing what I had planned for her."

Gabe snarled at her before she continued to taunt him. "She cried out for you the whole entire time I weaseled my way into her mind. I was able to warp her brain into mush, filling it with lies about our kind. It drove her mad. That was her own fault, though. If she hadn't resisted, it would have been so much less painful for her. After that it was easy. She did all the dirty work herself. I just had to kick the chair out from under her."

She ran a nail across Gabe's neck, indicating Claire's demise. I choked back another sob as she did it. Gabe's face fell instantly as she dangled the memory of Claire in front of his nose. The woman standing there was cruel—she was no mother of mine.

"What is the council's verdict, Mother?" The words felt like acid on my taste buds, but they broke her away from torturing Gabe with the memory of Claire any longer. "I could take a guess if you want."

"Well, there is no need to play guessing games. It is simple. You have two options, one being you join your brother and me to train in front of the council. They want you to hone your powers with the Elders' guidance. You would, of course, have to leave your boy toy behind along with all of these miscreants that you have been hanging around; none of them are a part of our world anymore. Or the second, my personal favorite, you are sentenced to however many years I see fit in purgatory. At the rate your disrespectful attitude is going, you'll be rotting there for years with dear, old Daddy sitting right next to you." Rowen's eyes bored into mine, a wicked smirk playing against her pink lips. "The choice is yours, flower. You could be a god like your mother or rot away in hell like your father."

I felt my knees buckle underneath me, but luckily Asher's grip held me upright, not letting them crash against the hard ground. Neither of the choices were pleasant, but I knew for a fact I would never stand beside her and the tyrants who called themselves a council. They only wanted me to be another one of their playthings to toy with when they got bored. Protests were being yelled out after her announcement, causing an uproar of commotion for the local bystanders standing close by to watch as the drama unfolded.

Then everything around us seemed to go up in flames in a matter of seconds.

Mallory stepped forward in the direction of where Rowen stood. It all happened too fast for anyone to reach out and stop her. Mal gripped Rowen's arm, trying to gain the upper hand on the Angel's visionary power, but Rowen was quicker than her. Rowen's hand reached up, latching onto Mallory's shoulder tightly. I could see her nails digging into Mal's skin as blood began to trickle down her back in long drips. I cried out, knowing exactly what came next.

Rowen began to speed up Mal's internal clock. Everything about the girl began to age at a rapid pace, her skin started to turn a grayish-blue color as she clawed at her lungs which had begun to collapse against her spine. Mallory's body was shutting down as Rowen's talons held tight onto her. I could hear the gasp of the last breath of air her body would ever inhale over the screams of terror that surrounded me. My mother had made Mallory Manson a corpse in seconds flat.

Delaney reacted quickly, darting towards Mallory, only to be close lined by Gabe's forearm. He swung it around, holding her back from trying to go back after Rowen. Laney screamed for her sister, but there was nothing any of us could do for her. Mallory was dead. Rowen dropped her lifeless body to the ground like it was a rag doll a child played with daily. It landed in front of Tabitha, lying in the mess of her sister's broken wings. The last light in Mallory's gray eyes left as they stared into the distance, meeting up with the triplet who had a matching pair. My heart felt like it had given way as I looked down at her body, which was contoured in an inhuman shape.

Gabe wasn't able to hold Delaney back any longer as she leaped towards her dead sister. In that second, Rowen made a quick getaway back into the crowds of people. Like a snake, she slithered back in her hole, hiding after the kill. It made me sick that part of my DNA was attached to that monster. Tabitha reached out in shock, watching her sister sob over the other. Her face was hollow, no emotions running through it. She craned her neck in the direction of the woman who had just murdered her sister, debating whether she should follow after her. In one fell swoop, Rowen had destroyed the Manson triplets, taking something from each girl tonight. An arm wrapped around the top of Tabitha's forearm, stopping her from doing something stupid.

Tabitha's eyes glanced up at Gabe, who was crouched down next to her. I watched the girl melt down into hysteria as what had just happened began to set in. Tabby let herself fall to the side, wincing at the pain in her back. Catching the girl in his arms easily, Gabe let her cry into him. Aspyn curled herself against Finley, trying to block out the agonizing cries coming from both sisters. Finley stood, holding on to her in shock which was plastered across his face.

I hadn't realized I was screaming until Asher's hand covered my mouth, pulling me away from the scene as I kicked against him. I felt numb, watching the group fade away from sight, knowing I would never see Mallory's sweet, bubbly smile ever again. Never hear that cheerful voice light up the entire room when she spoke. This was the worst pain I could ever imagine feeling. I wanted to rip my mother's throat out for this pain she had caused all of us. A red sheen covered my vision when I thought of the monster behind Rowen's face. Mallory was the only light in the darkness that hung over our group, and Rowen had just ripped it away from us. Nothing could replace Mallory. Now there was no telling what would happen to all of us.

"I need you to listen to me carefully, Lily," Asher's voice whispered in my ear, his hot breath tracing the inside of my earlobe. He spun me around, making me face him. We stood on the edge of the forest that surrounded Idelwood. I could barely make out his face in the moonlight that refused to shine for us. Tears leaked from my eyes as I tried to focus on the words that were coming out of his mouth. "You need to take a deep breath."

He demonstrated breathing in through his nose and out through the mouth, once making me copy him the next time he did it. After a few deep breaths, my breathing evened out, and I could see him clearly through the dark.

"I need you to run, straight into the forest. Do not stop until Aspyn, Finley, or I come and find you. Do you understand me?" I nodded numbly at him. Asher's hand reached up to run through my now messy curls that hung down my back. "They cannot catch you. I won't let them take you away from me to be tortured again."

"I don't want to leave you. What if something happens to one of us?" My breathing began to become uneven again. The thought of leaving him right now made me panic. We had just lost Mallory. I wasn't losing someone else tonight. Asher's hands came up, grasping the sides of my face. He pulled me close to him.

"Shhh, Lily, nothing will happen if you run. I will always find my way back to you, love." I took in Asher's green eyes for a minute. Memorizing every inch of them, exactly where they sparkled and how his irises blended together with the deeper green that swam through the vibrant coloring.

I smashed my lips against his, not knowing the next time they would be on mine. His hands found their way down on my hips as I gripped hard on to his baby hairs sitting at the nape of his neck. I pulled him closer into the kiss—not even the wind could pass between us as we melded our bodies together. My kisses were desperate, wanting him to know exactly how much I loved him in this moment. I could feel how worried he was about the seconds that were to follow. None of that mattered in this moment—all that mattered was us. Goodbyes were never my favorite thing, and I didn't plan on this being ours.

Asher pulled away from the kiss, leaning his forehead against mine. My words trembled out against the quiet forest. "Ash, please don't say it. Just stay with me, and we will figure all of this out."

"You have to run, Lily."

We could hear the commotion of the party die down, replaced by screams of horror. The council must have realized I had gone missing, and now they were willing to take out any mortal who stood in their way to track me down. I could hear glasses being smashed around the dance floor, causing chaos to erupt around it. Innocent locals were shouting, not understanding why their Founder's Day Ball was being interrupted by so much madness. Even after the madness, they would go back to being clueless about the monsters that sat next to them daily.

"I love you," I whispered to him before picking up the green dress from the dirt floor it rested upon. Kicking off my high heels, I sprinted away from him.

Hot tears streamed down my face as the cold air whipped around the shadowed forest. A flurry of snowflakes began to fall against the dark dirt floor. Each one stuck together, signaling the first snowfall of Idelwood this year. I could hear a faint "I love you" as I ran deeper into the darkness.

The only sounds that followed me were the light sounds of violins mixed with screams, which carried through the trees as I ran into the night, leaving everything I loved behind me once again.

CHAPTER THIRTY

My feet hit the hard ground again and again until they were numb, both from the cold and the constant pain radiating through them. I kept running just like Asher had told me to. The minutes continued to tick by with every step I took. My feet were cut from the sticks and rocks that lay against the forest floor, and I had managed to run face-first into one too many trees in the darkness, leaving me with large scratches on every inch of my body. They stung as the cold air ran over them.

The once-beautiful dress was tattered at the bottom. One long rip stopped around mid-hip on the left side of my body, exposing more of my skin to the below-freezing temperature. I could feel myself growing weaker every step I ran. Not knowing how much longer I could keep at it, I turned my head to check behind me. No one had followed me into the woods, leaving me only with the wildlife that resided here. I was the intruder in their home tonight. Asher had told me not to stop until someone came for me—that was the only thing pushing me farther into the trees.

Turning my head forward again, I missed the sight of a large rock that was stuck out from the mossy ground. I tumbled over it, sending myself plummeting down a large hill. I hit the bottom of the mound hard, and the force of impact knocked the wind from my lungs, leaving me gasping for air. The snow had caused the air to thin out around me, making it harder to gather enough oxygen. Pushing myself up, I struggled to crawl across the forest floor. All I needed to do was find my feet again to start my journey back into the darkness.

Don't stop running.

Asher's words rang out around me as I slipped again on a frozen-over puddle, face-planting into the dirt once more. The cold was restricting my muscle movement, making me feel like a baby deer first learning how to walk on an ice pond.

A hand landed on my lower back, startling me out of my thoughts. I threw my arm back, landing hard on my spine again. My elbow connected with the intruder's face, causing them to cry out in pain. I scrambled backward with my hands, trying to put distance between me and the person clutching their face in pain.

"Man, Aspyn wasn't wrong. You do know how to pack a punch." Finley's voice spoke out in the silent forest. I paused, looking at the boy, not sure if he was actually real or another one of Rowen's tricks. Finley watched me closely, clearly seeing the fear on my face. "Hey, Lily, it's me. You're safe with me."

He took a step forward, kneeling down in front of me so I could see his face in the darkness. Finley's right eye was already starting to bruise from my elbow. I reached out, running my thumb over the wound. "Sorry about that."

"It's fine, I've had worse." The boy chuckled at me. I never thought I would be so happy to see this boy's face in my life. I don't really understand why I did it, but I threw myself straight into his grasp, lacing both of my arms around his neck. I groaned inwardly as the pain of the crash from falling down the hill started to take over. Finley ran his hand over my back, trying to cause some friction against my exposed skin to warm me up. I shivered against him, now starting to feel the effects of the drop in temperature.

"Come on, let's get you back to the group." Finley laced his arm underneath my legs, picking me up to carry back to the others. His eyes roamed over my body. "That ankle looks pretty bad. It might be broken. I'll have Mal—"

Finley's voice cut off, his mind remembering that the girl he wanted to ask for help would never be able to help ever again. He sighed, continuing his sentence. "We'll have someone look at it when we get back. Hopefully, it just needs to be wrapped and elevated."

"Why are you helping us? I thought you hated me." I looked up at him, my words starting to slur together. I tried my best to keep my eyes open, but the lack of adrenaline was replaced by exhaustion. Opening one eye, I watched for his reaction to my question.

"I never hated you, Lily. The council had strong opinions on what you would be. None of them are what you actually are, which isn't surprising. They painted you out to be a cruel, vicious creature that would expose us to the world. Boy, were they wrong about that one." Finley chuckled at the thought.

"I don't know, you haven't seen me in the mornings. I'm pretty cruel and vicious then, just ask Aspyn." I cracked a smile towards him, liking the fact that for once we were not actually at each other's throats.

"As for your other question I got tired of playing on their twisted playground. Losing my wings would be better than being a puppet on a string for them." I could tell he was holding back the truth, his eyes staring straight ahead at our path back towards the group.

"You came back for Aspyn. Let's be honest with ourselves here." I pried into his mind, watching his face drop at the mention of the raven-haired girl's name.

"Yeah, I guess I did. I didn't realize she told you about us," Finley mumbled his words, slightly annoyed at the fact that their secret was out.

"I am her best friend. You do realize that we tell each other everything." He eyed me curiously. "Okay, almost everything."

Snuggling deeper into his chest, I yawned as my eyelids grew heavy again. "Did Asher make it back to the group?'

"He will be back when we arrive to the others." Finley's voice wavered as he spoke, like he was telling a lie. I was in too much pain to argue with him. The adventure in the woods added on more wounds to the ones Rowen had inflicted on me earlier in the evening. Asher could handle himself—I knew that it was only a matter of time until I was back in his arms. Letting the darkness consume me, I prayed everything would be all right in the end. This was only the beginning of our troubles. Rowen would come out of hiding once again, and when she did, I would be ready. She would pay for the destruction she had caused in all of our lives.

Something dark had laid dormant in my soul for so long now, and it was coming out to play. I couldn't help but love the electrifying feeling it gave me.

I wasn't the Night Monster they all imagined, but I would be the monster they feared.

THANKS FOR READING!

PLEASE ADD A REVIEW ON AMAZON OR GOODREADS AND LET ME KNOW WHAT YOU THOUGHT!

AMAZON AND GOODREADS REVIEWS ARE EXTREMELY HELPFUL FOR AUTHORS. THANK YOU FOR TAKING THE TIME TO SUPPORT ME AND MY WORK! DON'T FORGET TO SHARE YOUR REVIEW ON SOCIAL MEDIA WITH THE HASHTAG **#DARKSACRIFICES** SO I CAN FIND IT AND OTHERS CAN READ THIS STORY TOO!

ACKNOWLEDGMENTS

Every reader has that one book that startedit all. For me, it was a book and a person combined that launched me back into my love of reading. After coming home from a movie, I was asked to get the mail by my mom, and I was pleasantly surprised to see she had a package with the return address name E. Cullen written at the top. Inside that package was a copy of Twilight, and I caught my reading itch once again. My mom's best friend since middle school was named Stephanie, and she created magic no matter where you were. From having a waiter send a gift directly from Edward Cullen himself at dinner to creating a beautiful piece of art, she made every second spent with her special. I will never be able to thank her enough for her part in setting me on this path of being an author.

Mom and Dad, words don't suffice when I think of how to thank you. From encouraging words to creating a dress for an author event, you are always there to support and push me to be the best I can be. Thank you for everything you do.

Elijah Selinsky, your support for my writing means more than you know. I hope you know I am never letting you go and dragging you to every book event I attend. Thank you for reminding me the eye color of my characters and dealing with my at least twice-a-day freakouts. I am so glad the universe placed you in my life!

Kales Hickey, oh darling Kales, thank you for being such a light in our chaos trio. From the hilarious memes you send to having the best reactions to books on voice chat, I am eternally grateful for you! Thank you for always encouraging me even when I allowed others to make me feel like I did not belong. Now I just need to get the strawberry scene book in my hands.

And thank you to all the readers who have fallen in love with my characters. I would be nothing without you guys! You are the heart of this story, and I hope you loved book two as much as I loved writing it for you!

Allison Aldridge is an Arizona native who currently resides in Georgia. With a love for all things that have to do with storytelling, she continues to be an active member of the online book community. When she is not writing, you can find her watching hockey with her family or talking about her newfound fictional crush that has appeared in her life on her social media accounts. Allison graduated from Arizona State University with a Bachelor's in English with a concentration in Literature.

CONNECT WITH ALLISON ON:
Website: www.allisonaldridge.com
Instagram: @authorallisonaldridge
Twitter: Alli_Nichole96
Tik Tok: AuthorAllisonAldridge
YouTube: www. youtube.com/allisonaldridge